LONG REACH

LONG REACH

PETER COCKS

**WALKER
BOOKS**

First published 2011 by Walker Books Ltd
87 Vauxhall Walk, London SE11 5HJ

2 4 6 8 10 9 7 5 3 1

Text © 2011 Peter Cocks
Cover story test (pp 44–47) © Crown copyright 2005
Cover design by Walker Books Ltd
Image of running figure © 2011 Stephen Mulcahey / Alamy
Image of bridge © 2011 Andrew Ward / Life File / Photolibrary.com

This book has been typeset in Palatino and Pahuenga Cass

Printed and bound in Great Britain by Clays Ltd, St Ives plc

British Library Cataloguing in Publication Data:
a catalogue record for this book is
available from the British Library

ISBN 978-1-4063-2475-4

www.walker.co.uk

PROLOGUE

Donnie gunned the Mercedes back across the Medway bridge. It had been a busy old night and he took a nip from his hip flask to settle the early morning acidity in his gut. Heart FM gurgled out of the radio; comforting words and familiar tunes for the waifs and strays that found themselves going to or coming from their crap jobs at this hour.

Wage slaves. Bean counters. Shit shovellers.

Losers.

Donnie knew that none of them would ever know the kind of job satisfaction he felt now. If he put his foot down, he should be back in time for breakfast.

He had dropped Dave off in Plumstead, then had been all the way down to Thanet to ditch the tools in a bit of the creek where they would never resurface. Then he had cleaned the blood and the mess out of the boot and switched the Vauxhall at one of the family-owned garages in Chatham. Replaced it with the Mercedes, which he'd left there the previous morning.

Tidy job; all done and dusted in twenty-four hours flat.

Donnie knew the mood at the firm would be good today, that they would all be relaxing and congratulating themselves. Glad to have the heat off for a bit; pleased that they had found where the leak was. And fixed it.

The boss might even have something lined up for them. A day at the races maybe. A nice bit of nosebag somewhere posh.

The thought of a rare steak and the other four or five courses got Donnie's juices really flowing. Twenty minutes later, he pulled out of the Blackwall Tunnel and turned left into Greenwich, where he stopped at a greasy spoon and ordered the Breakfast Special: two eggs, bacon, sausage, tomato, beans and fried slice. He ordered black pudding as an extra and sat down in the steamy café with a mug of tea and a copy of The Sun.

He turned to page three, looking for something to whet his appetite. The girl was good-looking, he thought, if tit-jobs were your thing, but he had seen nicer. No disrespect, but the one he fancied was real, better-looking – curvier – but you wouldn't catch her getting her threepenny bits out in the paper. Donnie shuddered at the thought. Not a chance. Just as his huge breakfast arrived, he looked out through the steamed-up glass and saw a black shape hovering like a spectre over the Mercedes, which he'd parked on a double yellow right outside. Donnie jumped up and opened the door to see a traffic warden about to issue him with a ticket.

"Oi," Donnie bawled.

The traffic warden went to say something, then saw who was doing the shouting and kept his mouth shut.

"Now piss off," Donnie shouted. The warden did as he was told, and Donovan Mulvaney went back in to his breakfast.

1

Eddie

ONE

"We found him face down in the mud at Long Reach."

It was only 7 a.m. and you rarely see a copper in tears so early in the day. Even off-duty.

My mum looked wide-eyed at Tony Morris as he tried to get the words out, but his face collapsed like a leaky balloon, and the sentence turned into sobbing, snotty gibberish. Mum pulled Tony in by the arm. He dragged his sleeve across his eyes to try and staunch the flow of tears and get control of his voice.

"He's dead. Steve's dead."

My mum had known the instant she'd opened the door, and so had I. The feeling had been growing between us, unspoken, for days. She had just needed to hear the words and then she began to cry, throwing herself back against the wall in the hall and banging her head rhythmically against the wallpaper.

"He was down river. Place called Long Reach. Near the Dartford bridge. Looks like he might have jumped off." Tony looked at me through wet, red eyes. "I'm so

sorry," he said. "Sorry, mate. Your brother was a hero."
His voice dissolved into sobs again.

The emotion hit me like a fist to my stomach, but no
tears would come. Mum and Tony were clinging to each
other in the hallway and I pushed past them, through the
open front door and out into the wet street.

I ran across the road and over the railway bridge up to
the park, past a couple of hardcore joggers and commut-
ers heading towards the station. From the empty park I
looked out over the misty outskirts of London, my breath
coming in gulps. The gulps quickly turned to sobs and a
loud, animal wail forced itself out of my throat.

The realization hit me that I would never see him
again; breathe the smell of his leather jacket when he
hugged me, catch the beer on his breath and feel his stubble on my cheek.

Never again.

I looked across at Canary Wharf, twinkling with early
morning lights, and on to the Dome and the sluggish grey
flatness of the river as it widened out on its way down
through Kent. Looked out at the stretches of mud where
they had found *my* hero, my brother.

Steve's funeral was a month later. No fuss and bother: just
a simple service at a crematorium with a few words from
a vicar who had never known him.

Our old man didn't even turn up. Although possibly
he didn't know Steve was dead. Mum had kicked our dad
out years ago, when I was only a toddler. He was always
pissed apparently, drifted from job to job, until eventually

he went a bit nuts and became violent. Steve had had a big fight with him: beat the crap out of him until he'd left. I'd only met him a couple of times since, shabby and unshaven. Once he turned up to a family wedding; the other time I saw him asleep on a bench in Lewisham. I hardly knew him.

Steve had looked out for me.

It had taken them that whole month to do the post-mortem and all the paperwork. It was a nightmare, not just because of the way that Steve had died, but because officially it had been difficult to prove that he ever existed. Because, it seemed, Steve Palmer had worked on something a bit hush-hush, with various false identities, and it was hard to work out that he actually was the real Steve Palmer. It made my head ache. He was Steve. I knew he'd been light on his toes, but his aliases were new to me. A secret he'd never shared.

And then there was the coroner's verdict to swallow.

Suicide.

It struck me at the funeral that I didn't know *much* more about my brother than the vicar did. Steve was twelve years older than me, for a start; he'd always been at home when I was small, but I was just "the kid". He wasn't easy to know, but I knew he was smart. That he was the first one in our family to go to university. He'd done an industrial chemistry degree in Essex, or some-where, ten years ago or so. I also knew that around that time he'd got into a bit of trouble with drugs, organized raves and house parties, and had got caught knocking out cannabis to other students.

According to Mum, Steve had made a deal with the police, working for them as a trade-off for a sentence. Poacher-turned-gamekeeper; feeding back information here and there, giving them leads on drug deals, illegal raves, that kind of thing.

Tony Morris had sorted it out for him.

Tony had always been there for us, as far back as I could remember; the loyal family friend. He was plain clothes or CID – as far as I knew – and he'd drop round from time to time, just to make sure Mum and I were OK after the old man went. He'd be there to reassure Mum whenever Steve went on the missing list for a few weeks.

I knew that Steve hadn't been whiter than white, and I knew he could be difficult. I just couldn't understand how he had got to a place where topping himself was the best option.

I couldn't understand and I was angry. How could he do it to me … to Mum?

We drove back to the flat in the hearse. Heavy rain drummed on the big, black roof and our breath steamed up the windows, protecting us from the stares of passers-by. I hugged Mum close to me in the back of the car. Suddenly she felt very small, as if the month grieving and preparing for the funeral had shrunk her. She'd bought sandwiches and snacks from Marks & Spencer. They didn't look anything like the ones you see on the telly: *These are not just sandwiches, these are M&S funeral-pack sandwiches, dried-up and curly in the central heating.*

They didn't seem to put anyone off, though. Tony

Morris and some of Steve's mates tucked in, cracking cans of bitter and laughing and talking in loud voices that disguised their grief.

I felt very alone.

There was no one else of my age there. Plenty of people gathered around Mum, making the right noises, but nobody seemed to know what to say to me. Tony must have noticed me standing there on my tod, looking pissed off, and he came over.

"Beer?" he said, passing me a can.

I tipped it at him and took a swig, lukewarm and metallic. Tony shuffled awkwardly.

"Been back to school yet?" he asked.

I shook my head. I'd never been a big fan of the education system and I'd had my fair share of trouble at school. I figured that being fairly average in a massive South London comp wasn't going to secure me a six-figure City-boy salary or a degree in rocket science. As soon as I could, I wanted to be off.

"Well, you've got a pretty good excuse for skiving off for a bit, I'd say."

"I'm not going back," I said.

The previous year, I had finally stopped mucking about, buckled down and done a few GCSEs. It would be fair to say I hadn't broken any records, but I had the basics under my belt. I'd done all right in maths and English, got decent grades in drama and French. But ICT was my thing. Technology came as second nature to me. I'd gone back to do an A level in it, but school was really doing my head in now.

Tony stared at his shoes. "You sure? Bright bloke like you…"

"I've had enough, Tony," I said. "It's not been a great year. I thought I might get a job."

I could almost see the cogs turning in Tony's head. "What sort of thing?"

"Dunno. Something with computers maybe."

There was a moment's pause.

"I've been thinking about you over the last couple of weeks," Tony said. "How old are you now?"

"Seventeen," I replied. I felt defensive. Where was this leading?

Tony considered a moment. "Listen, I've got something of Steve's I'd like you to see." He went over to where his briefcase was sitting on a chair and pulled out a padded envelope. "Here you go, old son," he said. "Don't show this to anyone, it's still a bit sensitive. Just have a look and let me know what you think."

He took a card from his pocket and handed it to me. "When you're ready, give me a bell." Then he grabbed me in a bear hug and when he released me I could see the tears pricking his eyes.

"I might have a job for you," he said.

TWO

I emptied out the envelope onto the bed.

There was a certificate and a small box. I opened the box and inside was a medal, bright as if it had been made yesterday. It was silver with the Queen's head on one side and a crown on the other, with the words *The Queen's Gallantry Medal*. I unfolded the certificate. It had a royal seal at the top and underneath it declared that the medal had been awarded to Stephen Palmer, "for acts of great bravery".

Tears began to blur my eyes.

Tony was right. Steve had been a hero.

I held the medal in my palm as if somehow it would connect me to my brother – to explain – but I felt nothing. I carefully folded up the certificate and put the medal, warm from my hand, back in its box.

I kicked back on the bed and closed my eyes. It had been a long day and my brain was struggling to absorb this latest piece of information. I tried to sleep, but my mind was running too fast. I kept rewinding and going over the past month – the way my life had changed, the gloom that had infected the flat and settled like a damp, grey blanket over me and Mum. She hadn't spoken much for days and just sat for hours on end, staring at daytime telly with the curtains drawn; watching naff celebrities giving people's houses makeovers or changing their lives for a grand.

I pulled the thin duvet up around my neck and caught a whiff of my own smell. The sheets hadn't been changed for a month and that, added to the mess in my room, brought me up sharp. Unless I pulled my finger out and did something about it, we were heading for some kind of meltdown. I couldn't expect the old girl to snap to it and miraculously pull everything together. I wouldn't pretend that it was all happy families before Steve went, but losing him felt like we'd lost our anchor.

I finally began to drift off, but the very thoughts I was trying to banish from my mind kept coming back: Steve playing football with me … the three of us on holiday in the Isle of Wight … Steve sparring with me in the garden, grinning, telling me I was a loser who punched like a girl, before leaving himself open to a sucker punch and pretending to be knocked out, declaring me the champion of the world.

Every image seemed to be bathed in sunlight. I seemed to have blotted out the bits where Steve had come home looking starved and shagged, and had slept for days on end. Or the days when he prowled around the flat, doing nothing except smoking and peering out from behind the net curtains. Or, more recently, the times when he'd turn up, unexpected, pissed and talking fast, his hands shaking.

I remembered that holiday. About six years ago Mum had found us a place to stay in Ventnor. It was a flat in a big Victorian house that smelt of old books and damp from being so close to the sea. Steve had cooked us a fry-up for breakfast every morning and we'd spent every day on the beach, swimming and throwing stones at Coke cans, which Steve set up on the breakwater. I don't remember it raining, but it probably had.

Tony Morris had come down for the night halfway through. He'd had some business in Portsmouth and thought he'd pay us a visit. He took us for dinner to a pub overlooking the sea where we'd eaten prawns and crabs, and I'd been allowed to drink cider. I remember Mum being happy, and Steve a bit pissed and cracking jokes. To anyone looking in, we'd have looked like an ordinary family of four.

Steve and Tony had stayed on in the pub for another one while Mum took me back to flat. I remember seeing the two of them, huddled together over a table as we left, their talk suddenly dark and serious as they sipped whisky chasers.

Tony went back the next day, but after that we ate out every night. Steve paid for everything; said he'd had enough of eating tinned soup and toasted sandwiches in the holiday flat. He took me out fishing on a boat and to a waxworks museum, which had a chamber of horrors showing people being tortured with hot irons and a moving skeleton playing a church organ. That really freaked me out.

Of course, when I got back to London I acted to my

mates that drinking cider and looking at torture was part of my daily life with Steve. I'd big him up to them until he was at least ten feet tall with a punch that would fell Mike Tyson.

Happy days.

I woke up about four. It was still dark and the duvet was twisted around me in a knot. I was thinking good thoughts for a second, caught up in happy memories. And then the reality came back to me; a thump, low in my guts. I tried to go back to sleep, but lay with my eyes open until it became light. I got up and took a dump, trying to ease the knot in my stomach, then stood outside the door of the small bedroom that Steve had stayed in when he was home.

Neither Mum nor I had even touched the room since he'd gone, let alone had the heart to chuck anything out. I pushed the door silently across the carpet and stepped into the early morning light that streaked through his window. Another dawn that Steve would never see.

There were no surprises. It was what it was: Steve's room. The sofa bed that he slept on was folded up and boxes of his things still littered the floor. It smelt of Steve. I shut my eyes, took a deep breath and he could have been in the room with me. I flicked through the stack of CDs: mostly classic seventies rock dinosaurs and eighties bands that I'd never heard of.

I searched through the boxes: weights, some lads' mags, a glass bong. Nothing personal, just stuff. Nothing that told me any more than the little I already knew about my brother.

I opened the wardrobe, put my face into the clothes hanging there and inhaled leather jacket and faint after-shave, and he came back to me again. I searched his pockets and found nothing but empty fag packs and train tickets to and from New Cross.

And then I found a plastic wallet, tucked inside one of his jackets. There was no money in it, just another train ticket and a card. It was a membership card for a club in New Cross, The Harp Club. It had a picture of a harp and a shamrock printed in green. There was a photo of Steve a couple of years ago, with a beard. I remembered him growing the beard. Mum hated it. Steve had laughed – said it hid his double chin.

Next to the photo was his name. Not Steve Palmer, another name. James Boyle. Another identity. Jimmy.

I shut the bedroom door and went into the kitchen to make some tea and toast. I stared at the card again, and tried to read the blank, passport-photo look on Steve's face. It was giving nothing away. I glanced at my watch; it was nearly nine. Another day about to drift away, so I made a decision. I picked up the phone.

"Tony Morris," came the voice on the other end.

"It's me," I said. "You mentioned a job."

THREE

I don't really know what I was thinking when I walked into Tony Morris's office. I hadn't got a clear idea of what his job was about. I guess I was more interested in asking him exactly what my brother had been up to.

Getting there was the maddest bit about it. He gave me an address in town near Leicester Square and when I found it, it turned out to be a music shop. In fact the whole street was music shops, with instruments hanging in the windows and heavy guitar riffs strumming out of the shop doorways. I checked the street number again. It was definitely right, but the shop was chock-full of electric guitars.

I walked in. A bloke wearing a Jack Daniels T-shirt and a scrubby beard was noodling on a guitar. He looked up and nodded. I nodded back and he stopped playing.

"Hey," he said.

"I don't know if I'm in the right place," I replied. "I'm looking for Tony Morris?"

Jack Daniels grinned and put down his guitar. He went to an area of the wall that was covered with paper packets of guitar strings, found a handle and pulled a door open.

"Down the end and up the stairs," he said, pointing through the doorway.

I walked up the stairs and came to another door marked *Sugacubes Model Agency*. It was the only door there was, so I pressed the buzzer and was let in. A good-looking, dark-haired girl glanced up as I walked in. She smiled. She looked to be in her twenties and was wearing quite a lot of make-up. Pictures of other hot girls were framed on the wall behind her.

"Hi," she said.

"I think I've made a mistake," I said, embarrassed. "I'm looking for Tony Morris?"

"Is he expecting you?"

"I think so, yes."

The girl got up from behind the desk. "I'm Anna. Anna Moore." She held out her hand and I shook it. Her handshake was surprisingly firm. "Come this way."

She walked across to another door and pressed a code into the lock. The door opened and she ushered me through before heading back to her desk, closing the door behind me.

Tony Morris's office was small and unremarkable, save for the stacks of CDs that lined every shelf and covered every surface. Posters for recently forgotten bands covered the walls and a sign over Tony's desk read: *Tin Pan Alley Music Publishing*.

"Sit down, mate," Tony said. "Coffee?" He filled two grubby mugs with water and instant coffee and handed me one and a sachet of sugar. "Milk's off, I'm afraid."

"I'm fine," I said. I looked around at the crowded walls. "What's all this record-business stuff, Tony?"

"It's a front. I'm sure you guessed."

I hadn't, but I nodded anyway.

"A front for what?" I asked. "I thought you worked in a police station."

Tony laughed. "What? 'I arrest you in the name of the law'?" he asked in a comedy policeman voice. "Truncheon-meat sandwiches, Letsby Avenue and all that?"

I shrugged.

"OK," Tony said. "I don't work for the police *exactly*. Neither did Steve. We operate somewhere in the gap between the police and the more covert government agencies. We're a self-contained, intelligence-gathering department."

"What about the model agency next door? The music shop?"

Tony put a finger to his lips. "Too many questions, old son. All in good time. So what did you think about the stuff I gave you?"

"I never knew. About the medal. Did Mum...?"

Tony shook his head.

"What did Steve do?" I asked. "I mean, to earn it?"

"He cracked a terrorist cell up near Willesden," Tony said. "They were planning to blow up half of Oxford Street. Would have killed thousands. Steve went in by himself. We created a gas scare in their block of flats and he went in disguised as a British Gas employee and wired the place right under their noses. He even hacked their computer and found the explosives under the sink. That takes some balls when there are three Al Qaeda suspects in the room while you work. Steve was good. Then he went back in and bust it single-handed, before the heavy mob piled in and shot two of them. High-risk strategy. He really put his cock on the block for that one."

I felt my chest swell with pride.

"Did he get the medal from the Queen?" I asked lamely.

"Steve couldn't go to pick it up from Her Maj. It would've made him conspicuous. That's the trouble with this job. You don't get the glory, you just have to be content that you're doing some good. You can't even tell your family, because any information could put them in danger. Steve never let on much, did he?"

He hadn't. Now I wished I had asked more.

"It's work for a single man, like Steve … or a man like yourself. Not too much in the way of dependants to worry about."

I felt proud to be referred to as a man. At school they had still been giving me the boy treatment.

"So James Boyle was his alias for this work?" I asked. Tony looked taken aback.

I pulled out the membership card from The Harp Club and lay it on the desk in front of him.

"Where did you get that?" he asked, rattled.

"It was in one of Steve's jackets."

"Bit careless." Tony sighed. "That was part of the trouble. Steve was getting a bit sloppy. I think the stress was getting to him."

I remembered Steve sitting in our lounge only a few weeks ago, smoking like a chimney, chewing his nails down to stubs and drinking cans of beer. For breakfast.

"That level of stress is dangerous," Tony explained. "That's why I was worried when he went missing this time."

"Does going missing usually include topping yourself?" I asked.

Tony scratched his nose.

"He was under a lot of pressure," he said finally. "Quite a few people were on his back."

"So now he's 'gone missing' for ever, what happens?"

"Well, that's where you come in, old son. If you're up for it, you might be able to help us by doing a bit of background work."

I felt fear bubbling away queasily in the pit of my stomach. What was he going to ask me to take on? The worry must have shown on my face because Tony stood up and put his heavy hand on my shoulder.

"Look, mate. If you have any doubts about this whole thing, we can forget this conversation ever happened and just carry on as we were. No problem."

"I want to help." The fear was still gnawing away, but I knew that the shame of not honouring my big brother's memory would be far worse.

"Good man. I knew you would." Tony squeezed my shoulder. "A young guy like you can get to places where people like me would stick out like a turd in a swimming pool. I'm glad you're on board. Now, there's a couple of people I'd like you to meet."

FOUR

We walked down Charing Cross Road and across Trafalgar Square. If there was a straight line to be walked, Tony never took it. He would cross from one side of the road to the other, dipping into bookshops and leaving by another door; taking little side alleys and backstreets, cutting through Soho across Chinatown then behind the National Gallery and out into the side of the square. It was as if he was trying to shake someone off with every move he made. I struggled to keep up.

"Get used to it, mate," he said with a wink. "It's good practice. Means you can 'disappear' when you need to."

We stepped into a pub tucked away on the south side of Trafalgar Square. Tony seemed to know the barman, who served him a large Scotch without waiting to be asked. I had a cold bottle of beer. Tony scanned the half-empty bar and downed his whisky.

"C'mon," he said. We had been in there no longer than five minutes. I left most of my beer and followed Tony through the back of the pub and into a yard surrounded by high, grey buildings spattered with pigeon droppings. Steam billowed from the back of one of them and half a dozen men in chefs' outfits barely looked at us as they stood around, smoking their fags. Tony climbed the metal fire escape that zigzagged up the back of another of the buildings and I followed him. We arrived at a steel door and Tony swiped the lock with a card.

We came into a corridor: white and lit with fluorescent tubes. It smelt of school dinners. Opposite us was a heavy brown wooden door. Tony knocked.

"Come in…"

The room was large and sparsely furnished: a worn carpet, several lumpy-looking chairs and a big, battered desk. Not exactly built for comfort. The single dirty window looked out at Admiralty Arch that led down to Buckingham Palace.

The man behind the desk was reading something, lit by a lamp with a green glass shade. I followed Tony in and the man looked up. He must have been about fifty. His face was lined and tanned, and his hair was gingery, cut short. He looked hard.

"Hello, Tony." He sounded posh.

"Sandy," Tony replied. He gestured for me to step forward. "This is Sandy Napier."

Sandy Napier stood up and extended a hand. I saw a gold signet ring and cufflinks on a striped sleeve that shot out from a well-cut suit. Rolex Submariner diver's watch on his right wrist. I notice that stuff.

"How d'you do?" His voice was clipped, the

handshake was crushing. His eyes were cold and blue and locked on to me.

"I'm good. Pleased to meet you."

I'm sure I saw him suppress a smile as he flicked a glance towards Tony. "Sit down," he said, gesturing at the chairs in front of his desk, and Tony and I sat. Napier observed me for a moment. "You're very young."

"Yes, but I'm growing out of it," I quipped.

Napier glanced at Tony again. Had he delivered him a clever bastard? I decided to answer his next question straight.

"I'll be honest," he said. "I think you're too young. *Legally* you're too young to be working for us, but I'm following Tony's hunch here. I knew your brother, of course. I'm sorry for your loss." Napier paused, twisted the signet ring on his little finger. "Tony thinks you've got some of what Stephen had."

My feelings were still mixed. But I was chuffed that Tony had talked to Napier and put me in the same bag as my brother.

Napier looked at the notes on his desk and thought for a moment. "You look good on paper," he said, pushing them across the desk for me to look at. On three sheets of A4, my life was mapped out in detail: my date of birth, the appendix operation I'd had when I was five, my schools, my exam results and sporting achievements. Then the more personal stuff: a list of two or three girlfriends – the name of a long-term one I'd split up from last year. Finally, pictures: me as a kid on a bike; sweating in boxing shorts holding up a cup; in judo kit getting my brown belt.

29

"Where did you get all this?" I asked, looking at Tony.

"Child's play." He smiled.

"And what do you think this shows about you?" Napier asked.

"It looks pretty straightforward to me," I said. "I've not been in any trouble."

"You're alone in all the photos," Napier pointed out. "All the sports you participate in are one on one."

I'd never thought about it before. I had mates, but I was happy enough with my own company.

"I guess I'm not a team player," I said after a while.

"That may be no bad thing as far as we're concerned." Napier picked up a phone on his desk and punched in an extension. Although he said nothing more to me, I felt I had passed some sort of test.

"Can you come in, Ian?" Napier barked into the phone.

I took an instant dislike to the tall, sinewy man who entered the room a few seconds later. He must have been in his early thirties but looked as if he didn't shave yet. His skin was smooth, sallow and tight on his narrow face. His hair was short and crinkly, and his lips thin. He stood behind Napier at the desk and looked down at me without cracking a smile.

"Ian," said Napier, "Tony Morris you know, and this is…"

He looked at my details in front of him. Used the name that I was about to lose.

The thin man nodded at Tony and then looked back at me.

"This is Ian Baylis," Napier said. "Ian will be your case officer."

I wasn't sure what a case officer was exactly, but it looked to me as if Ian Baylis was none too pleased about being mine.

"Bringing us children now, are you, Tony?" Baylis said. He allowed himself a minimal mouth movement that passed for a smile.

Napier held up a finger to silence him: it was clearly a discussion they had already had.

"He's made of the right stuff," Tony said, coming to my defence. "He can look after himself. Besides, we're not going to send him out into the wilds on this one, are we?"

I felt I needed some input into this conversation.

"Where *are* you going to send me exactly?" I asked.

"First things first," Napier said. "Before you do anything, you'll need to look at this." He pushed a form across the desk to me. A glance at the heading told me that it was to do with official secrets. "You'll need to sign it. And you'll need to get used to this."

He passed me a brown envelope, which I emptied onto the table. There was a passport and various other pieces of ID: a credit card, a driving licence, gym membership.

Each piece of documentation had my photo on it and someone else's name. Eddie Savage.

"That's my granddad's name," I said. "My mum's dad. He's dead."

"So you won't forget it when you're in the field," Baylis said sharply. "Will you?"

"Why? Where am I going?" I pressed.

"We'd like you to make friends with a girl," Napier said. He smiled. "Shouldn't be too hard, should it? She's called Sophie Kelly."

I felt relieved that I wasn't being sent into a terrorist hotbed like my brother.

"So, where do I find this Sophie Kelly?" I asked.

Napier pushed a photo across the table. It was a picture of a very pretty blonde girl. I couldn't help smiling myself.

"Nice easy one for you, this, Eddie," Napier said, using my new name for the first time. "We'd like you to go back to school."

FIVE

Things moved fast in this world.

As soon as I'd said yes and signed on the dotted line, Sandy Napier shook my hand and I was in.

Up to my neck.

If I'm honest, what choice did I have? To say no and creep around for the rest of my life, wondering if I could have done something useful, ashamed that I hadn't honoured Steve Palmer's memory in some way? It wasn't an option.

When we stepped out into the bright day in Trafalgar Square it seemed like a new London: everything looked super-real, sharply detailed in the sunlight. I felt as if everyone was looking at me: people on buses, men in hats, road sweepers. Everything looked like a clue. I held out my hand. It was trembling, as if all my nerves had been wound up a notch. I felt Tony's firm grasp on my shoulder.

"Feels weird, doesn't it?"

I nodded.

"It's a big leap," he said. "I remember what it's like.

The paranoia. You get used to it but, I tell you what, it's a valuable tool. Keeps you on your toes. You trust no one and look for signs on every street corner. Nine times out of ten, that suspicion pays off. That's how it works in this game."

Tony hailed a black cab, which squealed to a halt in front of us. I got in while Tony gave the driver my address, then he sat down beside me. We rumbled down the Mall past New Scotland Yard and all the ministry buildings. The cab turned left over Westminster Bridge and as I looked across at Big Ben and the Houses of Parliament, I suddenly felt part of it all. Scared and proud. I had never really felt part of *anything* before.

My eyes darted left and right as we crossed the Thames, watching every car that passed, checking the registration of a motorcycle despatch rider as he pulled up alongside us.

"Blimey, you are jumpy." Tony chuckled. "Take a deep breath and relax."

"Does this really get better, Tony?" I asked, trying to make myself comfortable in the cab seat. "I feel a bit sick."

Behind us Big Ben chimed two and I realized how much I had already crammed into the day.

"It does," Tony reassured me. "I promise. It becomes second nature, a part of you."

My stomach gurgled as if in reply. Nerves, probably.

"You must be starving," Tony said. "Let's get some lunch."

He got the cabbie to stop at a drive-through on the Old Kent Road. A quarter-pounder with cheese, large fries and half a litre of Coke. The food seemed to settle my stomach

34

a bit and the sugar hit from the Coke helped. Soon we were burrowing back into the grotty, leafy backstreets of South London and I felt safer. We drew up outside Mum's.

Home again.

The old girl made us both a cup of tea, then Tony talked to her in the kitchen. They spoke quietly, but every now and again I could hear Mum raising her voice in protest, then Tony calming her again. I plonked myself in front of the TV in the lounge and watched a repeat of *Friends*. The familiar, attractive faces, the colours and the studio laughter made me feel secure. Whatever was thrown at the characters, their problems always got sorted by the end of an episode. No matter what the scriptwriter had dreamt up for them, they all had each other in the end. I wished I had the safety net of their script. And Rachel as a girlfriend.

After a while, Mum came in and sat beside me on the sofa. Her eyes were red and she looked at me with a down-turned smile and her lip trembled again. She hugged me close and I could feel the sobs shake her entire body.

She had known this would happen, and she didn't want to lose another son. Tony had told her it wasn't safe for her here now that I was involved too. It had been risky enough when Steve was around, and his death was bound to draw some attention. My background had to be concealed, all traces of my previous life brushed over.

Mum was going to stay with her sister in Stoke-on-Trent, and I could go up and see her whenever I wanted. Tony explained that he had found me a flat. He would take me there tomorrow.

Tony ordered a takeaway curry and the three of us ate around the kitchen table. The telly was still on in the background filling in the silences, but we managed a few laughs. I kissed Mum goodnight and she squeezed me tight, like she was never going to let go, and I went up to my room, stuffed with tikka masala and poppadoms.

I couldn't sleep. My mind was racing and my belly was full to bursting. I scanned through my iPod for something relaxing and selected "Steve's Playlist", which was nothing of the sort: Clapton, Bowie, Led Zeppelin, Queen, Sex Pistols, Iggy Pop, Primal Scream, Public Enemy, Gorillaz. Tracks that spanned twenty years or so, each one bringing back a different memory of Steve – a particular weekend or a Christmas past. Tunes I had grown up hearing in the background or from behind a closed door. I was wearing one of Steve's jumpers and as I took it off, I caught that faint smell of him again.

I don't believe in ghosts, but as the tunes washed over me I realized that if you keep enough of someone – their smell, their favourite food and the music they loved – then you can almost re-create a sense of them. You can feel them in the room. I could feel Steve with me, watching me.

I looked up at the ceiling of the bedroom that had been my boyhood refuge for as long as I could remember, every crack and cobweb familiar and comforting. And it occurred to me that, after tonight, I was leaving my boyhood well and truly behind.

SIX

Tony was picking me up at ten. I got up early and packed my bags. I still felt pretty sick. I don't think it was the curry, just my nerves. I had kept waking up all through the night, staring at the ceiling, worrying.

Ma cooked me eggs and bacon, but I didn't have much of an appetite. I forced it down to please her and washed it down with a mug of strong tea.

When Tony arrived, Mum did her best not to make a scene and so did I; she told him to look after me, or he'd have her to answer to. Tony promised he would, then we both kissed her and left.

The rush hour was pretty much over, but New Cross was still clogged up with traffic as we cut down into Deptford. The cars were mostly scruffy vans on local business, or shiny Beemers with black blokes flexing their muscles and their stereos. I couldn't help noting faces, wondering what sort of work other people were doing, and got steely stares in return.

I would have to be more subtle, I thought.

Tony turned down towards the river, humming along to a terrible tune on the radio that was beginning to get on my nerves. He pulled up outside a block of flats along the riverfront: a new development, faced in steel, glass and wood. To one side there was a scrapyard piled high with the rusting wrecks of old cars. On the other side, a second new block, shiny and metallic, that stretched upwards, with a neat line of glossy, prestige motors lined up outside. It was like the new world colliding with the old, and it wasn't clear which was winning: whether the shiny and new was taking over the scrapyard or whether the scrapyard was rotting the new stuff with rust and corrosion, dragging it down to its level.

"Welcome to your new home." Tony presented the block to me with a wave of his hand.

"You what?" I said.

"Your flat." He laughed. "But you won't have much company, I'm afraid – the block's half-empty. It was built for all the yuppies and City boys who were supposed to be flooding this area."

"So where did they go?" I asked.

"They either didn't exist in the first place, or they've gone skint in the meantime…" He grinned. "Merchant bankers," he added with a gesture of his wrist.

Tony punched in a code on the heavy steel and glass door. There were no numbers on the buttons, but they made different tones.

"No numbers?" I asked.

"No. It's more secure without. You'll have to remember the tone sequence, but don't worry just yet. Early

38

days." The door clicked open and we walked across a cool, marble-floored hallway towards a steel lift door. It hissed open.

"This is your safe house," Tony explained, pressing the button for the fifth floor. "The people who buy this kind of gaff like their security, so you'll be safe as houses, so to speak. It's quiet down here. Just be discreet and don't get too chummy with your neighbours. You probably won't see much of them anyway. They tend to go to work early and come back late, and none of them are families."

He passed me a piece of paper with the PIN tone sequence for the outside door and another number combination for the flat. The lift stopped at the top floor.

"Memorize the numbers, then eat that," Tony said.

The look on my face made him laugh.

"Only joking, mate." He slapped my shoulder. "Just don't leave it anywhere silly."

I pressed in the code to open Flat 501 and walked through the door. The trapped air hit me in the face and everything smelt new. Tony flicked on the lights and I felt a tingle of excitement as I took in the big, open space.

There was a comfy-looking sofa and a couple of leather armchairs. A thick, modern rug covered the floor between them, and there was a glass coffee table with a stack of books and a fruit bowl. There was a large, framed vintage film poster on the wall: James Bond – *Dr. No*. Tony saw my reaction and winked at me.

"My house-warming present," he said. "A bit of a joke."

Underneath the poster was a desk with a silver Apple

laptop on it. Tony lifted the lid and booted it up. In the toolbar at the top, my new name was already entered: Eddie Savage. The screen saver was the same as the view from the window that ran the width of the flat; the Docklands skyline, Canary Wharf towering in the middle. Tony clicked on my name then on *Guest Account* and the whole screen swivelled around, revealing a second desktop. Tony typed in another password: 3dd13.

I frowned. How was I going to remember all these codes and numbers?

"3dd13, Eddie … get it?" Tony asked. "Thought of that myself."

"Catchy."

"It'll be your pass for all the work you do for us, OK?" I nodded.

"This desktop is for all the confidential stuff. It has a separate email, web browser, everything." He clicked on my name again and the Canary Wharf skyline spun back into view. "This desktop you can do with what you like. Just make sure it looks like the desktop of an average seventeen-year-old bloke."

"Sure, Tony." I was pretty chuffed with the laptop. I'd only had shared use of the clunky old Dell at home and this was state of the art, thin as a wafer and sleek as a Ferrari.

"Fill it up with rap music and porn, if you like, but just remember, both sets of emails and web histories will be under surveillance, I'm afraid."

I must have blushed a little because Tony looked out of the window and coughed, sorry that he had embarrassed me.

"Anyway, don't get comfortable just yet. Dump your stuff and bring your overnight bag."

He helped me take my cases into the bedroom, just off the main living area. The bed was vast and white, more than twice the size of my bunk at home. It looked like a cool hotel room, with bedside lights fixed to the wall either side and another picture over the bed. This was a piece of abstract art, the poster for an exhibition that had been on at the Tate Modern a couple of years before. There was a sliding door that led out onto a balcony that faced directly over the river. I slid it open and stepped outside. The midday sun was bouncing off the futuristic city opposite, and upriver I could see the outline of the Gherkin and the dome of St Paul's. Below me, the river ran by, slow and murky, making pools and eddies around the slippery green legs of the small jetties that stuck out from the riverbank. Despite the unfamiliarity of my new place, I felt a feeling of warmth spread through me and wanted to do nothing more than throw myself back on the big white mattress, switch on the widescreen TV at the end of the bed and chill out for the rest of the day.

Tony had different ideas. He looked at his watch and made noises about getting going, so I put my stuff in the overnight bag while he packed up the laptop and, five minutes later, we shut the door of my new flat behind us.

SEVEN

We cut down through Greenwich, past the park and the National Maritime Museum then through the Blackwall Tunnel. The industrial landscape north of the river was pretty foreign to me. I'd had no reason to go there before. Eventually Tony swung off left into a slip road and we drove into a run-down residential area, the streets lined with Indian groceries, kebab shops and Mediterranean delis.

"Where are we, Tony?" I asked. I looked out at the mix of people spotted around the streets.

"Dalston," he said.

Although it could have been no more than a few miles from where I lived, I'd never heard of Dalston before. It felt different from south of the river. Don't know why. Just not my territory perhaps.

"Rough as arseholes round here," said Tony. "Not like the leafy avenues and boulevards of New Cross and Peckham," he added, grinning.

We drove on through Hackney and Islington, then up

the Holloway Road until signs began to signal the North Circular.

"So where's this place we're going?"

"Out towards Beaconsfield," Tony replied. "But the less you know about it, the better. Should have blindfolded you."

Tony seemed to be enjoying himself today with his lame jokes. I suppose he was just trying to make light of my nervousness. We sat in silence for the remainder of the drive.

The building looked like a school. It stood at the end of a long drive with modern blocks dotted around it. We were checked by security then waved up to the main building where Tony parked in a bay marked *Staff*. At a reception desk we signed in and a woman in a uniform gave me a badge in a plastic sleeve.

It didn't feel exciting or glamorous, it was more like signing on the dole or getting a tetanus jab. The walls were covered with government posters and health-and-safety warnings. My shoes squeaked as we walked down a corridor with a polished lino floor. No one acknowledged us, or gave any sign that they knew Tony as we walked out of the main building and across a yard into one of the modern blocks. Sitting behind a desk, surrounded by computers and piles of files and papers, was Ian Baylis. He didn't look particularly pleased to see me.

"All right, Ian?" Tony asked cheerily. Baylis gave his thin smile and looked at me.

"Better get started," he said. "We haven't got all that long."

"I'm going to leave you in Ian's capable hands," Tony told me, and I suddenly felt the urge to grab hold of him, to keep him there, as if I were a kid on his first day at school. Tony patted me on the back.

"I'll check up on you in a few days."

"A few *days*?" I asked. "How long will I be here?" I was shocked; I had thought it was just overnight.

"A week," Baylis said. "Just about long enough to knock you into shape."

For the rest of the day, Baylis had me in front of a computer, doing IQ tests and tests of initiative. He checked my results and timed my responses, but it was hard to tell how well I was doing.

One test was to remember a cover story and the details of a new identity, not my own. Ian gave me exactly two minutes to read the cover, then ten seconds to answer each question. I clicked the mouse and turned the page on the computer:

Your cover story:

You're stationed in Transeuratania. You're a vegetarian and the food isn't especially good in Metropoligrad – unlike the coffee, which costs less than a shilling for a pot at the best hotel. Your name is Stephen Johnson. You were born on 14 December 1974 in Skegness. At A level, you gained an A in Geography, an A in French and a B in Economics. You have two sisters and a brother.

You studied Geology at university and now work as a management consultant for a company called British Coal Associates.

I read the cover story again and again, and tried to put pictures to the words – like visualizing a carrot for the vegetarianism. I knew Skegness because we'd stayed at Butlins there, so I formed a picture of the holiday camp in my mind. My brother's name was Stephen, so that was easy... I tried to remember the exam grades... A for Geography, A in French... Time up.

The page disappeared and a map of the imaginary country of Transeuratania popped up. Numbers were pinned to the map and I could answer the questions in any order... I clicked on number one.

1. What is your name?
A: John Stephenson
B: Stephan Johnston
C: Stephen Johnson

Easy one. I chose C as the clock ticked down from ten. Three seconds. Question 2...

2. What is the currency of Transeuratania?
A: Transeuratanian rouble
B: Transeuratanian zloty
C: Transeuratanian shilling

I remembered the coffee. Pressed C. Next question...

3. What is your favourite meal?

A. *Mushroom Risotto*

B: *Duck à l'Orange*

C: *Roasted Vegetables with Lamb*

Got to be risotto – I remembered the carrot image and clicked on A. Next question…

4. What were your grades at A level?

Once more the clock ticked down from ten at the side of the window. The letters began to swim in front of my eyes.

A: *ABB*

B: *CAB*

C: *AAB*

I nearly pressed A. No, it's C. I think. Look again. Four seconds left. I stab C with one second on the clock. Begin to sweat a bit…

5. What company are you working for?

Oh, no. An acronym. More letters. I know it was something to do with British and coal, but which one…?

A: *CBA*

B: *ABC*

C: *BCA*

I'm sure it was C. Or was it B? Time's running out. Three seconds. I pause too long and press B. Sure I'm wrong... Move on.

6. What was your degree in?

A: Geology
B: Geography
C: Management

I know this. It's A. Move on...

7. What's your brother's name?

Easy.

A: John Stephenson
B: John Johnson
C: Stephen Johnston

I click on C then instantly regret it. C is supposed to be *my* name ... and the surname shouldn't have a T. I've fallen into an easy trap.

8. What's your date of birth?

A: 17 December 1974
B: 14 December 1974
C: 19 December 1974

I've gone to pieces now. All the letters and numbers are beginning to look the same and the clock is already down to three seconds … two … one. I click on A.

"Pathetic," came Ian Baylis's voice from the other side of the office, where he had been noting my answers and timings on his own computer. I looked up in time to see him mime an imaginary pistol with his index finger and thumb and shoot it at my head. "You're dead," he said. "You got five out of eight. On a simple one like this you should have got them all right. Even one slip could have blown your cover."

"I'm sorry," I murmured. "I'm just a bit nervous. It was quite confusing."

"Don't apologize to me, you twat," said Baylis. "I'm not the one who'll be getting the bullet in the head or who's being filmed while he's carved up by terrorists and posted on the Internet. We're going to have to work harder on you than I thought."

EIGHT

Ian Baylis was true to his word. I didn't like him any more now than I had at first, but I had to admire the way he coached me. The memory games, tests, random questions, going over my cover story again and again:

"What's your name?"

"Eddie Savage."

"Date of birth?"

"23 May."

"Born?"

"Lewisham Hospital, London."

"Parents?"

"Both dead. Dad cancer, Mum too."

"What sort of cancer did she have?"

"Breast."

"Brothers and sisters?"

"No."

"School?"

"St George's, New Cross."

"What's your middle name?"

"Arthur, after my granddad."

"Brother's name?"

"I…"

"You hesitated. Start again."

And on he would go, asking questions about my childhood; about pets I never had and holidays I never went on. He kept going until I began to believe all the stories myself. I could even picture my imaginary childhood and the house that I never lived in.

They had created a new me.

There were other tests, physical ones, on the treadmill and in the gym. Pulse rate, blood pressure, recovery time. There was often another man hovering around – Ian Baylis just called him Oliver. Said I would see him around. He just seemed to be in the background, observing.

On the evening of day four, Ian took me out to the pub, somewhere in the country near wherever we were. He bought me a pint and we sat there, sipping Guinness and crunching handfuls of nuts. He didn't say much at first, but then he seemed to relax a little. After a while he looked at me and told me I wasn't a "complete bloody disaster", which, coming from him, I took as a compliment. Then he asked if I played pool. I said I did, so we played best of five and he thrashed me.

"You need to improve your tactics," he said. "Think about the game a bit more instead of knocking balls all over the table. Set up traps. Make things a bit awkward for your opponent."

The following morning Baylis introduced me to the martial arts instructor, who said much the same. I had done a bit of judo and boxing as a kid, but this guy told me I couldn't fight my way out of a wet paper bag. That aside, his advice was never to start a fight. To walk away if at all possible but, if I had to engage, to make sure I got the upper hand quickly – and by whatever means. He showed me stuff that would never go down in judo or the boxing ring. Streetfighting tactics, like how to punch and ram your thumb into the other bloke's eye, how to bring the heel of your hand up under someone's nose. How to hit with your fist going forward, and again with a slashing motion on the backstroke. To stun with an elbow in the solar plexus or the temple; a knee to the heart. To stab someone in the windpipe with a ballpoint, to garrotte them with pen and a shoelace.

In his hands, he said, a ballpoint pen was all he would need to survive in the department of dirty tricks. He went into some detail about how much pain the sharp end of a pen would cause if rammed into someone's ear, how fatal it would be if you hammered it home with the heel of a shoe. Equally, if you pushed the pen or even a sharp pencil into the eye hard enough, it would burst through the orbit and penetrate the brain.

Nice. Dangerous things, pens.

The instructor was stocky and flat-nosed with a head like a bull terrier. He shouted at me in a rasping Welsh voice as I punched the heavy bag and threw hooks into pads that he held up. He bawled at me as I worked the speedball and insulted me as he dropped medicine balls on my tensed stomach.

He didn't tell me his name. Too personal, he said. He

didn't want any mateyness, and he didn't give – or get – any. The only name he called me was a four-letter one I would never have used in front of my mum.

I held my temper as he chased me around a muddy assault course, screaming at me as I skinned my knees and elbows crawling across corrugated iron sheets. I didn't flinch as I cut my legs on brambles and broken glass, scraped my back to ribbons crawling under barbed-wire fences. And I didn't complain when he loaded me up with a backpack full of rocks and told me to run round the whole circuit a second time, twice as fast.

I went round again, his voice roaring in my ears the whole time. In fact the more he shouted and screamed, the stronger I began to feel. The pain dissolved as my determination not to break increased. I threw myself across ditches and up rope walls, the rocks digging into my back and making me yell with angry resolve. My hands burned down to the raw flesh as I swung on a rope across a ditch crammed with shopping trolleys, shit and sump oil. At the other end, I smashed my face into a wall, making my nose bleed and my eyebrow swell instantly.

When I made it back to the start – in double-quick time – my breath was hot and rasping in my dry throat, and blood, sweat and drool poured down my face. So when he called me a wuss who wasn't fit to lick his boots, let alone kiss his arsehole, I lost it.

I shrugged off the backpack and launched myself at him, letting off an explosive punch that I dearly hoped would spread what was left of his nose across his face. He caught my fist in a huge hand and sidestepped my blow, twisting me, causing me to lose my balance and fall back in the mud. I jumped straight back up and went for him again, this time anticipating his move and landing a smacking right-hander into his mouth, splitting his lip. This seemed to anger him a little and I was suddenly on the receiving end of a right backhand that caught me on the neck. It felt like being whacked with a tree trunk and I went down again. I was on my feet in an instant and at him with both fists when I saw his face. Through the blood trickling from his split lip, he was grinning from ear to ear.

Not taunting, but warm and friendly.

"Nice one, my son," he said. "You got balls of steel." He put his hands up defensively to catch the punches I was about to throw, but the fire went out of me. I dropped my fists and rested my hands on my knees, panting heavily, half laughing, half crying with pain, exhaustion and relief that it was over. He patted my back and I spat dryly into the wet mud, a smear of blood mixed in the spit. From the corner of my eye I saw Ian Baylis approaching. His mate Oliver was with him.

"How's he getting on, Jim?" Baylis asked.

"By Jove, I think he's got it!" Jim said in a mocking voice. Then, serious, "He's as hard as nails. I think he'd have killed me if I'd given him half a chance."

Oliver checked the stopwatch, raised his eyebrows and showed it to Baylis.

"Never seen anyone do the course that quick second time around," Baylis said, allowing himself a glimmer of a smile. "Well done, Eddie. Let's get you a hot shower and some dinner. We'll make a man of you yet."

NINE

I woke up the next day stiff with the pain in my bones. Every muscle and sinew in my body seemed to be screaming for help. I tried to roll over and make myself comfortable on the lumpy mattress, but wherever I moved, something else hurt. The sun was streaming through the thin curtain, so I knew I wouldn't get back to sleep. I swung my legs out of the bed, feeling my hips creak, and put my feet on the cold floor. Where I had been lying, the sheet was speckled with spots of blood. I looked down at the broken toenails and blisters on my feet, at the scratches that criss-crossed my legs, and suddenly felt proud that I had survived this far. Some inner strength had made me go the extra mile. I got to my feet and staggered across to the washbasin, found a couple of ibuprofen in my washbag and swigged them down with cold water. I splashed my face and looked in the mirror. In just a few days I thought I appeared leaner and fitter. OK, my face was scratched and cut, and I had a black eye, but – and perhaps it was just my imagination – there was definitely a new look of determination in my eyes.

Hard as nails, he'd said. Balls of steel. I could handle whatever they threw at me.

The fifth day was different from the rest. Ian Baylis eased off a bit, only throwing the odd question here and there to make sure I was still quick off the mark. If he called me Eddie, I jumped to it. I'd almost forgotten my real name. Like someone learning a foreign language in another country, I almost began to dream as Eddie. Different dreams, different places.

They gave me a crash course in driving. I knew the basics because I'd had a few lessons, but they gave me my test anyway. And I was pretty chuffed when I passed.

The day after, Baylis took me to a new part of the building. In a nasal voice, a thin man called Hamish Campbell talked me through some of the technology I would need. Most of it was pretty basic: two mobiles, one an iPhone for personal use, the other a small Nokia, a hotline to Baylis and his operatives. The iPhone had all the usual apps, but plenty of other extras like navigation stuff and an encoded keyboard I could use to send encrypted messages. This was top-notch gear, quite a few steps up from my T-Mobile pay-as-you-go.

I panicked, thinking I wouldn't know how to work it all, but Campbell assured me I would pick it all up in due course. He also instructed me to take out the SIM cards every night to cut down the likelihood of being tracked by anyone else. He gave me some shoes that had been adapted for me, so that if you lifted up the insole, there was a little hollow in the heel with specially cut slots for storing SIM cards and memory chips. There was also a USB stick that Campbell said had the memory capacity of half a dozen laptops, so I could copy the whole contents of someone else's computer if I needed to. It slotted neatly into the back of the other heel and could be easily pulled out without anyone noticing. He stressed the importance of removing the SIMs every night.

Campbell spent the rest of the afternoon explaining how to install spyware into someone else's computer, giving me a web address where I could download a bit of software that would track incoming and outgoing mail on someone else's account. He showed me how to install the download and activate it where the computer's user would never find it. He also backed up the software on my memory stick, so I had the spyware with me if I couldn't get an Internet connection.

There was lots of other stuff I would have to learn in due course, he told me: code-breaking, surveillance techniques, lock-picking and the rest.

After we'd finally been through the IT business, Campbell hauled a briefcase up on to the desk.

"Time for a bit of fun," he said. "I know it all looks a bit Secret Squirrel, but some of it might be useful."

"A bit what?" I asked, laughing.

"Secret Squirrel." He smiled. "You're too young to remember, I suppose. He was a sixties cartoon squirrel who was a spy. *He's got tricks up his sleeve...*" Campbell began to sing the theme tune in his nasal voice. "*Most bad guys won't believe, a bulletproof coat, a cannon hat, a machine-gun cane with a rat-tat-tat-tat!"* He mimed the machine-gun cane, tapping his foot to make the rat-a-tat. It was the most animated he'd been all afternoon.

There was a cough from behind us.

"Glad to see you're having fun, chaps," Sandy Napier said.

Hamish spun round.

"Commander Napier," he gulped, his mouth opening and shutting like a decked fish. "Yes, er, I was just showing Eddie some of our surveillance gear, sir."

Napier grinned and tapped the glass of his diver's watch.

"Well, get on with it, man, we're running out of time. We've got to get Eddie kitted out yet, and I'm gasping for a drink. You'll be joining us later, of course, Eddie?"

"Yeah, I mean, yes, sir." I didn't have a clue what I was meant to call him. Of everyone I'd met so far, Napier was the one who scared me most.

"Thanks," I added, and Napier left.

"If in doubt, always call him sir," Campbell offered helpfully. He rested the briefcase on the bench and opened it. The box of tricks included an ordinary-looking digital watch that could record up to eight hours of conversation in a five-metre radius. It had a push button that operated the stopwatch and also set off the voice recorder. There were also several magnetic tags that would fit inside the petrol cap or under the exhaust of a car to track it on a phone or a laptop. He showed me some small magnetic microphones that I could use to bug rooms. Said I'd be needing them pretty much from the off.

I nodded, impressed.

Campbell snapped the case shut. "Boys' toys," he said, then tapped his nose with his index finger. "I think you have an appointment with a lady next."

TEN

"Sorry I'm late, Eddie." Her hair was black and glossy, tied back in a ponytail, and she was wearing less make-up than when I'd last seen her. She wore jeans and a crisp, fitted white shirt over a vest.

She was stunning.

"Anna," she said, holding out her hand. I remembered the firmness of her handshake and the direct look in her eyes. The dimple when she smiled.

"I remember," I said. "From the model agency."

She smiled and raised an eyebrow as if she wasn't sure whether or not I was being serious.

"Looks like you've been through the mill." She touched my cheek in a matter-of-fact way. I flinched instinctively, and she drew away. I cursed inwardly. I wished she'd put her hand back and touch my face again. Touch anything she wanted.

"I remember my induction week well," she said. "I think that bloody sadist Jim Owen enjoyed putting me through it even more than usual, pervert that he is."

"You mean…?" The penny was beginning to drop. "You work as…"

"Yup, me too. You didn't think I really worked for that cheapo modelling outfit, did you?"

"Well, I…" I started to make excuses.

"Sugacubes Modelling Agency," Anna squeaked in a sing-song voice, mimicking a receptionist answering the phone. "Can I help you?" She looked at me, questioning.

"Of course I didn't," I lied. "I knew it was a front."

Anna gave me the benefit of the doubt. "Help me in with these things, will you?"

I went to the door of the office and helped her carry a dozen stuffed carrier bags and a clothes rail full of trousers, shirts and suits.

"It's taken me all day, two parking tickets and a near clamping to put this lot together for you," she said.

"How did you avoid the clamp?"

Anna put her hands on her hips and looked at me.

"How do you think?"

"Feminine charm?" I tried.

"Yeah, right." She grinned. "Actually, I broke the traffic warden's neck with a single blow." She laughed, mimed a karate chop across my own neck, then started unpacking the bags. She pulled out T-shirts, socks, pants and sweaters, and stacked them on the table.

"These all for me?" I asked incredulously as the pile grew.

"We'll see what looks right on you and ditch the rest," she said.

She considered me for a moment.

"Hm, Gap's OK," she said, feeling the edge of the grey hoodie I was wearing. "Nice and anonymous. But I think we want to go upmarket a bit and lose the skateboard labels."

"I like this Vans shirt," I said defensively. "I've had it for years."

"Looks like you haven't taken it off for years," Anna said, grinning. "C'mon, try some of these on."

She handed me a navy-blue Lacoste polo shirt and a pair of jeans. I looked around for somewhere to change, but there was nowhere to hide and Anna didn't bat an eyelid as I stripped down to my pants and put on the clothes.

"Better," she said, looking me up and down. "Pretty good."

She threw me more shirts: Paul Smith, Ralph Lauren, some soft knitwear, then deck shoes, Nike trainers and a pair of suede desert boots. I tried on other combinations and became less embarrassed at standing half naked in front of this hot-looking woman.

"I think it's all working, Eddie," she said. "You wear clothes well. But I'll take back the Calvin Klein stuff because it makes you look a bit gay."

"Cheers," I said.

"No, gay in a good way." She laughed. "It's just that I want you looking a bit rougher and tougher for this gig, a bit more casual. Queeny's not going to go down all that well."

"So how do I look now?" I asked. I had on a pair of washed-out vintage Levi's, deck shoes, a checked, short-sleeved Ralph Lauren shirt and a navy Aquascutum windcheater.

"Cool," she said, handing me some aviator sunnies. "Yeah, cool and a bit preppy. Possibly a bit indie band. Like a South London boy who spends all his wages on clobber *should* look. You look like Eddie Savage."

"I'll take that as a compliment."

"I chose them, you cheeky bugger," she said. She paused for a moment. "But your hair's still a bit too floppy."

"Floppy?" Defensive, my hand went to my fringe.

"Did I say floppy?" She grinned. "Sorry, I meant it looks a mess. We'll sort that out next."

A minute later she was pushing me down into an office chair with a scarf around my neck and snipping away at my hair with small scissors. After ten minutes she rolled the chair in front of a mirror and tousled my hair with her fingers.

"Gives it a bit more texture," she explained, admiring her work. She put her hands on my shoulders and squeezed.

"Like it?" she asked.

I looked in the mirror at my battered face and at the new, shorter hair. I had to admit, it did look good.

Rougher, tougher.

"Yeah, I like it."

"Good. OK, let's pack this lot away." Anna ruffled the top of my head again. "The boss wants to see us for a drink."

*　　*　　*

Sandy Napier gathered everyone together in the library: Ian Baylis, Oliver, Jim, Hamish, Anna and one or two other faces I had seen during the past few days. Everyone was drinking red or white wine except Sandy Napier and Jim the Pitbull, who drank whisky.

I chose white and regretted it; it wasn't very cold and tasted of old wood. After the first glass I switched to red, which wasn't much better, but I drank it anyway. I stuck by Anna and we chatted for a bit. Not only was she great-looking and had a sense of humour but, stupidly, I felt protected by her. I don't know why, she was hardly maternal. Maybe it was just the feminine vibe I got from her after living in a violent, sweaty world of blokes for a week.

Maybe it was just that I fancied her to bits and would have crawled over broken glass just to drink her bathwater.

Of course, all the other blokes tried it on with her in different ways. Ian Baylis came over and made what he thought were smart remarks, but which just made him look like the sexist wanker he was. His head wobbled a bit when he talked at her. Jim the Pitbull flexed his muscles and reminded her of how bendy she had been when she did her assault course. He looked like he might be about to drop and do some push-ups to try and impress her. Campbell the techno spod took a different approach and made silly jokes at the level of his Secret Squirrel song on the assumption that making a girl laugh was half the battle. He mostly chuckled at the jokes himself, snorting when he laughed.

Cool.

Only Sandy Napier stood back. He acted as if talking to girlies was a bit shallow. Or maybe they weren't his thing. Given the options available to Anna, I started to reckon I wasn't such a bad choice. I think the wine was getting to me. Just as I was fantasizing about my chances, Sandy Napier tapped his glass with a pen and called for silence.

"Thanks for coming, everyone," he announced. "I'm not going to say much. As most of you know, I never do. I just wanted to give a few words of welcome to our new recruit, Eddie Savage. Eddie is the youngest operative we have ever taken on – indeed, I have bent the rules backwards to make it possible. It was a risk, and I am glad to say that my gamble shows early signs of paying off."

I glanced over at Ian Baylis, who looked determinedly straight ahead. Anna smiled at me and winked. Napier continued.

"In terms of our organization, I would like to remind you all that Eddie does not become strictly legal for a while, so for most purposes he doesn't actually exist. Given that, I hope that you will all give Eddie what you can in terms of support and protection. That's all. I'm sure you'll join me in wishing Eddie all the best."

He raised his glass.

"Eddie Savage."

That's rich, I thought. I'm putting my cock on the block and, like Steve, I don't actually exist.

"Eddie Savage," they chanted.

ELEVEN

Once Sandy Napier had gone back to London, Ian Baylis rallied the troops together to go to the pub. We piled into a couple of official Jags and raced down the country lanes the mile or so to the village. Baylis and Jim were driving, and no one seemed too concerned about the amount they had already drunk. I guess they had a Get Out of Jail Free card.

I sat in the back and engineered it so that I was next to Anna. I already felt flushed with the wine, and the pressure of her body against mine on the back seat made me breathless. I opened the widow a gnat's.

In the pub they bought round after round and, although I was a bit slower than the rest, I must have had four pints of lager. On top of the wine, I was feeling quite pissed. There was lots of laughing and joshing, but I kept pretty quiet. I didn't want to make a prat of myself and, in particular, didn't want to behave like a prat in front of Anna.

"You're quiet," she said, sipping a pint of lager with

the best of them and with no apparent effect.

"It's been a busy week," I replied.

She smiled and patted my leg. I noticed the slight unevenness of her white teeth that made her lip curl sexily when she smiled.

Then it was all off for a curry in one of those dodgy Indians you find in villages all over the country. More beer and a chicken jalfrezi. I don't remember much about it, except that it was probably the worst curry I have ever eaten.

On the way back, I sat next to Anna again. She was wedged between me and Baylis, and as the car swerved round the country lanes, gravity pushed her against me, so close that her hair flew across my face and I could smell her faint perfume above the aroma of beer and fags in the car. As the car banked violently again, she steadied herself and her hand slipped accidentally across my leg into my crotch.

"Sorry, Eddie," she said, pulling away quickly.

"Don't mention it." I swallowed hard. She leant forwards and shouted at the Pitbull in the driving seat.

"Jim, will you stop driving like a complete see-you-next-Tuesday? Some of us have the rest of our lives to look forward to."

"Sorry, love," he said. "Bit fast for the girls in the back, is it?"

"Put a sock in it, Jim, you sheep-shagger," I said, half joking and cocky with the booze, "or I'll have to give you another slap."

Jim laughed. No offence taken. Anna laughed too,

which pleased me a lot, and Jim slowed down a little.

I don't remember much about going to bed. It was dark back at base and there were slaps on the back and drunken goodbyes and a kiss on the cheek from Anna. I remember crunching back across the gravel, hitting my bunk and closing my eyes. The room spun around for a bit, but I managed to hold on to the contents of my guts – which might have been a bad idea because as soon as I drifted off, I started to dream…

I was in a park somewhere. Greenwich? It was hot and sunny. My mum was there too and Steve, drinking cans of Stella: wife-beater. We were having a picnic and Anna was with us, lying in the sun in a bikini, looking pretty fit. I was feeling embarrassed because I was wearing these stupid swimming trunks, like Borat's Mankini, and I had trouble keeping my wedding tackle contained.

The sky seemed to darken over, as if there was a thunderstorm coming, and dogs from all over the park began to circle our picnic. Steve was drunk and started trying it on with Anna and she was doing her best to push him away, and the more she did, the more persistent he got. He pulled at her bikini top until it came off and she shouted at him. He wouldn't leave her alone, so I threw myself on him, rolled him over and began to smash my fist into his face again and again, blood spraying everywhere.

Then I noticed that he wasn't resisting and that my fist seemed to sink into his head. Like punching an overripe melon. I pulled my fist away and saw that his face was completely pushed in, dead and grey, filled with maggots, and his body was swollen and bloated as if it had been in the water for weeks.

I could hear my mum screaming and I looked around to where she was sitting, surrounded by dogs: Alsatians and mastiffs, all growling, and eating whatever they could find. Then my mum screamed louder as a big dog bit the sleeve of her cardigan and tore at it. I jumped up and tried to pull the dogs away, but they snapped and snarled, gnashing and baring their teeth, biting at her face, biting my hands.

Two dogs had broken away and were doing something to Steve's body. As I got closer I could see that they had torn his bloated stomach open and were eating his entrails, dragging out lengths of intestine on to the grass, their teeth and gums covered in his blood.

Then I saw Anna raise her head from Steve's body. She was on all fours and her mouth was covered in blood, as if she had been eating him too, the blood dripping down from her chin all over her naked—

For a split second I didn't know if I was still dreaming. The door smashed in and I was dragged from my bed in the darkness. A hand slapped gaffer tape across my mouth and someone blindfolded me. I was dragged away down the corridor. I could feel the shiny lino under my feet, and then the gravel as I was manhandled out of the building. There were no voices. Just grunts of effort as various hands lifted and pulled me this way and that, tying me up. The night air was damp and I could hear an engine running. I felt cold metal. I was bundled into the boot of the car. The smell of petrol. It became darker, the sounds muffled as the door of the boot was slammed and the car roared off.

What the—?

How could they let this happen to me? My heart was pounding and the adrenalin seemed to clear my head a little. I tried to think rationally. This place was supposed to be high security, yet someone – several people – had just dragged me from my bed. Unless it was someone on the inside? What was this? A hostage-taking? A kneecapping?

A warning not to get involved?

I bumped up and down in the boot, wrestling against the ropes around my wrists as the car sped along the lanes and round corners. Finally it stopped, and the momentum threw me against the back of the boot. I hit my head on something sharp. If I hadn't been fully awake before, I was now.

I heard voices, muffled, and then the boot opened. I was pulled out again. My feet were bare and I was only wearing a T-shirt and boxers. The night air felt chilly and I could smell woodland. I heard a wooden door creak open and I was led into some kind of building.

It smelt of hut: damp canvas, sawdust, wood preserver.

I was pushed down into a chair, and a light punch in the guts helped me sit down. I thought I was going to chuck up. The gaffer tape was ripped off and the nausea subsided.

"What's your name?" a voice came from the darkness. A voice I didn't recognize.

"Eddie Savage."

"What's your brother's name, Eddie?"

"I … I don't have a brother."

"You sure?" the voice said. "You don't seem too sure."

"I am sure."

"Tell me again, about your brother."

"I don't have a brother," I insisted.

"What about Steve?" the voice said, gloating.

"I don't know any Steve," I said.

"What's your middle name?" The voice came closer, hoarser, and I could smell alcohol on its breath.

"Arthur."

"After your brother?"

"No, after my granddad." I desperately tried to remember the details of my cover.

"So what's your brother's granddad's name?"

"Arthur." Shit. No. "I haven't got a brother."

The voice jeered and another voice joined in. Suddenly the chair was kicked from under me and I felt cold metal against my neck.

This is it, I thought. I've blown it and now I'm dead meat.

Terrified, I felt a tug at the waistband of my boxers. My mind reeled at the possibilities of the torture that might follow. Then I felt something wet splash on my face, heard the gurgle of an aerosol and smelt something perfumed, soapy and unmistakeable.

I was being drenched in beer and covered in shaving foam.

Moments later, with much joshing and beery laughter, I was bundled back into the boot of the car and driven a short way down the lane. Then I was pulled from the boot, dumped on a grass verge and left as the car sped off.

"You bastards!" I screamed after the car.

It took only a few seconds to wriggle my hands free and pull off the blindfold. I untied my feet, which were filthy. I was half naked, and my underwear was torn. Soaked in beer, ketchup, aftershave and shaving foam. Alone in a country lane in the middle of the night. The victim of some stupid initiation ritual.

"Perverts!" I screamed again, for good measure, though they were long gone.

I began to walk. Twenty minutes later the lights of the building appeared between the trees. The guard on the gate let me through with a nod. He'd clearly been expecting me. The clock on the wall of his hut made it nearly three-thirty.

I found my way to my room and went straight into the bathroom. As well as my already bashed-up face I had a fresh cut on my forehead, and not only did I stink like a dead ferret, but my face had been blackened with boot polish. I looked like I had been camouflaged to go on some mad night manoeuvre up the Amazon, smelling of aftershave, shaving foam, ketchup and beer to attract the natives and the flies.

I got into the shower and turned it up as hot as I could stand. As the needles of scalding water stabbed my shoulders I scrubbed at my face and body, trying to remove all the boot polish and the lingering smells. Trying to wash away the stains of my shame.

The horror of having been so comprehensively done over would be hard to live down. My cover had cracked under pressure. I stepped into the bedroom, naked. Shaken, but clean.

"What kept you?" The voice came from the half-light.

From my bed.

"Anna?"

She sat up and pulled the covers back, making room for me beside her.

"In you get," she said.

TWELVE

I woke up early, the sun already shining through the window. I woke up alone: she was gone. Only the indentation on the pillow and the light smell of perfume told me that she had ever been there.

Tony Morris came and picked me up at about ten-thirty. No one else was there to see me off. Apparently they'd all gone back to London already. I was quickly realizing that there was no sentimentality in this game. Anna hadn't even said goodbye, or left a note. What Tony had said about not getting too close to anybody, particularly other operatives, clearly held true. A note would have been concrete evidence of closeness.

I would have to adjust my way of thinking.

As I threw my bag in the boot, I had a momentary flashback to the small hours of the night before.

I got into the car. Tony looked genuinely pleased to see me.

"How are you, kid?" he said, throwing an arm around my neck and pulling me to him in a hug. "The boss said you did brilliantly." He squeezed tighter. "I'm really chuffed, Eddie."

"Yeah, it wasn't bad." My new name was beginning to sound normal to me already. "I could have put up with being brain-damaged by Baylis and near crippled by that Welsh sadist. But being abducted, terrorized and dropped in the woods with my pants round my ankles in the middle of the night was pushing it a bit. I felt like I'd been raped."

Tony's face dropped.

"Oh, they didn't, did they?" He looked pained.

"Well, not raped *exactly*…" I admitted.

"I thought they'd stopped that initiation stuff years ago. Boot polish and shaving cream all over, was it?"

I nodded. "Plus ketchup, beer, aftershave, gravy and possibly piss."

Tony shook his head. He pulled away and started off along the drive. "Who was it?"

"I didn't really see," I said. "But I suspect Ian Baylis was behind it. He still doesn't like me. There was another voice I didn't recognize – maybe that bloke Oliver?"

"Hmm. Could be. He's the man of a thousand voices, cracking mimic. Although it could have been any of them. Possibly people you haven't even met."

"OK," I said. "So if it's just an initiation prank, why did they scare me shitless? I thought I was going to be decapitated or something."

Tony pulled out on to the main road. "The charitable view is that they were just testing your cover under stress. Especially if you'd had a skinful."

"Nice of them to be so concerned," I muttered.

"Well, you can't always choose when your story's going to be tested," Tony said. "It's quite likely to take you by surprise."

"So why did they keep going on about my brother?" I asked.

"Did they?"

"Yes, every other question. Trying to catch me out."

Tony sighed. "Well, the *uncharitable* view…"

"Yes?"

"Is that Steve wasn't universally popular. And you might be taking a bit of stick for it."

"Great." Instinctively I felt protective of Steve. "Now you tell me. Why?"

"Everything I've told you so far has been true," Tony assured me. "He was a hero. But that's just it … the gong and everything, makes people jealous. Especially when they feel they've been working just as hard, or in equally dangerous conditions. And Steve went about stuff his own way. On his own. Which can make people resentful, like they're not being trusted or kept in the know."

"But he got results, right?"

"Sure," Tony said evasively. "On his terms."

"I see."

"I just thought you should know." Tony looked across at me.

"Cheers," I said. "Better late than never."

"So you got back all right afterwards?" Tony asked, changing the subject back to me.

"Yeah, half naked and covered in cack, but alive."

"Good, and you got cleaned up OK, and got some rest?" Tony threw me a sideways glance.

"Yeah, I was fine once I'd had a shower and got into bed," I said, feeling myself blush.

"Good." Tony indicated to overtake a slow old lady.

I put my head back on the headrest and shut my eyes, smiling at the memory: remembering a faster, younger one.

We got back to Deptford around lunchtime. Tony decided to push on into Greenwich and we drove up the hill and parked outside a nice old pub in the middle of a row of Georgian houses. Well, Tony told me they were Georgian. I should take notice of that kind of detail, he said. It can come in handy.

I still felt a bit wobbly from the night before, but I'd had a kip in the car and by the time Tony had forced a pint and a sausage baguette down me, I felt as right as rain.

"So, you still all right about taking on this job?" Tony wiped a smear of ketchup and mustard from the corner of his mouth. I shielded my eyes from the sun, which beat down brightly into the beer garden. Tony was wearing mirrored sunnies and it was hard to read his expression.

"Yeah, I guess," I said.

"You don't sound too keen."

I paused for a second, picking my words. "It's been quite a week," I said. "I've had to change the way I think about one or two things."

Tony nodded.

"Learned to trust no one," I said, then paused again. "And not to take anything or anyone on face value …

even my own brother," I added.

"Sure," Tony said, "that's spot on. So?"

"So, it's made me view the world as a pretty dark place."

Tony looked into his pint for a moment as if it were a crystal ball. "That much darker than before?" he asked. "Vagrant, alcoholic father, no money, dead brother?"

I looked up at the bright blue sky. Something in me had always been able to make a blue sky look black. "No, not that much darker, I guess."

"So, you got serious doubts?" Tony peered at me over the top of his specs.

"It's a bit late to back out," I pointed out. "Now I know the nature of the game."

"It's not too late yet," Tony said. "But I agree, it wouldn't look good for any of us to try and get you out now."

"So, I'm in."

"Good man." Tony smiled. "I can give you this then." He put his hand out across the table and gave me a memory stick.

"What's that?" I asked.

"Some of Steve's stuff," he said. "You don't have to use it, but it might give you a bit of insight, you know, into what 'James Boyle' was up to." He reached over and squeezed my shoulder, then drained what was left of his Guinness and lifted up his sunglasses. "One thing, mate," he said. "You can trust *me*."

"Can I?"

"Yes," he said. And I believed him.

*   *   *

Tony dropped me off at the flat after lunch. He said I should spend the weekend relaxing, and get to know the apartment and the area. Get up to speed with my new computers and phone before starting the job on Monday.

A new term.

I reminded myself of the codes and let myself in. The apartment still smelt brand new. My stuff was all there and the fridge had been filled in my absence. There was a good-luck card from Tony and a bottle of champagne. He really was looking after me. He'd also left a handful of black notebooks on the table. *Moleskine*, the label said, as used by Ernest Hemingway, Picasso and Bruce Chatwin, whoever he was. Tony had written in his note, "Use them, then get them back to me. Store in a safe place." I supposed it was up to me to find my own safe place – even Tony didn't want to know where it was.

I wandered around the apartment aimlessly for a few minutes, stared out of the big windows across at Canary Wharf, then took a leak in the brand-new toilet, like a dog marking its territory.

I got a beer from the fridge, enjoying the fact that I could. Then I walked over to the bedroom and lay back on the big, white bed, which smelt fresh and clean. I pointed the remote at the widescreen and a black-and-white movie came on. I caught a shot of Piccadilly Circus, then a sign that said *New Scotland Yard*. A police officer was talking to a woman wearing a great big bow and one of those ugly hats they wore back then.

"You're quate rate, madam," he said in a squeaky,

old-film voice, *"it's true that the air ministry has a new thing thet quate a few people are interested in, but they're puzzitive thet no papers are missing thet would be any use to a spy…"*

I laughed.

The next scene was in the London Palladium, where a greasy-looking bloke with a pencil moustache asked the memory man on stage, *"Look here! What* are *the Thirty-Nine Steps?"*

And the memory man went into a kind of trance and said, *"The Thirty-Nine Steps is an organization of spies, collecting information on behalf of the foreign office…"* Then he got shot by some villain in the balcony with a cap gun.

I sipped my beer and chuckled at the simplicity of it all. I didn't find out what happened in the end, because by the time the old jazz-band music kicked in, I was nodding off into a deep and dreamless sleep.

II

Sophie

THIRTEEN

It didn't take long to spot Sophie Kelly.

She was surrounded by a group of girls. Good-looking girls like her usually hang around with a couple of rough-looking ones who won't draw the attention away from the main attraction. But the girls surrounding Sophie Kelly weren't exactly dogs either: they were all well-dressed with good haircuts and a kind of polish you rarely see in my patch of South London. Taken individually, you would probably fancy any one of them, but together they all looked a bit ordinary compared with Sophie. She was naturally blonde, while the rest of them had expensive highlights or shiny brown curls. She wasn't small – she must have been five eight or five nine – and not thin either. She had quite an old-fashioned figure. Curvy. The others came in various shapes and sizes. There was a snotty-looking Indian beauty and a very tall, unsmiling black girl who could have been a tennis player or a model.

Sophie seemed to glow a bit brighter than the others, too. Her conversation looked animated and lively, and there were laughs whenever she said anything. It was as if she had a natural aura of celebrity about her.

I didn't gawp, of course. I used some of my newly learnt field craft to observe from afar, to keep a distance and remain unobtrusive.

I had caught the DLR from Deptford Bridge, then hopped on a bus at Lewisham Station that took me down towards Bromley, in the posher part of the suburbs. Even though the bus stopped directly outside Marlowe Sixth Form College, I got off a couple of stops early. I didn't want anyone to see me arrive at the gates. In fact I circled around the block and approached the college from the opposite direction. Quite a few of the students arrived in cars, and I was surprised by the number of Minis, Golfs and Beetle convertibles in the small car park. I didn't attract any attention: I was underdressed in jeans, a charcoal grey sweatshirt and black suede skate shoes, carrying a backpack that held my phone, laptop and some books. The idea was to blend in with the background.

Everyone was gathered in the large yard at the rear of the college building. It was the first day of term and students clustered in pairs and groups. The noise of their chatter was loud in the air, with that excitement that people have catching up after their holidays. I did a circuit of the yard but looking around vaguely, taking in all the groups, acting as if I was looking for someone. All the while I kept Sophie Kelly and her gang, all leggings, hair and Ugg boots, firmly in my sights.

Another unusual thing about them was that there were no males hanging around. Boys circled and watched, but didn't join in. I felt as if I was watching some kind of wildlife documentary. The girls surrounding Sophie Kelly knew the boys were circling and made gestures: playing with their hair, checking their lipgloss, putting their hands behind their heads, world-weary, as if they were already bored by the day. The looks they flashed at nearby males did nothing to encourage an approach. They were all protecting their queen bee.

Getting to know Sophie Kelly was already looking more difficult than I had anticipated.

"Sorry…" I'd stepped back straight onto someone's foot. I automatically apologized, but whoever was behind me must have virtually been breathing down my neck. I turned to see a geeky-looking bloke with a big head of curly hair just short of an afro.

"No worries," he said, grinning. "The Kelly Gang." He nodded towards the group of girls and I was instantly mad at myself. So much for my subtle surveillance – I had already been caught watching by someone watching me.

"You can look, but don't touch," the Hairdo continued.

"Oh, right."

"You're new," he said. "Benjy Fwench." He obviously had a problem with his Rs. He held out his hand for me to shake. I did and it felt limp and slightly damp, like a fish.

"Eddie Savage," I replied. "Yes, I am new."

"You'll be needing a friend to show you around then," Benjy French continued, as if I had no choice in the matter. "What subjects are you doing?"

"IT, Art History and French." I resisted the urge to say *Fwench.*

"Interesting choices," he said. "You'll be doing IT with me."

"What are the chances?"

Benjy grinned, uncertain as to whether or not I was being sarcastic.

"Best mosey on in then," he said finally. "It's first session."

Benjy French made sure he sat next to me during IT. Other lads pushed and jostled him on the way in, taking the piss and ruffling his curly hair. He was clearly the butt of plenty of jokes but seemed to accept his position in life, good-naturedly telling the others to naff off.

Wherever you go, it's always the needy freaks who run up and try to make friends first. They're either the ones that no one else likes, or they have worn out all their other friendships by being weird and demanding. They've tried everyone else, so you're next in line. Fresh meat.

I tend to think that people who are desperate to be your friend are best avoided, so although I felt a bit cruel, I tried to shake him off at the first break. But Benjy wasn't having it and followed me to the canteen, stuck like glue. I worried that his presence was already cramping my style – but then no one else had so much as looked at me, let alone spoken to me, so I decided Benjy French was a good enough place to start my enquiries. I grabbed a coffee and he sat himself down next to me, sucking from a bottle of water like a thirsty baby.

"First impressions?" he said, glancing around the canteen. It looked pretty ordinary to me: a few vending machines, some tables, a sandwich bar. Sophie Kelly and a couple of her girls were sitting over on the other side.

"Yeah, pretty good," I said, not wishing to offend.

"So, how come you're starting this year?" Benjy asked.

"I had a gap in my education," I said honestly. "A death in the family. I took time out, then got a place here."

"Sorry about that," said Benjy, looking at me sideways. He shut up for a moment, as if he was worried he might have upset me. I used his silence to take the initiative.

"So, what's the big deal with Sophie Kelly then?" I asked, nodding in her general direction.

"Don't you know?" Benjy almost squeaked, his voice then dropping to a conspiratorial whisper. "Her old man is supposed to be some major villain. Serious robberies, drugs, fraud ... the lot."

The way Benjy struggled with his Rs made the list sound almost comical and I had to stop myself from smiling. His voice got lower still. "He gets people sorted ... you know, blown away."

I shrugged as if to say no, I didn't know. Of course, I had done some background reading on Sophie Kelly's family, but it was best to act ignorant.

"Sweet," I said. "So does she have a boyfriend?"

Benjy snorted. "Apparently there was one, a couple of years ago. The rumour was he was thrown off a multi-storey car park for trying to get her bra off."

Bwa... I had to bite my lip.

"So, even if she was interested in getting a bloke," Benjy continued, "no one would go near her for fear of her old man."

I glanced up and saw that Sophie Kelly was looking directly at me from across the room. My stomach lurched a little as I felt I'd been caught in the headlights. I attempted a tight smile and she turned away again. I kept looking for a moment longer.

She really did have a fantastic figure. Like I said, curvy. I wondered whether it would be worth the risk of the multi-storey…

FOURTEEN

I got back to Deptford about five. It had been my first day on the job and I thought I should start writing up my notes. I opened up a blank page in one of the new notebooks and stared at it for a while. Then fiddled with a pen and looked at the page a little longer. I didn't know where to start.

I had worked out a hidey-hole in the floor of the closet in my bedroom by levering up a plank that opened into a cable duct. There was a good space down there and once I had replaced the square of carpet over it, I reckoned it was pretty secure.

I lifted the carpet and pulled up the plank. Underneath were spare SIM cards and memory cards, my false passport and ID, and the memory stick that Tony Morris had given me. I plugged it into the laptop and double-clicked on the icon. There were several MP3 files, labelled *Classified* and dated two or three years ago. I clicked on the first.

My brother's voice.

It was a verbal account, a bit monotonous, but Steve's voice. I tried to concentrate on what he was saying, but all I could hear was the sound of him. I spooled the clip back to the start and listened again.

"Came back to Belfast a week before the start of term. Just to get into the swing of things, do some groundwork before the rest of the mob gets back to Queen's. The chemical engineering course attracts all the nutters and misfits… The chemists spend more time in the pub than students on any other course, and the ones who aren't learning to make explosives seem to be intent on making stuff to blow their minds…"

I scrolled forwards a bit.

"They've bought my cover as a mature research student on secondment from Royal Holloway. It all fits with what they know about London: my flat in Kilburn; my sympathy for the cause. My accent is pretty much London, but my 'parents' are Irish. I'm James Boyle to them. Jimmy. It all adds up, and none of them seem to be the suspicious type … I hope."

He went on to describe how he had gone out for an evening with the Irish guys on his corridor, Dessie and Paul. How they had taken him up to a pub in the Falls Road area:

"Paul ordered Guinnesses all round and we sat at a formica-topped table at the back of the bar by the pool table. Dessie racked up a game and broke. Paul never took his eyes off me. I was getting pretty uncomfortable. I sipped Guinness I didn't want, just to stop my mouth from being dry. This was all happening too soon. Paul finally spoke, told me that Dessie had seen me hanging around the college during the holidays.

'Sniffing around,' he said.

I repeated my story that I had come back early to revise for exams. Paul nodded and didn't say anything else, which made me more nervous. I needed a leak badly and went out to the toilets.

I heard the toilet door swing open behind me and felt the heavy thump of a fist on the back of my head.

I dropped forwards and hit my nose on the low windowsill above the urinal. Some training kicked in and I banged a leg out as I fell, catching Paul in the shin and bringing him down with me. We wrestled on the slippery tiled floor but he had the better of me. I was on my back and he held me by the collar and cracked my head against the floor.

'I don't feckin' believe you!' he spat into my face, and I could smell and taste the beer, the fags and the aggression on his breath.

I tried to blink my mind clear through the drink and the throb from the back of my head.

'I'm straight, I tell you. I'm feckin' straight.'

Paul punched me in the mouth and my head went back against the tiles again. I tasted blood. I hadn't expected everything to happen so quickly. It was supposed to have taken me months to get this far into their organization. I had to think fast. I didn't want to fight back too hard and reveal my training but I had no time to spare. I would have to play my joker now, or…"

The sound clip finished. I clicked on to the next one, my heart pounding. I felt sick just hearing about it. I sat on the edge of the bed listening to Steve getting it off his chest. How he had shown Paul his membership to The Harp Club in London and finally convinced them he was on their side. I scrolled forward again.

"Dessie came round the following morning and apologized: said that taking me up to the Falls was the only way to test me. To put me through the trial by fire with that animal Paul.

'What's with the man?' I asked. Dessie said he's got IRA genes that stretch back to Michael Collins, that he's spent years inside and on the run in Spain. He's only here now under an alias. The authorities know, but he has protection in some very high places. I need to work on finding out his real ID. He could be pivotal to cracking this one.

I asked Dessie what Paul was wanted for – what he'd done. Dessie said it was more a case of what Paul hadn't done. It was a very short list. I asked what might have happened if I hadn't belonged to The Harp.

Dessie chuckled grimly. Said he'd probably have cut my ears off first for fun, then kneecapped me with a power drill, castrated me and cut my throat with a bread knife before burying bits of my dismembered body all over the county. It made me feel a bit sick, as I think he was only partly joking, telling me in case there was any further doubt about whose side I was on.

And of course, I *was* on the wrong side."

Whatever side that was, Steve was a cool customer.

I looked again at my blank page. A tear had rolled down my nose and onto the paper. Hearing his voice again, I guess. What I was up to seemed so childish compared with the stuff Steve was talking about, but you had to start somewhere. I relived the moments of the day ... arriving at Marlowe College, surveying the yard, meeting Benjy French and locating Sophie Kelly.

I began to write.

FIFTEEN

Donnie did the pick-up at eight.

If he cut through the back of Sidcup and Chislehurst, avoiding the main arteries into town, he should make it by nine.

He got there for eight, but Her Ladyship kept him waiting a good ten minutes, which would put the pressure on if she wanted to be on time. Naturally, he forgave her everything when she got in the car. She gave him the old charm offensive as she climbed into the Merc: the white smile, the baby blues and a flash of cleavage. She always smelt so good too. Donnie breathed in her perfume and was as helpless as a kitten.

She apologized for being late and for the fact that her car was in the garage after her latest ding. Donnie didn't know how the boss put up with it. She'd only been driving a few months and had already mashed up a new Mini. But, it seemed, everyone forgave Sophie everything. Always had.

Donnie hadn't been so forgiving of Donna, his own daughter. He'd been a bit pissed off when she got herself tubbed up at sixteen. The drug habit and the black boyfriend hadn't helped matters, in Donnie's view. Sophie was cut from a different cloth altogether. Donnie didn't even think of her as the same species as his own daughter, never once connecting the way Donna had turned out with his own heavy-handed parenting skills and the black eyes he'd inflicted on his ex.

Donnie checked the rear-view mirror. Sophie looked comfortable in the back, leafing through a copy of Vogue, her blonde hair caught in the sunlight streaking in through the window.

The rest of his day would not be quite so pretty, he thought. Once he'd dropped Sophie off, he was going on to Croydon. He had some goods to pick up from one of their offices down there. Then there was the route up through South Norwood and Crystal Palace, picking up sums of money that were owing by some of their smaller-scale clients. The kinds of sums that generally took a smack in the mouth or a kick in the Jacobs to extract.

At 8.55 a.m. precisely, Donnie pulled up outside Marlowe Sixth Form College. Sophie asked him to drive on a bit, said she didn't want to be seen getting out of one of her dad's cars. Donnie felt a small pang of hurt: perhaps she didn't want to be seen being driven by him. The pain was soon forgotten, however, as Sophie leant forwards, thanked him and kissed him on the cheek before climbing out.

Donnie felt himself blush and unleashed a rare smile, revealing a mouthful of capped and broken teeth. He didn't smile very often. Which was probably a good thing.

At the end of my first week at Marlowe I got off the bus at the stop just past the college so as not to fall into a routine. The bus stop was occupied by a big, navy-blue Mercedes and the bus had to pull alongside to let passengers off, blocking the car in.

The car horn blared and the bus driver hooted back. The electric window of the car slid down and the big bloke inside told the bus driver to piss off. I hopped off the bus while the altercation continued and almost bumped right into Sophie Kelly, who had just got out of the Mercedes. She saw me and looked embarrassed, turned and walked back towards the college. I followed a couple of steps behind her. She looked as good from behind as she did from the front.

I had about a hundred paces to make up my mind.

If only she'd drop a hanky or a book or something naff like that, then I'd have an excuse. But she didn't, sod it. And in one of those mad moments, I just dived in. I quickened my step and caught up with her.

"Your taxi driver looked a bit hairy," I said, jerking my thumb back to where she'd been dropped off.

She barely looked at me but smiled, reddening, which I liked.

"Yeah," she said. "Really embarrassing."

I pressed on. "I'm new this term. I think we're in the same Art History group."

"Yeah, I think so." This was going well.

The conversation would have ended there, but the gates were getting closer and any minute Sophie Kelly would be swallowed by her gaggle of protective bitches. This was a rare gap in the defence.

So I took it.

"I was wondering if you'd like to go out some time?"

I couldn't believe it myself as the words tumbled out. Maybe it was easier to say because I was hiding behind a mask. It didn't feel like it was me who was saying it. A couple of months earlier I would never have dared. My words had an instant effect. Sophie stopped dead and looked at me.

"Are you asking me on a date?"

"Well, I don't really know anyone here," I began to explain. "And you look really nice."

She smiled. I was encouraged.

"Better than nice," I said.

Sophie burst into a laugh and put a hand over her mouth. "You *are*," she said. "You're asking me out!"

"Is that so bad?" I opened my arms so that she could look at me.

She laughed again and began to walk towards the gates.

"I don't even know your name," she said.

"Eddie." I caught her up and held my hand out for her to shake. She didn't take it but looked at it as if it was something strange, unknown. She smiled at me again and turned into the gates.

"I'm Sophie," she replied. "And I'll think about your kind offer ... Eddie."

Benjy French was straight on to me.

"Oh. My. God," he said. "You were *talking* to Sophie Kelly." He put both hands to the sides of his head as if his massive brain couldn't process the information.

"Talking's a bit of an exaggeration," I said. "I just opened my mouth and words came out."

"You were walking alone with her and talking," he went on. "You are one brave man."

"I asked her out."

Benjy walked over to the wall and pretended to bang his head against it. "Sorry," he said. "Not brave, just completely and utterly *mental*."

"She hasn't said yes yet," I told him.

"Well, let's hope she doesn't. Or her mum will be getting a pair of Eddie-testicle earrings for Christmas this year. Steer well clear."

"Thanks for the advice," I said.

SIXTEEN

Sophie had obviously said something to her posse.

At lunchtime in the canteen, her table of girls kept throwing glances my way, whispering. If I returned their stares, they tried to look bored and disinterested. Sophie was nowhere to be seen. Benjy stuck to me like a limpet. In a way, his presence gave me a sense of security. Hanging with the arch-nerd of my year made me less interesting to anyone else, which suited me fine, though I had got on to nodding terms with one or two other blokes who also sat on our table at lunch. Finally, one of Sophie's girls broke free and approached our group. The other guys' eyes widened at this unusual behaviour. Benjy French nearly wet himself and left the table. It was the black girl, Anita, who floated over and sat down opposite me, folding long legs around the chair.

"Hi," she said, without cracking a smile. "You Eddie?"

"Yup," I said. "Me Eddie. You Anita?"

She nodded. Still no smile.

"You're really confident."

"Am I?" I said.

"You must be. Do you know what you're taking on?"

"I don't get you." I didn't, really.

"Sophie wants to know what you know about her," Anita said.

It was as if an envoy from the Kelly Gang had been sent to negotiate a peace deal.

"Er, she's a girl," I started. "Not bad-looking…" Even Anita managed a smirk at this. "That's about what I know," I admitted. "I'm new here. I know nothing." I held up my hands in surrender. She looked at me, unsmiling again.

"I'll talk to Sophie," she said. "And get back to you."

"Cheers," I said, and from the corner of my eye I could see Benjy French across the room, shaking his head and mouthing *No!*

Donnie's day wasn't shaping up too well.

Ever since he'd dropped her off, things had gone tits up. First there was the altercation with a bus driver: not serious, but an indication of the way things were going. He'd sat in traffic all the way down to Croydon, then just when he was pulling off the main road, lighting a fag, some muppet on a bike had nipped out in front of him and gone across the bonnet.

Donnie had got out of the car and picked the bloke up off the road, all huffing and puffing. He wasn't really hurt, just had bloodied knees and elbows. Then Donnie'd picked up the bike and thrown it over to the pavement, its front wheel bent in half.

The cyclist had called him an idiot. Said he wasn't looking.

Called him stupid. Donnie tried to square it with a ton, but Bicycle Boy said he didn't want his money, he wanted his insurance details.

Donnie didn't do insurance. He was beginning to get hot and bothered, especially when he found the smashed lens on his headlight and the scratch on his bonnet. He told the cyclist it would cost a monkey to put that right.

The cyclist still went on – knew his rights. Probably a social worker or something, Donnie thought. He didn't like him, so he slapped him. Then Donnie got back into the car while the cyclist writhed on the pavement, a bloody nose added to his knees and elbows, and drove off.

It was late when Donnie arrived in Croydon. The offices of the Kelly management company, Goldaward Holdings, was on the seventh floor of an office block. Donnie bumped into the firm's accountant, Saul Wynter, as he got out of the lift. Wynter acknowledged him but said little. He could see Donnie wasn't in the mood for a chat. Donnie went to the safe in the back office, got out what he had come for and left.

He made several pick-ups and drop-offs in Thornton Heath, South Norwood and Crystal Palace. Two drops were to clubs, dark and smelling of stale beer in their down time, and one to a private address just outside East Dulwich. A smart house where he dropped a large quantity of stuff. Restaurant and wine-bar owners. Business was clearly good – paid cash. Two more pick-ups of monies owing went without too much grief and the morning's work was done.

Donnie stopped for a swift pint on Peckham Rye to take the edge off the morning's aggro. Then had another one for the road. And a Scotch. He finished with lunch at a pie and mash in

Nunhead to sustain him for the afternoon.

The sun had been shining on the car, and when Donnie got back in it made him feel warm and sleepy. He needed a livener. He reached into the glove compartment and took out a small bottle. He didn't skim off much as a rule, but saved enough from a larger consignment here and there to keep himself a ready supply for moments like this. The amounts were too small to be noticed, but enough so that Donnie never went short.

He pulled out the little mustard spoon attached to the lid and scooped up a small pile of the powder and sniffed it straight up his nostril. The movement was so well-practised and discreet that even a passer-by would have thought the big man in the Mercedes was just picking his nose.

Donnie sniffed and lit a fag, started the engine and headed off towards Catford. Now he was ready.

Hyrone Brown's club, Chilli Peppa, was halfway between Catford and Lewisham, tucked up a side road in what had once been an old music hall, then a cinema and more recently a bingo club.

Hyrone, of mixed race, drew a mixed crowd. His punters were not exclusively black, but included a few whites from the colleges and middle-class slummers from the fringes of Blackheath. He was close to the boundary of Yardie territory, but his clientele and their narcotic of choice meant that the Chilli Peppa enjoyed the security offered by the long arms of the Kelly family.

As long as Hyrone paid his bills on time.

Donnie pulled into the tight parking space round the back of the club. There were beer crates and barrels stacked against the chicken wire, and a new-looking, black Mazda CX-7 four-by-four. Black windows. Registration plate HYR0N3.

Twat. The money was going somewhere, Donnie thought.

He pushed open the fire door at the side of the building and stepped into the darkness. The smell was mother's milk to Donnie: stale beer, illicit fags, manky carpet, yesterday's hormones. His eyes adjusted to the half-light and he walked across to the office behind the DJ booth. A black girl with straightened hair and extremely long, painted fingernails was listening to an R & B station and half-heartedly looking at Facebook on a computer screen. Donnie hadn't seen her before. She glanced up as he walked in, and if she was frightened of him she didn't show it.

"Mr Brown in?" Donnie asked, in his most charming voice.

She looked at him with big, dark eyes.

"Who shall I say?"

"Ron Tiddlywinks," Donnie mumbled, using one of his many self-invented aliases. The girl got up and opened a door behind her.

"Ron Somefink," she announced. A voice grumbled from inside the office. "He's not in," she told Donnie.

"Tell him it's Mr Kelly's associate," Donnie said. He was already on his way into the back office. He shoved the girl out of the way and levered the door from her grasp.

Hyrone realized in a split second that it was an unwelcome guest. He was a big bloke and perfectly capable of frightening people or dishing out the odd stab wound. He'd done time for a shooting and knew how to handle himself. But he also knew he was no match for Donovan Mulvaney.

Donnie was a legend.

Hyrone Brown leapt out from behind his desk and, by the time Donnie was in, was trying to make his way out through the open window at the back of the office. Donnie grabbed the back of his shiny trousers and yanked Hyrone back in again, dumping him in the chair behind the desk. The club owner tried hard not to look terrified.

"Eager to get in your nice new motor?" Donnie asked. Hyrone wriggled in the chair.

"A mate gave it to me," he gabbled, mouth dry. "He owed me one."

"In that case you'll have some wedge, won't you?" said Donnie. "Because you owe me one."

"Business hasn't been good," Hyrone bluffed. He appeared to be regretting the brand-new, three grand's worth of Breitling chronometer that he was trying to retract into his sleeve.

Donnie grabbed his wrist. "Nice watch." Hyrone twisted his arm, but Donnie's grip was like a wrench. "I suggest you open the safe, Mr Brown, and withdraw the five large you owe my boss."

"I haven't got it."

"Show me." Donnie gripped the arm harder and pulled Hyrone across to the cupboard where he knew the safe was kept. He let go for a moment to allow Hyrone to open it. The heavy steel door swung open. Inside there was a large bag of white pills, some piles of papers and a couple of passports, but no money.

"See?"

"Oh dear." Donnie scratched his head theatrically. "I don't want pills, do I? We have pills. Remind me, who owns this club, Mr Brown?"

"I got a twenty-year lease, you know that." Hyrone's tongue was smacking noisily against the roof of his dry mouth as he spoke.

"So who owns it?"

"I do," Hyrone said.

"Well, I think from now on, Mr Kelly does," said Donnie. "And you will work for us, OK?"

"You're f—" Hyrone was about to protest, but Donnie shoved four fat fingers into his mouth, pressing down on his tongue. He pushed his middle finger into the man's throat and squeezed hard on his soft lower jaw with his thumb so that he was unable to speak.

Hyrone gagged and struggled against Donnie's grip.

"As I was saying…" Donnie increased the pressure on Hyrone's skull. "You're a shop. You take merchandise from us, sell it, and then you pay us. If you don't pay, we call that irresponsible. So we take over your shop and run it properly, and you keep your job. Simple. Oh, but we still need to be paid for goods sold so far…"

Donnie took his fingers from Hyrone's mouth and grabbed his left wrist again. Hyrone spluttered and choked, ready to vomit. Donnie led him back to the safe, as if he was about to take something out.

Instead, he lined up Hyrone's fingers against the lock and slammed the heavy door shut.

The terrible howl that came from Hyrone Brown brought the girl to the door. She screamed.

Donnie opened the safe again and, taking his wrist, lifted Hyrone's bloody hand and its pulped, half-severed fingers out of the opening. He gently unclipped the Breitling and took it off, dropping it into his own pocket.

"Call this a deposit," he said. "Interest, if you like."

Hyrone fell to the floor, whimpering.

"Now, have the five grand here for me next week, or I'll come back and do the other hand ... your wanking one."

He looked at the girl, shaking and open-mouthed in the doorway.

"Where can I wash my hands, love?" Donnie asked politely.

At 4 p.m. sharp Donnie parked the Mercedes in the bus stop where he had stopped that morning. Three minutes later Sophie Kelly opened the door and jumped into the back. She looked lovely.

Radiant, that was the word.

"Had a good day, princess?" Donnie growled in his best-behaved voice.

"Yeah, pretty good," Sophie replied. Donnie looked over his shoulder. She was smiling, as if she was keeping something to herself. Then she remembered her manners.

"Oh, and how about you?" she asked. "Good day?" Donnie revved up and roared away from the bus stop.

"Yeah, not bad," he said. "Not bad at all."

SEVENTEEN

"Sophie says OK."

"Sophie says OK, what?" I asked. Anita looked down at me as if I was mad. As if I was questioning her authority.

"She says OK, she'll go on a date," Anita said.

"Will you be coming with us?" I asked. Anita cocked her head and gave me her "whatever" look. "It's just I thought Sophie might have told me herself. Call me old-fashioned…" Anita handed me a piece of paper with a number on it.

"Text her your number and she'll contact you," she said.

"Cheers, Anita, you're a star." I winked at her and she sort of shrugged, screwing up her face. Sense of humour wasn't up there on the list of Anita's life skills. Diplomacy and reaching for things from high shelves were obviously more her thing.

I hid away in an empty classroom and called Ian Baylis.

"Ian, it's me. Eddie."

"I know."

"I've spoken to her. I've got her number."

"What took you so long?"

"I've only been here a week," I protested. "And she's pretty hard to get close to."

"OK. Text it to me. Then keep me updated on your progress. Over and out."

"OK," I said, but he had already cut me off. I punched the number into the Nokia and sent it. Then I put the same number into my iPhone and typed a text:

Hey Sophie. Eddie Savage mob… Call me?

I watched the progress bar as it sent, then put the phone back in my pocket and felt it vibrate almost immediately with an incoming message. It was from Sophie:

No. Call me @ w/e. S ☺

I smiled. It wasn't exactly a come-on, but it was contact. No "x" at the end, but I guessed it was early days.

Saturday morning: I was sitting on my bed watching TV. A couple of blokes from a has-been boy band were trying to be funny and clever as they were talking to the presenter, and failing badly. I got up and made some toast and a cup of tea, but I couldn't settle.

The idea of contacting Sophie Kelly was making me jittery.

Apart from anything else, I was confused. I was supposed to be getting to know her as part of a job. Supposed to be taking a purely professional interest in her. But now I had made contact, I found my confidence deserting me a bit because I really, really fancied her. She was hot and I had her number, and the thought of her made my stomach flutter. It was ten-thirty, still too early to call. I kicked my heels and waited till twelve. At twelve-thirty I couldn't wait any longer. I fired off a text:

Hi. Can you talk?

The message came straight back:

No. Call me @ 5. S x

It was a knock-back, but at least it came with an instruction to make contact later. And an "x", which was an improvement. Or maybe I was reading too much into it. The afternoon dragged by. I sat out on the balcony and watched barges chugging slowly up and down the river. The skyscrapers of Canary Wharf sparkled in the sun and I must have watched twenty or more planes swoop down into City Airport, each of them looking as if they might collide with Canary Wharf Tower. I checked my watch. Four-thirty.

It had been four twenty-nine last time I looked.

Eventually five came around, and then I didn't want to look too anal by calling right on the button, so I waited three minutes. It went straight to voicemail: "*Hi, this is Sophie. Sorry I can't take your call. Please leave me a message."*

I didn't. Instead I hung up, cursing myself that I hadn't called at five sharp.

Then my phone rang.

"Eddie? It's Tony. Can you talk?"

The disappointment was clear in my voice.

"Tony," I said. "Listen, I want to talk to you, but I'm waiting for a call from Sophie Kelly."

"Nuff said." Tony was quick on the uptake. "Good work. Call me back." He hung up.

I waited ten more minutes and tried again. Voicemail. This time I left a message, pissed off, but trying to sound light and cheerful.

"Hi Sophie, it's Eddie. Give me a call back when you have a minute. Or I'll try again later. Cheers."

Cheers? I slapped myself on the head. Why did I say that?

Then my phone rang again.

"Eddie?" It was her.

"Hi, how are you?"

"Good, thanks." No apology then.

Awkward pause. I was going to have to do the talking.

"Listen, I was wondering if you'd like to do something later? A film or something?"

"I can't tonight. Sorry, I'm out."

My heart sank.

"Tomorrow then?"

"I've got this big family Sunday lunch thing…"

"Oh," I said flatly. "OK, maybe next weekend?"

"I could meet you in Greenwich Park later tomorrow afternoon, if you like?"

She sounded as if she was trying to come up with a compromise. Good sign.

"That'd be great. Where shall I meet you?"

"There's that statue by the observatory. I'll be there at four."

"Four. Brilliant," I said, as if her coming up with a time was itself an act of genius. I felt a complete plum. "I'll see you tomorrow then."

"OK," she said. "See ya."

"Bye." *Bye?* The epic phone call I was expecting was all done and dusted inside sixty seconds of pauses and single syllables.

But I had a date.

I rang Tony back.

"You are speaking to the man who has a date with Sophie Kelly," I said, bursting with pride.

"Nice one," he said. "Top stuff. Have you let Ian know?"

My heart sank.

"Do I have to, Tony?" I groaned. "I don't want him crawling all over it."

"He's your case officer, mate, you don't have a choice. He'll probably just let you get on with it, but you have to tell him."

I sighed. "OK, I'll let him know."

"Nip in and see me on Monday morning. Let me know how you got on." Tony sounded like a kind uncle again.

111

"We could do with a quick catch-up."

"I'm supposed to be at college."

"Hospital appointment."

"What shall I say is wrong with me?"

"Make something up," Tony said. "Dose of clap, maybe? Genital warts?" He laughed gruffly. I was a bit embarrassed, and he sensed it over the phone.

"Sorry, Eddie." He coughed. "Asthma clinic maybe?"

"OK, Tony," I wheezed. "See you Monday."

EIGHTEEN

Sunday was beginning to drag as much as Saturday had. I'd got up at ten and made myself a bacon sarnie, then started to get antsy again. I listened to some more of Steve's recordings and they scared me, so I watched some comedy on YouTube for a bit, then went for a walk along the riverfront.

I cut up past an old church towards Creek Road. It was called St Nicholas's and had an ancient, crumbling gateway with two worn stone skull and crossbones mounted on the gateposts. Maybe it was a pirates' cemetery, or just a grim reminder of what was in store for us all.

I was feeling shaky and paranoid, like I was being watched, though I was sure I wasn't. I took deep breaths to calm myself down. All I was doing was meeting a good-looking girl in a park. Get over it, Eddie, I told myself.

I walked up past the market. One or two places were open. Deptford High Street is a real mix: African shops, selling everything from coconut milk to dried mudfish, sit next to white-painted art galleries showing pictures by local artists. I bought a paper and sat outside a Portuguese caff that did good coffee. I had a small custard tart as well and tried to read the headlines, but I kept reading the same sentence over and over again. The caffeine hit was only making me jumpier, so I left the rest of the coffee and continued on to Greenwich.

At ten to four, I started to make my way up the hill to the top of the park. I panted up towards the statue of General Wolfe, who looked out over the National Maritime Museum and across the river to Docklands. Five minutes later I joined the gaggle of tourists and Sunday walkers gathered around the foot of the statue, admiring the view. Ten minutes after that I was still circling the base, beginning to doubt I was in the right place.

I checked my watch: 4.25 p.m. It was going to be a no-show, I was sure. I looked at my phone. No messages. I wasn't going to send one either: that would have been too sad and needy.

Then I saw her. A green-and-cream Mini screeched into a parking space and Sophie got out. Tall and blonde, she looked like a model. As she ran across the car park, tight jeans, leather jacket, swinging ponytail, heads turned. She was *running*. In a hurry. To see me.

I took a deep breath. Be confident, I thought. Be Eddie. Relax.

"I'm really sorry," she said, breathless. "I couldn't get away, then there was a load of traffic and roadworks up the A20."

"No worries," I lied. "I haven't been here long myself. Shall we walk?"

We strolled along towards the flower gardens. The sun was shining and everything was beginning to look golden as autumn approached.

"So d'you live near here?" I asked.

"Not really, we're down just inside the M25," she said. "Country. You?"

"I've got a flat in Deptford," I told her.

"With your parents?"

"They passed away," I said, pleased at how easily my cover came to me. It had an effect on Sophie. Her features visibly softened.

"I'm really sorry. That must be tough."

I nodded. My lips set tight as if holding in emotion.

"Have they been ... I mean, passed away long?" She looked genuinely sympathetic. I might have found my way in, I thought cynically.

"A couple of years," I said. "Cancer. Dad first, then Mum not long after. Unlucky, eh?"

"My dad says you don't really grow up until you lose your parents. He lost his early too."

A mention of her old man on our first date. Real progress, I thought. I chanced a question.

"How did he get over it? Throw himself into work?"

"Sort of," she said. "He's always worked hard."

Going well. I pushed it one step further.

"What sort of work does he do?" I saw her stiffen immediately. She looked at me sideways, stared at me strangely.

"You mean you don't know?"

I shook my head. Tried to look as innocent as I could.

"He's a businessman," she explained. "Self-employed. But people say all sorts of things about him. They're jealous of his success."

"Often happens," I managed, uncertain how to respond.

"Don't believe everything you hear," she said.

I sensed that the subject stopped there and didn't push it any further. We came to a kiosk.

"Fancy an ice cream?" I said, smiling.

She grinned back at me. Perfect white teeth. My heart lurched.

"I had a massive lunch a few hours ago," she said, rubbing her stomach. She weighed it up. "But, yeah, why not?"

"I like a girl with a good appetite," I said.

"Do they have pistachio?"

"Flake as well?"

She nodded and we both laughed.

"Crushed nuts?" I added, pushing it.

"You'll have to wait and see," she said, and let out a peal of earthy laughter.

NINETEEN

I walked through the guitar shop and up the back stairs towards Tony's office.

Anna was there in the Sugacubes reception.

"Hello, handsome," she said. I felt myself blush. Last time I'd seen her was during my induction, and things had moved so fast since.

"Hi," I replied. "How are you?" She got up and leant over her desk, kissed my cheek and squeezed my arm.

"Busy. How are you getting on?" I remembered my date with Sophie. It had gone pretty well, I think. The ice had certainly been broken and, once she'd warmed up a bit, we had a laugh. She actually had a pretty down-to-earth sense of humour, which was great to find in a girl who looked that good.

"Yeah, OK." I scratched my head. "It's all a bit new." I felt slightly uncomfortable. After all, the last time I'd seen Anna she hadn't had any clothes on. "Look, about the other night…" I began. But Anna just smiled and put a finger to her lips.

At that moment the door opened and Tony Morris came out of his office. "Ah, Eddie Savage Esquire," he said. "You've met Anna?"

I nodded. "We met when I first came here. And then again on my induction week."

Anna winked at me and sat down, went back to her screen.

Tony ushered me through to his office.

"Tea?" he asked. I looked at the mess of unwashed mugs and dried-out teabags and politely refused. "Something going on out there?" he asked, gesturing back towards the reception area.

"No," I lied.

"Well, if you're sure." Tony scratched his stubble. "Just thought I detected a bit of an … atmosphere?"

I shrugged. "She is pretty fit," I admitted.

"Hm. I had noticed. But don't get involved, Eddie." Tony waggled his little finger in his ear then inspected it. "Not with her, anyway. She takes no prisoners."

I told him I wouldn't, keeping my fingers crossed behind my back. Tony delved deeper in his ear.

"And don't get involved with anyone else, for that matter. Keep it professional."

I nodded, feeling guilty on all counts.

"So. Sophie Kelly?"

I drew a deep breath. "Well, I met up with her yesterday in Greenwich Park."

"You got on pretty well, it seems." Tony pushed a ten-by-eight black-and-white photo across his desk. I picked it up. It was blurry, taken on a telephoto lens, but it was definitely me and Sophie. Walking along in the park, chatting and smiling. The body language was obvious too. At the time I had felt that we were walking along some distance apart, but in the photo we looked close, like boyfriend and girlfriend.

"I thought you said Ian wouldn't put anyone on my tail?"

"I know, I said not to, but he insisted. He thinks it's too early not to keep an eye on you."

So I *was* being watched. My instinct had been right.

"Listen, Tony," I said. "It's hard enough not to feel self-conscious doing this at all. But if I think I've got a camera up my arse every time I step outside, I'll feel even more paranoid."

"It's a safety net," said Tony. "You'll get used to it. Now, what did you find out?"

"Not much. They live just inside the M25 somewhere off the A20, so I'm guessing down towards Brands Hatch or somewhere like that. She says her dad's a businessman and that people say all sorts of stuff about him that isn't true."

Tony smiled to himself. I didn't know how much he already knew.

"She's a crap timekeeper."

"Crap, or playing hard to get?" he asked.

"Bit of each maybe. She's also got a sympathetic side, warm. She doesn't worry about what she eats, which is pretty healthy, I think. I can't stand girls who whinge about diets all the time."

"Maybe she's got a fast metabolism," Tony said. "She's in good shape."

I nodded, agreeing with his assessment.

"And she's actually quite a laugh, once you get her away from that bunch of witches that form a protective cordon around her."

"Excellent," Tony said. "I'd say you've found out quite a lot about our Miss Kelly. You've watched and listened and made some reasonable deductions. She's even talked to you about her old man. Good sign. Shows she trusts you."

"You think so?"

"I do," he said. "Keep it up at this pace. Leave it a few days and ask if she wants to go out again. Looks like you didn't make a complete Horlicks of your first outing, so it should be OK."

"Cheers." I grinned.

"Anything else?" Tony tilted his head back. Looked at me through narrowed eyes. "You holding something back?"

Tony must be some kind of mind-reader, I thought. Could he detect that I was already taking more than a strictly professional interest in Sophie Kelly? But that wasn't it. My mind was filled with what I'd heard on Steve's debrief. The fear had been chewing away at me. Tony kept looking at me.

"That memory stick," I said finally. "Steve's voice. It freaked me out a bit."

"Hm." Tony considered a moment. "I wondered if it might. I wanted you to listen to it so that you know what the work is about. Perhaps you should stop."

"That's the thing, Tony," I said. "I can't."

Tony had hit the nail on the head. Since my first night at the flat, I had played and replayed the voice clips each night. To begin with it was just to hear my brother's voice, but then I became obsessed with listening to the reports of how he was getting deeper undercover, into more and more jeopardy. How he had come back to London from Ireland, made some contacts with Paul's associates, and met with them in South London dives and clubs. Then bugged them. Was this what I was getting into?

"They scare me, Tony," I said. "But I keep going back to them."

"Do you want me to take them away?"

"No, I needed to know what Steve was up to. But I won't listen to them any more."

"They're a mixed blessing, but I don't want you to be ignorant of the risks involved," Tony said. "You're right, though, don't shit yourself up. It's not productive. Stash them away somewhere safe."

"Why was Steve in Ireland?" I asked. I couldn't let it go just yet. "Wasn't the army over there?"

"They were," Tony confirmed. "But army intelligence tended to stick out like a sore thumb. The IRA knew everyone and everything. We needed more of a maverick operator, with a deeper cover. Someone a bit left of field."

"Like a mature student?"

"Exactly," said Tony. "Chemistry faculties are always good places to contact potential terrorists, meet overseas students. Great places to learn how to make bombs. And Steve was good with explosives."

"Right," I said. "Wasn't all the trouble about religion and stuff … Catholics and Protestants?"

"Originally, yes, but more recently the organizations over there have become less interested in religion and more like fronts for organized crime: drugs, gun-running, protection. The big stuff. Steve got right into the thick of it."

"So that's where your lot come in?"

"Exactly," Tony said. "Not so much because we're interested in the politics – although that's part of it – but more because once the crime gets to that scale, it tends to link up. Steve was a genius at uncovering those links."

"With what?" I asked. I didn't really get it.

"With other crime organizations; anyone else who's interested in drugs, guns, bombs."

"Terrorists?"

"Yes, terrorists." Tony took a glug of tea. "But also mafia: Russians, Italians … our own home-grown mobsters and their bent mates on the Costa del Crime. The thing about crime is that it *all* links up. The junkie who shoplifts to feed his habit is all part of the same game as the City fraudster and the Bolivian drug baron. And any intelligence we can get at any level is all useful."

"Including making friends with Sophie Kelly?"

"Yeah," Tony said. "From little acorns…"

"But I'm not getting into heavy stuff like Steve, am I?"

Tony suddenly found the polystyrene tiles on his ceiling interesting.

"No, no," he said. "Light duties. Different area."

"Got to start somewhere, I suppose."

"Exactly." Tony got up from his chair and squeezed my shoulder. "You're doing good. Keep it up and try not to worry too much about what Steve did. We're your safety net; you have back-up. Steve tended to walk the tightrope without a net. And it's a long way to fall."

"Thanks, Tony," I said.

But I didn't feel reassured. I just couldn't shake the image of my brother spinning and tumbling, falling through the air to his death.

TWENTY

I wasn't popular with the rest of the girls. News of Sophie's "date", innocent as it was, had put their noses right out of joint. Anita and her friend Nazeem could barely look at me the following morning, as if I had taken what was rightfully theirs.

All I'd done was buy her an ice cream.

When Sophie did eventually turn up, she gave me a cheery "Hi" as she crossed the yard to join her friends, casting the odd glance in my direction, keeping it discreet.

Benjy French was beside himself. Apparently one of Sophie's friends had told one of his mates that we'd gone on a date. Of course, the story had become exaggerated, starting with cocktails at the Met Bar, followed by dinner at the Ritz, a show and then a late night at Stringfellows. Or some such bollocks.

I put Benjy straight.

"We just went for a walk in the park," I told him. "End of."

"That it?" Benjy said. "Didn't you snog her? Put your hand up her shirt?"

I dead-armed him.

"What, and get chucked off a multi-storey, you perv?" He writhed, rubbing his arm to restore feeling. "No, I didn't."

"Fair enough. No hard feelings." He gave me another cheeky glance – couldn't resist the joke. "Or *were* there?"

I dead-armed him again.

My next date with Sophie was arranged by text. Just between the two of us, without go-betweens. I felt that I'd scored an important point.

She agreed to go to a movie. Neither of us was too concerned about what to see. On offer was an action movie, a chick flick and an American comedy with Steve Carell. So we settled for the comedy.

Sophie picked me up at Deptford Bridge DLR station, almost punctual this time, and we drove down to Greenwich. I felt bad as I fixed the magnetic tracker to the underside of the passenger seat without Sophie suspecting a thing, but it had to be done. It had been drummed into me as standard procedure.

We'd arranged to go an hour early to get something to eat, and decided on pizza. We both chose the same one, Fiorentina, with spinach and an egg on top, so I changed my mind and ordered an Americano with pepperoni so we could have half and half. And a glass of house red. The waiter was Italian and was all over Sophie. She thought it was funny as he waved his big pepper pot around, until

I started to get a bit humpy and he got the hint and went away.

"Easy, tiger." Sophie smiled.

"Sorry," I said. "He was getting on my tits waving that thing around."

"Actually, I think it was mine he was trying to get on," Sophie joked, and we both giggled.

I offered to pay – I had a decent allowance to cover my expenses – but Sophie insisted we went halves.

I tried to concentrate on the film, but the close proximity of Sophie made it difficult. I could almost feel an energy coming from her, and every time she moved, I got a whiff of a faint, clean-smelling perfume. There was something quite physical about her: animal. Once or twice as she moved, her arm or leg brushed mine and my concentration went completely as I got butterflies in my stomach and my breath started to come in short bursts. It was all I could do to keep my hands off her.

Sophie didn't seem to have quite the same difficulty focusing on the film, and she laughed out loud at some of the gags. At one point she turned to me and grabbed my arm, asking me whether I found it as funny as she did.

"Yeah," I said. "It's a scream." She left her arm resting on mine and it was an easy progression from there to holding hands, which we did through the rest of the film. I don't remember much about the ending; I just remember the dry warmth of Sophie's hand. I remember trying to detect any change in pressure, any small signal that I might read as encouragement. I made no further move.

Don't rush it, I thought.

Afterwards, she offered me a lift. I couldn't let her see the flat, so I refused. Said I'd be fine walking back along the river. Sophie seemed a little disappointed and asked me to see her back to the car anyway. We walked through the backstreets that ran down to the park until we found the Mini, parked in the shadow between two streetlights.

"I'll drop you off at the bottom of the road," she said. So I got in.

It was quite dark by now and all I could see was Sophie's hair, lit by the lights from the park and the profile of her nose and mouth. The curve of her lips in silhouette.

"I like this," she said. "Being with you. I feel comfortable. It's never really happened for me before."

"Dunno why," I said, though really I knew that everyone was shit-scared of getting close to her. "But I like being with you too."

The moment comes when you know that kissing someone is inevitable. My heart beat a bit faster and Sophie leant towards me, and I felt her lips part as she pressed her face into mine. Felt her teeth and her wet tongue. We must have kissed for half a minute, then pulled away. Then kissed again, this time for longer. I sat back in the car seat, feeling giddy and unreal.

She dropped me off at the end of Church Street, chucked a U-turn before beeping, waving and screeching back off towards the A2.

I walked back along the river feeling like I was six inches above the ground. I was even singing to myself. The last thing I was feeling was professional: I'd almost forgotten my business – the evening had turned into pure pleasure.

I got back to the flat. The checks before I went in and the PINs were pretty much second nature to me now.

Even though I was floating on air.

I switched on the lights and booted up the Mac. There were a few messages – encoded stuff from Ian and Tony asking about the evening. I replied that all was well and I would detail my report in the morning. Then my phone buzzed with an incoming message. Sophie:

Had a great evening, Eddie. I like being with you.
Let's do it again. S xxxx

Four kisses.

I remembered the real ones. At the rate they were multiplying, I would have enough to cover me from head to toe within a few weeks. I went to bed with that thought.

TWENTY-ONE

Several weeks, several more dates.

Sophie and I were getting increasingly easy in each other's company. She was happy to hang around with me, and I couldn't believe my luck every time she made contact. Even at college there had been a major shift. She still talked to her gang of girls, but I seemed to be more her confidante than any of them were. She would leave them behind to sit with me. Likewise, Benjy French and the others began to keep their distance. They started talking to the girls.

Talked behind our backs.

I was still wary because I had got close to Sophie under false pretences. I expected her to rumble me as a fake at any time. But the longer it went on, the less fake I felt. I was behaving like the new me – and the new me was what she liked.

I much preferred the new me too. After all, what was I except a better, more confident version of myself? Better-dressed, with a bit of money and a great flat. I started thinking of it less as a new identity and more as a makeover, and as our dates became more frequent, each time I was a little less surprised that I had managed to pull this gorgeous girl.

Conveniently, I had almost forgotten her background.

I had also forgotten to make notes. Well, I had written them up at first, but my entries were pretty dull: *Went out, Sophie drove, had a drink, ate Chinese in Greenwich, snogged, home.* After the first few entries I felt ashamed that they were so safe and easy compared with the missions Steve had been set, so I stopped writing them until, I imagined, something interesting might happen.

We were leaving college one Thursday, some weeks after our first date, when Sophie said, "I can't do this Saturday. Dad's taking us sailing over to France."

"Oh." The disappointment was clear in my voice. "I didn't know you were a sailor."

"I'm not, really," she admitted. "When I say sailing, I mean we're going on the yacht. It's a big thing with an engine. You don't really get wet."

"Cool," I said. "How big is it?"

"Dunno. About sixty foot maybe." She looked embarrassed. "As big as a bus."

"Big. Where are you going?"

"A place called Honfleur," she told me. "It's really pretty. We're going for dinner."

I nodded, impressed.

"Maybe you could come next time." She looked a little guilty. "This trip is a load of Dad's business friends. Mum and I have to smile nicely and pour them drinks and listen to their boring golf stories."

She was trying to put a negative spin on it, but sailing to France for dinner sounded pretty smart to me.

"My brother's coming too," she said. "I don't know if you'd like him, he's a bit flash."

"I didn't know you had a brother," I said. Although I did. Jason Kelly had featured in my briefing notes.

"There's a lot you don't know about me," Sophie said, smiling. She kissed me on the cheek and tapped my nose with her finger.

"So, where d'you sail from?" I asked. "Dover or somewhere?"

"Portsmouth – well, Gosport's where the boat is. We'll drive down on Friday then sail on Saturday morning."

"What's the boat called?"

"Guess."

"*Sophie*?" I guessed.

"Close. It's *Lady Sofia.* It was called *Seawolf.* My dad just renamed it."

"Isn't it unlucky to rename a boat?"

"I hope not." She laughed. "I might drown."

"Wear a life jacket," I said. "And I'll see you when you get back, yeah?"

"Maybe I could come round to your flat?" she asked. "I'll bring you a present." She put her arm round my waist and batted her eyelashes at me.

"I'll look forward to it," I said.

"She wants to come to the flat." I was on the phone to Ian Baylis, filling him in on my progress.

"She can't. It's a safe house," he snapped.

"I know that. But it makes sense that she might want to, doesn't it?"

"I'll think about it. Anything else?"

I searched my brain, looked at the notes I'd made. I'd told him the Kelly boat had been renamed, plus the point of departure and approximate time. Told him who was going and where. It was his guess as to why. If he knew any of it already, he didn't let on. I felt I had dished up a lot of information for Ian Baylis. He could have someone down in Gosport Harbour tonight, putting a tracker on the boat. Someone could be posted to look out for them when they arrived in Honfleur. Based on what I had given him, the whole trip could be under surveillance, but he still asked if there was anything else.

"That's it," I said, a bit pissed off that he wasn't more appreciative of my efforts. At last I'd had something to report and, to be honest, Baylis was so unresponsive when I did tell him, I felt undervalued. I thought he might have encouraged me more. Also I didn't like him, but I did like Sophie, so it felt strange giving information about someone I liked to someone I didn't. Against my instincts.

He'd had his pound of flesh for this week and I was ready for a little time out. I rang off.

An hour later, Tony rang. "Good stuff," he said. "Ian's filled me in. You're making great progress."

"Thanks, Tone. I'm glad you think so. I wouldn't have a clue from talking to Baylis."

"You know what he's like," said Tony. "He's a pretty

serious bloke. Doesn't make a song and dance about it. But he thinks you're doing good."

"Did he mention the flat?" I asked.

"Yeah, he did say something. To be honest, I hadn't factored in that you might have got so close to her so quickly."

I felt myself flush at the other end of the phone. "It's pretty normal to invite people round, isn't it?"

"Course it is," Tony said. "But I can't risk anyone seeing the apartment. Especially anyone … well, connected."

"So, what am I supposed to do? Tell her she can't come to my flat? I think that would bring things to a pretty dead end, wouldn't it?"

"You're right," he said. "I'll sort it. I'll talk to Anna. Get her to call you."

TWENTY-TWO

"Eddie?"

"Yes?"

"It's Anna. Hi. Can you meet me at Deptford DLR at twelve?"

I looked at my watch, it was ten-thirty and I was still in my boxers. It was Saturday, and I'd been drinking tea and scratching my nuts most of the morning, channel-hopping.

"Sure," I said.

"Don't do a big meet and greet," she replied. "Just follow normal protocols, and when you see me, follow me towards the high street. We'll disappear in the market."

Something in her tone made me a little wary. I don't know whether it was the tension I detected in her voice or if it was because Sophie was away and I was seeing Anna alone. I got showered and dressed, and an hour later I was on the street. I did a routine check on the cars parked there. Nothing unusual, so I began to walk along the riverfront.

After a few minutes I was aware of someone behind me. I quickened my step, then took a side path into the green behind the church. I ducked behind the gatepost, waiting for the figure to pass. It didn't. The man turned in straight after me and we almost collided.

"Sonny?" he said. It was a childhood nickname I hadn't heard for years.

I couldn't remember the last time I'd seen my old man. I think it was when Steve kicked him out for hitting Mum. My immediate instinct was to look around to make sure no one had seen us. The churchyard was empty save for a wino asleep on the far bench and a few crows.

"How did you find me?" I asked under my breath.

"Accident," he said. "I wasn't looking for you. I thought I saw you the other day. Going towards Greenwich."

"Last I heard, you'd moved down to Hastings, or somewhere."

"I did. Now I'm back. Full of old people, the seaside. And junkies and queers. I'm a City boy at heart: know where I am with the drunks and the coons."

I winced at the terms he used. Remembered his voice and the expressions from my early childhood.

His hair was longish and greasy. He was unshaven and sunburnt – not tanned, but as brown as a turd. Like he sat outside a pub all day. Which is probably what he did, judging by the beer belly that stuck out from his otherwise scrawny frame. I felt a bit guilty that I didn't have a scrap of feeling for him. But then I guessed his long absence showed that he probably didn't feel much for me either.

"You know Steve's dead?" I asked.

He rubbed a grimy hand across his eyes, like he was trying to work up some emotion, or at least make his bloodshot eyes water.

"I heard," he said. "Bad news." He took out a pouch and rolled a fag. I looked at my watch: 11.50 a.m.

"I've got to be somewhere," I told him.

"Looks like you're doing all right for yourself, Sonny," he said, lighting his roll-up.

"Ducking and diving," I answered vaguely. "Listen, don't call me that. I've moved on. Everyone calls me Eddie now."

"I'll still think of you as my Sonny-boy," he said, trying to sound sentimental, wiping an imaginary tear from his eye.

I didn't buy it for a minute. "Well, don't," I said. "Better if you don't think of me – or see me – at all."

"Only myself to blame, I suppose." He shrugged. "Couldn't lend your old man a couple of quid till next week?"

I fished in my back pocket, pulled out my wallet and found a twenty.

"Here's a score," I said. "Have it. Don't owe me, then I won't have to see you again."

He weighed up the possibilities. Looked at the note.

"Make it fifty and you won't see me for dust," he said.

I peeled off another two twenties and handed them over.

"Good lad," he said. "Always knew you'd do well … Eddie." He clapped me on the shoulder, turned on his heels and headed off across the churchyard.

I was a few minutes late for my rendezvous with Anna. She was sitting on the opposite, eastbound platform, wearing a white belted raincoat.

I strolled along the westbound platform as if I was waiting for a train. Then, as soon as she had seen me, I went back down the stairs to the ticket area. Anna came down the stairs on the other side. Once she had left the station, I followed her along the busy high street and down into the market, which was throbbing with assorted people and the sound of reggae from a CD stall. She was dressed down, but still one or two stall-holders called out to her, always up for a chat with a good-looking girl.

"Hello, darlin', have a look at my lovely plums…"

"Cheer up, treacle, it might never 'appen."

The lairy banter of a South London market.

She wasn't very inconspicuous, I thought. She must have thought the same thing because she ducked between the stalls and walked behind them for a while. She continued down the street until the stalls thinned out and then went into a grey-fronted, modern gallery. I went in after her and looked at the pictures, circling in the opposite direction to Anna until I was standing next to her, looking at the same painting.

"I quite like this one," she said. It was a large, colourful image of a cartoon character in a cowboy hat, with graffiti on the wall behind him. Big splashes of acrylic paint stuck out from the canvas.

"Yeah, it's not bad." I did actually quite like it. "Sorry

I was a bit late. Ran into someone I didn't want to see."

"Who?" Anna sounded worried. She didn't take her eyes off the picture. Spoke as if she was still talking about it.

"My dad," I said.

"Shit." She looked around. "Did anyone see you?"

"I don't think so. No. I'm pretty sure."

"I didn't know you had one," she said.

"I'd almost forgotten myself."

Anna passed me a sheet of paper. Estate agent's details for a flat.

"Meet me there in twenty minutes," she instructed. "Get a cup of coffee, go round the houses a bit. I'm the estate agent, by the way."

She seemed edgy.

Anna left the gallery and the girl behind the desk didn't even look up. I spent another couple of minutes looking at paintings and then left myself, heading back down the high street in the opposite direction to Anna. I walked down to the end of the road and then turned back, under the railway bridge, taking a back lane up past a pub until I arrived at the address she had given me.

The flat was above a dusty row of shops, accessed by a back alley. I climbed up an outside steel staircase to a rear door on the first floor: 1a. I pressed the buzzer and found the door open so I went inside.

It was scruffy – certainly nothing like my apartment by the river, only ten minutes away. Curly-edged carpets, a shiny laminate floor, white woodchip walls, a couple of Ikea chairs and a saggy sofa. Anna was looking through a net curtain out on to the street below. A bloke was just finishing some wiring, as if he was putting in a phone line or TV aerial.

"All done," he said. He handed Anna a wiring diagram and she signed a worksheet and he left, nodding to me on his way out.

"Putting a phone in?" I asked Anna.

"Among other things."

"Who lives here?"

"You do," she said.

My heart sank. I had quickly got used to my smart bachelor pad. She saw my disappointment.

"Don't worry," she said. "You can stay put in the safe house. This is a place for your assignations with Sophie Kelly."

"*What?* She'll blow me out as soon as she sees this pile of shite."

"Don't hold back." Anna laughed. "Say what you think about the place. I think you're underestimating either your own attraction or the kind of girl Sophie is."

"You think so?"

"I know so," she said. "The game would be up the minute she saw the place by the river. This makes you credible. Young bloke, not much money, making his way. It'll bring out her protective instincts, believe me."

She lifted the curtain and looked out of the window again.

"You seem a bit…" I hesitated before I found the right word. "Jumpy." I didn't want to sound cocky. She'd been doing this for a while and I was still a rookie.

"I am a bit," she admitted. "There's something going off this weekend."

"Is it to do with the Kellys?"

"Not sure. Probably. This is still their manor and I can smell trouble. It's all connected." She looked at me. "I just don't like it when something unexpected happens. Like you meeting your dad. We should have known about that. About him. That's exactly where slip-ups happen."

I agreed. Slip-ups had always occurred around the old man.

"Does he know anything about this? Where you live? About your brother?" Anna asked.

"He knows Steve's dead," I told her. "Nothing else."

"Sure?"

"Sure. And even if he did, you could buy his eternal silence for a couple of drinks."

"You don't think much of him, do you?" Anna softened momentarily.

"Less than not much," I said. "He's a stranger to me."

She nodded; understood.

"I've tried to make this feel a bit like home," she said. She turned back from the window to face me. "I've put some beers in the fridge. Crack us a couple, will you?"

I went through to the kitchenette, just inside the entrance to the flat, opened the fridge and pulled out a couple of cold Buds.

"Make sure that door's shut," Anna called from the living room.

I checked the catch. A couple of new Banham locks

had been added to the bolt and chain on the door. It was like Fort Knox. The locks were secure. I went back in with the beers.

Anna had taken off her raincoat and was wearing a sort of business suit. I say "business", but the skirt was quite short. It was navy blue and pretty tight and she wore it with a thin, white blouse. When she took off the jacket you could see her bra straps – she definitely had more buttons undone than a real estate agent would. Unless it was an estate agent trying it on with a client. She walked through into the bedroom. It was nicer than the sitting room, with French windows that opened on to a little balcony. A floor-length curtain blew in the breeze from the open window and, although the decor was grotty, the bed had been made up with clean sheets and a puffy duvet. Anna took the beer from me and took a glug. She reached back into her jacket, pulled out a pack of Marlboro Lights and stuck one in her mouth.

"You don't, do you?" she asked. I shook my head. She sat on the bed and lit the cigarette, inhaling deeply and blowing out. She seemed to relax instantly.

"Feel better?" I said.

"A cold beer, a fag, the door's locked. I'm alone in a flat with a fit-looking bloke on a sunny afternoon. What's not to like?" She looked at me and smiled.

"I just asked if you felt better," I said. I could feel my breath coming faster.

"I will do in a minute," she said. She patted the clean bed beside her and undid the zip on the side of her skirt. "Come here."

"Is this place wired?" I asked nervously, looking at the corners and the light fittings for hidden cameras.

"Not yet," she said. "Sit down."

I took a swig of my beer and sat down beside her.

Who was I to argue?

TWENTY-THREE

"How was your trip?"

"Complete disaster," Sophie said, shaking her head.

Tuesday. I'd given her the address and she'd come round to the flat. She'd looked around. Said it was nice.

"Did you sink?" I asked, but she didn't look in the mood for a joke.

"We got there all right, but we had this big fat Russian bloke who Dad does some business or other with. He was getting pissed on vodka all the way there and started groping me and Mum, even though he'd got some twenty-year-old tart with him who didn't speak a word of English."

"Sounds like fun."

"Yeah, right," she said. "It didn't end there. When we got into the harbour, he and the mate he was with started singing and showing us up. And if there's one thing Dad hates, it's drawing attention to himself. He's very ... discreet."

"So how did your dad react?" I asked. The picture I

143

had in my mind was not of someone shy and retiring at all.

"He just goes really quiet. But Mum and I know he's bubbling up and everyone should watch out. Then the Russian started picking a fight with the posh American client…"

"There was an American as well? Quite a party."

Sophie looked at me; paused for a moment. "Yeah. Dad was introducing his American client to the Russian… Anyway, it all kicked off."

"What sort of business were they doing?" I asked, knowing I was pushing it. Sophie obviously realized she was saying too much and brought the shutters down.

"I dunno," she said. "Just business. You know, like blokes in the City do. Deals. Art and stuff."

She gave me her sideways glance and I knew not to push it further. But then she carried on with the story, as if she needed to tell me something to compensate for cutting me off. "And if that wasn't enough, we got pulled in by a customs boat on the way back and towed into Portsmouth. They turned the boat over completely. We were there till four in the morning. Nightmare."

"Did they find anything?"

"Not a thing. I think we had a few bottles of champagne over the limit so they took them away. They were pretty embarrassed."

"What do you reckon they were after?"

Sophie fixed me with her innocent blue eyes. "Search me."

"Hey, and what about the present you promised me?" I reminded her.

Sophie smiled and put her hands on my shoulders.

"Search me…" she said again. She patted herself, then held her arms out as if she was waiting to be frisked and laughed.

Donnie hated boats at the best of times. He even got dicky on a boating lake. He had chucked his breakfast up over the side of the ferry on the way over to France, and now he had spent most of the night up on the deck of the yacht, honking his way across the Channel while Dave, Jason and the skipper sat below, smoking, laughing and drinking rum and Coke.

They had slipped out of Dieppe early Sunday evening, just as most of the other yachts were coming in. Just as Lady Sofia *was being given a tug off the English coast, creating a useful diversion. Her Majesty's Revenue and Customs wouldn't be looking for two Kelly boats in the Channel at the same time.*

Donnie had taken the ferry to Dieppe, where he had hooked up with Dave Slaughter, the boss's driver, who had arrived the day before to set up the van hire. They had driven out on the ring road to an English-owned bonded warehouse on an out-of-town industrial estate. The warehouse sold booze at rock-bottom prices and was a regular stop-off for English publicans and club owners.

Donnie rapped on the shuttered door and an unshaven Eastern European-looking man poked his head out. "We're here to see the Bish."

The man jerked his head in place of asking who they were.

"Tell him it's Jonathan Toothpaste and Duncan Donuts," said Donnie. Dave sniggered.

Seconds later, steel shutters rolled up and Kenny Bishop – the Bish – rolled out. He was tanned and rotund, his belly pushing tautly over his white trousers and against his pink shirt, which was unbuttoned halfway, revealing white chest hair and an assortment of chains. White Italian shoes finished off the look.

"Donald ... David," said the Bish, holding his hand high and sweeping it down in an elaborate handshake. He laughed loudly and bobbed and weaved in a display of shadow boxing as if he was an old sparring partner.

"Donovan," Donnie growled, "not Donald." Donnie couldn't stand Kenny Bishop. Not that he liked anyone all that much. He knew one of his farts would knock the Bish over – and spoil his carefully coiffed grey hair.

"Come on, Bish, you silly old ponce," Dave said. "Get the friggin' doors open, we haven't got time to talk about the old days."

The Bish stopped smiling and looked chastened. He pressed a button that rolled up the steel shutters on the goods entrance. Behind him, the engine on the hired van started up and the Bish looked alarmed. He glanced from Dave to Donnie and back again.

"I thought it was just you two," he said.

"And a driver," Dave replied. "It's expensive merchandise. Can't have one of us distracted by driving. We have to keep our eyes open."

The van reversed into the goods entrance, the driver obscured by the darkened windows. Stacked just inside the doors was a pile of boxes. Cases of champagne marked with the label of a well-known champagne house. The Bish got his Eastern European boy to load the van while Donnie and Dave took a case into the office to check the merchandise. Donnie levered it open with a crowbar from the van. The bottles were packed in papier-mâché moulds, just as they should be. Dave took a bottle out and examined it.

"Very good," he said. "Classy work. Looks just like the real thing." He handed the bottle to Donnie, who examined it and tapped it with his blunt fingernail.

"Cushty," he said. "Top-dollar job, don't you think, Bish?"

The Bish held up his hands, already looking guilty. "I dunno, Donnie. You know me, I don't touch the stuff. It's just for buying and selling as far as I'm concerned. Could be tins of sardines."

Dave nodded reassuringly.

"The geezer from Marseilles just dropped it off as is, and here you see it." The Bish was gabbling, waving his hands around, trying too hard.

"What's up, Bish?" Donnie said. "You're sweating like a paedo in a paddling pool."

"Nothing, Don, honest. I just want the deal to go right. Smoothly, you know."

"Eager to please, aren't you, Bish?" Dave said.

"That's it, Dave," Bish gushed. "I paid up quite a bit of my capital to secure this transaction, so I'm keen to get the gear sold and off my stall." He gave them a sickly grin.

"That's fine then," said Donnie finally.

The Bish looked instantly relieved, his eyes flicking from one to the other, and laughed again. Just like they were old mates in a pub back in Woolwich, Donnie thought. Instinct told him that Kenny Bishop was up to something. Maybe he hadn't taken an extra cut from the consignment – after all he was being paid, on *top of his stake in the merchandise. But he was a blabber, Donnie knew that. Probably why he didn't like him.*

This consignment was too high-risk for blabbing.

"Well, we'll be off then," Dave said. "If you're happy, Don?"

Donnie nodded and loaded the crate they had opened with the forty-seven others in the van. Multiples of twelve.

The Bish looked expectant. "When will I see the wedge?" he asked.

"All in order," said Dave. "Cheque's in the post. Your money back plus the fee."

The Bish looked disappointed, about to say something, then thought better of it.

Donnie slammed the back of the van shut and locked it. The Eastern European stood around, looking as if he was waiting for a tip.

So Donnie put his hand in his pocket, pulled out a small pistol and shot him in the face.

Dave looked away in distaste as if he'd just trodden in dog shit. The Bish blanched as the fountain of blood that squirted from the man's head spattered his white shoes and pooled on the concrete floor.

"Czech's in the post," Donnie said with uncharacteristic wit.

"Oh no, Donnie … no … no," the Bish stuttered. "What am I gonna do now?"

"You're not telling me he was legal, are you?" Donnie asked. "Get rid. And if you squeak, you get some of the same. Right?"

Dave and Donnie got into the van and told the driver to leg it.

Jason Kelly looked in the wing mirror, where he could see Kenny Bishop standing over the body of the dead man.

"Go, Jase," Dave shouted. "What you hanging about for?"

"You just going to leave Kenny Bishop there?" Jason put on the brakes. "You know that as soon as he gets his money, he'll be down in a bar in Puerto Banús spouting about the deal he's pulled off, like he's Billy Big Bollocks. That's if he hasn't already tipped someone off."

"He's not getting any money," Donnie said. "He just thinks he is."

"So, if he doesn't get it, he'll be in a bar in Calais telling anyone who'll listen how we turned him over," Jason said.

"Jason's right," Donnie agreed with a sigh. "He's high-risk. He's got form for spouting. Both ways, we lose."

Kenny Bishop looked surprised when he saw Donnie get out of the van again with the third, younger man in the white track-suit and the big Rolex.

It didn't take him long to realize why they had returned. Ten minutes later he was swinging by the neck from an RSJ by his striped Gucci belt, his life draining away with every twitch of his blood-stained moccasins.

By four in the morning they were off the south coast of the Isle of Wight. Donnie had just about stopped throwing up and was sip-ping sweet tea out of a tin mug. Just past Ventnor they saw a light flashing from the shore and the skipper flashed a light back. Ten minutes later a motor launch piloted by the skipper's brother drew up alongside and they transferred forty-eight cases of champagne. While Jason, Dave and the skipper sailed the charter yacht back to Portsmouth, Donnie jumped on to the launch and accompanied *the cargo ashore, where it was loaded into a goods van that was going across to the mainland on the six o'clock ferry.*

Donnie was happy to be back on dry land by seven-thirty, and by ten he was unloading the champagne cases into the cellar of a wine bar in Orpington owned by Saul Wynter.

Bish, bash, bosh, he thought. Job all tied up by the time Tommy Kelly and his family were putting their pretty heads down after their comfortable trip. France and back without getting their hands dirty. Not that he was complaining. He would protect Tommy, Cheryl and Sophie with his dying breath. They had been good to him.

He wasn't quite so sure about the other one.

Hearing his empty guts begin to gurgle, Donnie's thoughts turned to breakfast, so he locked the van and went off down the high street in search of a packet of fags, a cup of tea and something to settle his stomach after a busy night.

III

Tommy

TWENTY-FOUR

"Mum wants to meet you," Sophie said. "And Dad."

My guts dropped through the floor. "What?" I said. "They can't, I mean I can't, I…" I didn't know what to say. I felt an extra surge of panic.

Sophie just laughed. "Course you can," she said. "They don't bite." I had imagined that they did. Hard. "I've told them all about you."

It had been a few months now, I had to admit. I'd been seeing Sophie at college most days and then at the weekends – Friday night maybe, and Saturday. Sundays she was usually at home, which gave me a bit of time to catch up. I supposed they were getting curious. I knew that I would have to enter the lion's den one day but had banished the thought from my mind. Although I had done plenty more research on the Kelly family's activities, I'd mostly drawn blanks.

It had to be done.

I was able to feed snippets back to Ian Baylis about stuff that Sophie told me. I'd filled him in on what I knew about the sailing trip: about Russian businessmen and insulted Americans. About art. About them being hauled in by customs. But beyond that very little had happened, so when I called Baylis from the flat and told him that Sophie's parents wanted to meet me, he sounded almost excited.

"Yesss!" he hissed. "Nice one."

"Glad you're pleased," I said. "I'm filling my pants."

"Look, you're just a nice young man going to visit his girlfriend's mum and dad. Pretend her dad works in a bank if it makes you feel any better. Imagine him sitting on the toilet. That usually brings people down to size, I find."

"Thanks for the tip. He probably robs them, doesn't he?"

"Toilets?" said Ian, humourlessly.

"Banks," I said.

"Not quite his style."

"So I'm just a boyfriend going to meet my girlfriend's mum and dad, and her old man works in a bank. Right." I tried to convince myself.

"Yes. Except you're a boyfriend who's also going to plant bugs in the kitchen, the lounge and the old man's study if you can."

"You're pulling my chain." I laughed. "You expect me to bug the place on my first visit, when they'll be watching me like a bloody hawk?"

"Never know if you'll get the chance to go back again," said Ian. "We have to take the opportunity when it presents itself."

*   *   *

"He wants me to bug the place. On my first visit." I was whining down the phone to Tony Morris. There was no negotiating with Ian Baylis.

"Ian's right, mate," Tony said. "You have to strike while the iron's hot. We haven't had anyone get this close to Tommy Kelly before. Use your tradecraft, think what your brother would have done."

His words took me back for a moment. It was the first time Tony had sounded anything but sympathetic. Reading between the lines, he was telling me to shut up and get on with it. Telling me to be a man.

Steve's were big shoes to fill, and I realized that I was about to try them on for size.

TWENTY-FIVE

My legs were already trembling when Sophie picked me up in the Mini. I'd been waiting at the top of Greenwich Park for about twenty minutes and although the sun was shining, it was a chilly morning and the damp had worked its way through the soles of my shoes, freezing my toes. It was hard to tell where the shivering from cold stopped and the shaking from nerves started.

Whichever way you look at it, I was shit-scared.

Sophie kissed me on the lips. She smelt great and I got a taste of something like cherry lip balm and felt a little better.

"You look pale," she said.

"Bit cold," I said. "Not feeling a hundred per cent."

She rubbed the back of my head, combing her fingers through my hair, and I felt better still.

"You're not nervous, are you, Eddie?" Sophie challenged me, smiling.

"Course not," I said, as if it was the craziest thing I'd ever heard.

"Liar! It's only my mum and dad."

"I know, I know. But your dad does come with a bit of a rep, doesn't he?"

"You don't want to believe everything you hear." Sophie smiled. "He's a teddy bear underneath it all."

I nodded. Yeah, right. From everything I'd heard about Tommy Kelly, "teddy bear" was a long way down the list. Only one or two higher than "fairy cake" and "fluffy bunny".

A *long* way from "ruthless killer" and "psychopathic crime lord".

We drove across Blackheath and out on to the motorway, through the ribbon of semi-detached houses to where red bricks gave way to greenery. Past a golf course and an outdoor ski centre. Sophie turned off after a few miles and threw the Mini round country lanes with more confidence than she should have had, seeing as she'd only passed her test a few months before. I put my hand on her leg and felt the soft muscle of her thigh tense and slacken through her tight jeans as she pumped the clutch.

The house wasn't what I'd expected. Yes, there were electric gates. Yes, there was a camera. Yes, there was a long gravel drive. But the house at the end of it was lovely. Old. Pretty, with ivy on the walls and neat white windows that looked out over a tidy lawn surrounded by high hedges. I suppose I'd expected a big, flash villain's bungalow fenced in by barbed wire and guarded by Rottweilers, with a hot tub and a drive full of four-by-fours.

For want of a better word, Kelly Towers looked smart. The kind of place you'd expect a rock star to live. Mick Jagger, or someone old-school like that.

My heart was in my mouth as we crunched up the drive. The only other car visible was a silver-blue vintage thing that looked like an old jet. "What sort's that, Soph?" I asked, slightly embarrassed by my ignorance.

"It's a Bristol," she said. "He's mad about them. They used to make planes in the war. Bombers. Fighters. You should ask him."

"Nice one."

We walked round to the back of the house, where a bigger lawn stretched down to a lake where swans were swimming. A couple of peacocks strutted across the grass, snaking their necks down and pulling up worms.

Sophie opened the back door and pinched my bum as I entered a cloakroom lined with green wellies and shooting jackets. A pair of lazy red hounds jumped off their bed when they heard us and showed their appreciation by licking Sophie's hand, barking and jumping up at her.

"Hello, babies," Sophie cooed. "Eddie, this is Starsky and Hutch."

"Nice dogs," I said. I didn't know enough about dogs to say anything more about them. Actually, they scare me. "What breed are they then?"

I stroked the smooth coats without much enthusiasm.

"Hungarian vizslas," Sophie said. "Mum breeds them."

The dogs showed their appreciation by sniffing my nuts and returning to their beds as if they had decided I was no threat to them. They were right. My nuts had shrunk by three sizes and I had never felt less of a threat to anybody.

Sophie led me into the kitchen. It was vast, practically

the size of our old flat, with flagstones on the floor and one of those cookers that looks like it should be in a restaurant. Something that was simmering on top smelt really good and my stomach rumbled.

"Hungry?" Sophie asked.

Before I could answer, a woman came into the room. I guessed she must have been around fifty, but her hair was straight and blonde, and made her look ten years younger. She was tanned and beautifully dressed in soft grey and black, which looked expensive. She wasn't wearing anything revealing, but there was enough on show for me to see that she still had an impressive cleavage. She was definitely fanciable for an old girl.

Definitely.

She squealed and put an arm around Sophie.

"Mum," Sophie announced, "this is Eddie."

Sophie's mum stood back and took me in. "Soph's told me about you." Her voice was warm and the accent South London. When she smiled, she looked a lot like Sophie. Good teeth.

I shook her hand. "Only good things, I hope. Pleased to meet you, Mrs Kelly."

"Cheryl," she said. "Of course they were all good. We wouldn't want Sophie hanging around with bad lads, would we? Can I get you a drink, Eddie? Sophie, get him a drink."

"Beer?" Sophie asked.

I nodded. Anything to calm the nerves. Sophie handed me a San Miguel from the big American fridge and I took a glug.

"Where you from, Eddie?" Cheryl asked.

"New Cross originally. I live in Greenwich now – well, Deptford, really."

"Me and Tommy were in New Cross for a time when we were first married," she said.

"Bit rough now," I said, not knowing what else to say.

"Always was." She smiled. "You living with Mum and Dad?"

"I'm afraid they're both dead," I told her. "I've got a flat."

Cheryl Kelly's face softened immediately. She stepped towards me. "Ah, I'm sorry. I didn't mean to put you on the spot, babe." She hugged me, the wool of her dress warm and soft. "We'll look after him, won't we, Soph?"

Sophie looked at me over her mother's shoulder and rolled her eyes, giving me the thumbs-up – like I'd given the old sob story and had got the right reaction. Sophie's mum squeezed me again and kissed my cheek, and from that moment I knew I liked Cheryl Kelly almost as much as I fancied her daughter.

"Now, why don't you go in and see your dad while I get dinner on the table?" said Cheryl. "He's been dying to see you all morning, Sophie."

The good feelings I had from meeting Cheryl evaporated on the spot.

TWENTY-SIX

The guv'nor wasn't quite what I had expected either.

Sophie took my hand and led me out of the kitchen into a big entrance hall, which smelt of cigars and furniture polish. A girl was cleaning out the fireplace. She visibly brightened when Sophie walked in.

"Hey, Daska," Sophie said.

"Hello, Sophie, how are you?" Daska grinned. Her accent was thick and sounded Polish or something.

"I'm good, thanks. This is my friend Eddie. Is Dad in there?" Sophie pointed to a door off the hall. Daska nodded and then smiled at me, like we were all part of some big, happy family.

The room that Sophie took me into was long, bright and airy, looking out across the garden. The floor was covered in what looked to me like antique rugs and there were paintings, mostly modern, on all the walls, like a gallery. There was a big, wooden desk stacked up with art books and cigar boxes, and beyond the desk, sitting on a black leather sofa, was Tommy Kelly.

He wasn't nearly as tall as I'd imagined. In my mind, I'd built up an image of a gorilla of a bloke, but when Tommy Kelly stood up he was no taller than me, maybe five nine or ten. When he saw Sophie, his tanned face broke into a big smile, showing expensive white teeth.

"Hello, baby," he said, grabbing Sophie in a bear hug and kissing her. I could see that his body was compact and strong, but softened by the yellow cashmere sweater that was now wrapped around Sophie, owning her. Sophie kissed him back, then wriggled from his embrace, tickling his ribs with her polished fingernails. He let her go, putty in her hands.

"Daddy, this is Eddie." Sophie looked towards me. I was rooted to the spot.

Tommy turned his attention to me, the smile fading a little. "Eddie?" he said.

"Eddie Savage," I said. "Pleased to meet you."

He looked at me for a moment. His eyes were bluish, but pale. His hair was gingery blond, quite long, and swept back from his forehead. He was neat and immaculately groomed with a tidy goatee beard. He had an expensive smell about him, like leather and cigars and lemons all mixed together. When he finally held out a hand for me to shake, it was warm and soft. Not the manly crushing I was expecting.

It was as if he had nothing to prove.

"Any relation of Billy Savage?" he asked. "Camberwell? Light-heavyweight?" His accent was also South London, but faint, and the edges had been polished off.

"Not as far as I know," I replied, already feeling like he

could see right through me. "I'm a bit short of relatives."

"Really? Why's that?"

I looked across at Sophie, aware that I was trotting out the same old story. "My mum and dad passed away," I said. "They were both only children, so I don't have any uncles or cousins or anything."

Tommy nodded. "Mine were both brown bread by the time I was fourteen. It can be a bit lonely, can't it? Less aggro at Christmas, though." He gestured over to the sofa. "Come and sit down."

He turned down the volume on the flat-screen TV that was tuned to Sky's History Channel. Black-and-white images of Winston Churchill and fighter planes flashed across the screen. He tugged at the creases of his trousers and sat down, examined the toes of his brown suede shoes. They looked as if they had never been worn outside.

"So, how do you get by, Ed?" he asked. "You know, without your mum and dad."

"Dad..." Sophie said, with that reproachful whine only teenage girls can make.

"It's OK, Sophie," I said. "I don't mind, Mr Kelly. I was left a little bit of money, so I've got a flat. I'm still at college for a while, but during holidays and stuff I duck and dive a bit. I help out on a market stall."

"Good way to learn the ropes, on the market," Tommy said. "Done it myself. Do you know anything about art, Eddie?"

He pointed at a large, abstract picture, which took up most of the wall in front of us. To me it looked like a big red rectangle with an orange oblong painted in the middle.

"I don't, really," I said.

"It's a Rothko," he said. "One of the great American artists of the twentieth century. What do you think it represents?"

I shook my head. Didn't want to make a prat of myself by having a stab in the dark. "I don't know."

"Me neither. All I do know is that the longer I look at it, the more I see. I get a feeling off it, like I know what Rothko felt when he was painting it. Amazing, isn't it?"

I nodded, not wishing to disagree, but I could feel the sweat trickling down between my shoulder blades. He was making me nervous … more nervous than I was already.

"That's how I judge things, Ed," he told me. "I don't listen to opinions. I take a good old look and work out how I feel about it. In here." He patted his stomach.

I couldn't work out if he was trying to tell me something – that he could see through *me*. I continued to stare at the painting, waiting for something to happen, and it did. The edges of the inner shape began to shimmer a little, one colour pulling against the other, and it began to live in front of my eyes. "I think I can see what you mean," I said finally.

Tommy smiled. "You can tell a lot about someone by what they hang on their walls," he said. "By having a good look and making your own mind up." He clapped a hand on my shoulder and squeezed.

"Mum says lunch is ready," Sophie called from the doorway. She had left me alone in the lion's den for a minute. It had seemed like an hour. She winked at me. I was doing OK.

Tommy Kelly guided me out of the room, his hand still on my shoulder. "I'll take you for a spin in the Bristol after lunch," he said. He squeezed my shoulder again till it almost hurt. "Show you a real car."

TWENTY-SEVEN

Lunch was smoked salmon, then a rich beef stew. I think it was French. It was made with red wine, and had a thick gravy full of tiny onions and mushrooms. Herb dumplings on top. I realized that it was the most delicious thing I had ever eaten in anybody's house. Not that I had eaten in that many houses anyway, and those dinners had been mostly limited to fish fingers, beans and burgers.

Yes, it was *definitely* the best food I had ever eaten outside of a restaurant, so I told Cheryl. She smiled and told me that Tommy had made it. I was momentarily taken aback, but my comment went down well with the boss, who grinned at me and said how simple it was to make: cubed beef, bacon, button mushrooms, shallots and a bottle of cheap burgundy. He enthusiastically went through the motions of making it: browning the beef, sautéing the shallots and bacon.

"Tommy's pretty good in the kitchen, aren't you, babe?" Cheryl said.

Tommy shrugged. "Can't do puddings, though, can

I?" He looked at me. "Great in the pudding department, my missus." He rubbed the small paunch that swelled beneath the cashmere. "I've got Cheryl to thank for this, haven't I, darling?"

She made a few self-deprecating noises and he grabbed her leg under the table. Cheryl gave a squeal and shot him a look that made me think that they were still at it, given half a chance. I must have blushed or looked away at their moment of intimacy, because Sophie jumped in.

"Dad!" she squeaked. "Eddie's here, you're embarrassing him."

"Sorry, Ed," said Tommy.

"No, I don't mind, honestly," I replied. "It's nice to see a bit of love in the house."

They all laughed, and I covered the moment by collecting up the dishes.

"He's well trained, Soph." Cheryl smiled, watching me. Sophie slapped her mum playfully on the arm.

I *was* well trained. Well trained enough to stick a magnetic bug underneath the dishwasher when I went to retrieve a dropped fork while I was stacking. I sat back at the table, trying to look calm, my heart going like a steam hammer. Tommy Kelly poured me more wine.

"You like this plonk, Eddie?" he asked. "It's a Rioja. Spanish." I took another sip. "I'd like to say it came from my estate in the south of Spain, but actually Cheryl picked it up from Sainsbury's. Should be about twelve quid a bottle and they're knocking it out at six ninety-nine. Can't argue with that."

"I don't really know anything about wine," I admitted. "But I like it."

"What does it taste of?" Tommy asked.

He fixed me with pale-blue eyes. Another test. I thought hard, trying to identify the sensation in my mouth.

"Wood?" I suggested.

"Very good," said Tommy. "Aged in oak barrels. Bit of vanilla in there, too?"

I took another sip, and there it was, like the taste you get from sponge cakes. "I see what you mean."

Tommy nodded, and looked at me for a moment while Cheryl began to dish out a rhubarb crumble. "Did you know that the first rhubarb ever sold as a fruit was just down the road from you, in Deptford Market?"

"I didn't," I confessed.

"Eighteen-twenty. Bloke called Myatt. Started with seven bundles. They laughed at him because up till then it had only been used as medicine. By eighteen-fifty he was shifting ninety thousand bundles a year. He stuck his Gregory Peck out. Took the risk. Had a vision."

Cheryl poured custard on the crumble and placed a bowl in front of me.

"Here's your medicine crumble." She winked. "Tommy's full of useless facts like that."

"So you lot have only got a few terms left at college, haven't you?" Tommy continued.

Sophie nodded as if she was bored of hearing about it. Alongside a million other parents, he was clearly wondering what the hell his kid was going to do outside full-time education.

"What are you thinking of doing after, Eddie?" he asked.

"Haven't really thought about it," I said.

"You should. You seem like a bright bloke." He looked at me, longer than was strictly comfortable. Not that I was feeling all that comfortable to start with. I felt the need to expand.

"I'm not bad with computers," I told him. "And languages. I just haven't had a lot of guidance, really. What with my mum and dad not being around."

I got a tingle up my spine as I trotted out the lie because I could see Tommy Kelly was falling for it. His eyes twinkled and he patted my hand. "I don't know nothing about computers or languages," he said, "but it's not held me back too much. The only computer I know how to use is this one." He tapped his head, "but if you know your way around the things, maybe you could help me."

He scraped the custard from his bowl and gulped down a cup of black coffee.

"Now let me show you the Bristol before I get too pissed."

The car smelt of ancient leather and that deep, tarry oil and petrol smell you get from old garages. It was basic inside, not like a padded modern car. The dash looked like the control panel of a plane or something: black dials with luminous numbers and letters. I could feel the springs on my arse through the leather seats.

Tommy started it up and the engine roared. He looked at me and grinned as if his excitement on powering the car up never got any less. He had wrapped a thick red scarf around his neck and pulled on a special pair of driving gloves, punched with holes. When he finished it off with a checked cap, he looked like something from an old film about motor racing. The car clunked into gear and across the gravel, down the drive and away from the security blanket of Sophie and her mum. He roared off down the lane and within minutes we were on a slip joining the A-road, where Tommy really opened up the accelerator.

"Goes like a bomb, doesn't she?" he said. "Still got plenty of grunt for an old bird built in the fifties."

"Fantastic," I said, not really knowing what he meant.

"I'm not a big fan of these new motors with all the bells and whistles. They're OK for hairdressers and Flash Harrys. I prefer an older model with better upholstery and a few more miles on the clock." He paused and glanced at me. "Like my missus," he added, and roared with laughter.

I didn't know how to respond and looked out of the window. He seemed to be waiting for me to say something.

"Don't take this the wrong way, Mr Kelly," I said, "but I think your wife is lovely."

Tommy laughed again and grinned to himself, pleased. In just a few hours, Tommy Kelly had turned from a fearsome ogre into someone warm, friendly … cuddly. I almost began to forget who he was.

"The daughter's not bad either," he said after a moment, and I remembered again. I didn't know the right answer, so I attempted something harmless.

"Goes without saying," I said.

"She's a beautiful girl," Tommy said. "She likes you. Be nice to her."

"I will."

We drove on in silence, the hum of the Bristol's engine the only music Tommy needed. My heart started beating like a drum as I fished in my pocket for a bug and tried to fix it under the seat. Tommy glanced in my direction as I shuffled around, and I adjusted my trousers and coughed as if I was uncomfortable in the seat.

"OK, so you might want something better sprung for a long journey," he conceded. I nodded and managed to find a hold for the bug with my left hand. I wasn't confident it was on properly, but it was the only chance I had. We turned off the A-road then back across some fields past an oast house and over a stream. In ten minutes we were back in the lane leading up to the Kelly home. As the electric gates closed slowly behind us and the Bristol purred up the drive, Tommy spoke again. This time his voice was quiet, measured, and I realized what our drive had been about.

"While we're on the subject of Sophie," he said, "she's my life."

I gulped, about to agree, but he continued.

"And anything ... *anything* ... bad you do to her, I will do to you ten times over. Get it?"

I nodded.

I briefly recalled Benjy French's legend of the bra and the multi-storey. I wondered where Tommy Kelly's definition of bad started. If it included kissing, I was already in the shit. I might get kissed to death.

By him.

We got out of the car and the doors slammed with a heavy clunk, bringing our conversation to an end.

TWENTY-EIGHT

"We're pulling you out," Baylis said. I was confused. An instant feeling of relief washed over me, followed by a kind of dumb panic. What? Why? How?

"You mean I'm off the case?" Sophie had become part of my life and I felt I had passed the initiation of meeting the family. Of meeting the boss and coming out alive.

"No, you twat," Ian replied with his usual charm. "You're sunk to the nuts in the case. I mean we're taking you out of sixth-form college."

"Oh. Why?"

"For a start, you've made contact with Miss Kelly – the aim of the exercise. Some would say you have made *too much* contact." He chuckled in a leery way and I found it hard not to tell him to eff off. "You only have a couple of terms left and, to be frank, you're better off working out-side now. Anything you need to learn, we can teach you."

As the idea sank in, I began to agree with him. My mind was not on the college work, and as a result I wasn't learning anything. I hadn't really made any friends: Benjy French had pretty much moved on once I had started seeing Sophie, and none of her friends could stand the sight of me. I pictured myself lying in bed in the safe flat, only getting up to watch reruns of American sitcoms on TV, nipping out for a spot of lunch, meeting Sophie a few evenings. Could be worse.

"We'll have to find you some other work to do, of course," Ian added, shattering my 'gentleman of leisure' illusions.

"Like what?"

"Well, you told Tommy Kelly you'd done a bit on the market stalls, so that's probably a good way to make your story stick."

"You heard that?" I asked, incredulous.

"I hear everything," Ian said. "Except when the dishwasher's on, you plum. Then we can't hear jacks-hit. Didn't anyone tell you not to put devices on noisy machines?"

"I didn't get much of a chance," I protested.

"Put that one down to experience," Ian said. "At least it's in the kitchen and we can hear it some of the time."

"So what about this market stall?" I asked glumly, picturing stupidly early mornings and stacks of cheap white socks, batteries and three lighters for a quid.

"Tony wants to sort it out for you," Ian said. "He'll meet you tomorrow morning. A couple of days absent from college will work before they chuck you out."

He gave me the name of a café near Tower Bridge, where I was to be at midday the following day. I decided to take today off college too if I was getting chucked out,

174

so I got back into bed and flicked the telly on, determined to make the most of my short-lived life of leisure.

I took the bus along the Lower Road from Deptford to Bermondsey and around twelve found the caff, an old eel and pie shop, on the road that led to the Elephant and Castle.

Tony Morris was hunched over a bowl of pie and mash smothered in a thick, green sauce.

"What's that you're eating, Tony?" I asked, joining him at the table. "Looks like a bowl of snot."

"Thanks for that, mate," he said, unfazed. "Pie, mash and liquor. It's a dying art. Best in town. Lovely job." He splashed more vinegar and pepper over his bowl and gestured towards the thin, bearded man who had just come into the caff and slid onto the bench beside me.

"This is Danny," said Tony. He waved at the man with his fork. "Danny Croucher, Eddie Savage."

The man held out a wiry hand, an anchor tattoo just visible at the wrist of his waxed jacket. He wore a good watch, a vintage TAG Heuer Carrera, and a couple of interesting-looking rings.

"Danny works with us. He's going to sort you out some gear for your stall," Tony explained. He wiped a smear of liquor from his chin. "He'll set you up with a bit of stock and introduce you to a few places to buy stuff."

"So, what am I flogging?" I asked. "Socks?"

"Antiques," Danny Croucher said. "Antiques and collectables. Pictures. It'll be a mixture of good gear and old toot. I'll show you what's what."

We went to a warehouse by Tower Bridge and Danny helped me to choose some bits: a couple of chairs that looked like nothing special to me, a leather suitcase, a couple of old tin toys. Tony peeled off tenners and we soon had enough to fill a stall. We added it to some bits and pieces that Danny already had in the back of his Transit.

"Right," said Tony. "Just need to call in on an old friend of Danny's and you should be set up ready for Friday."

TWENTY-NINE

Our next call was to an ordinary-looking house off Camberwell Road. A hunched old man with a paint-spattered shirt invited us in. He was bald, with wisps of white hair on the sides of his head and a straggly white beard. His accent was foreign, German maybe. Danny introduced him as Barney Lipman. He waved a paint-stained hand at me and Tony, and eyed us up for a moment through thick glasses. Then he led us through a kitchen piled high with dirty plates and jam jars, and out into an overgrown garden.

At the end of the garden was a large shed, tatty and patched up with sections of corrugated steel. It was hot inside, warmed by a fan heater, and smelt of putty, meths and smoke. Canvasses and frames were stacked every-where. There were pots bristling with dirty brushes and ashtrays stuffed with cigarette and cigar stubs, their packs scattered on the floor. On an easel, buried among paint rags and newspapers, was a large picture I sort of recog-nized. Something I'd seen on a poster for an exhibition.

Or rather a half-finished copy of it. There was an orange background and a grey, snake-like figure reared up its head, baring human teeth.

"Francis Bacon?" Danny asked.

"That's right. Study for a figure at the base of the Crucifixion," said Barney. He sounded like a museum curator. "The missing study. Damian Hirst bought the other one for twenty-five mil. This one has been painted to order for a Russian gentleman."

"Spot on," Danny said. "What have you got for me?"

"Depends what you're after."

"Dunno, something small to slip in at Bermondsey. Nothing too flash."

Barney pressed his finger to his lips for a moment, then flicked through a heap of pictures on the floor. He came up with a small one, about thirty by thirty centimetres, framed under dirty glass. Danny looked at it closely and then showed me. It wasn't much of a picture, just a bit of creamy paper with a bus ticket and a couple of numbers cut from newspaper. In the corner it was initialled *KS '47*. I turned it over. There was some faint pencil writing on the faded brown tape that held the picture in at the back. Whatever it was, it looked as if it had been in this frame for a long time.

"What do you reckon?" Danny asked me. I shrugged. It meant nothing to me.

"Kurt Schwitters," Barney said. I assumed he was talking a foreign language and looked blank. "Kurt Schwitters," he repeated. "The Dada artist. He came over here to escape the Nazis. Worked in the Lake District for several years till he died in the fifties. Gave bits of work away."

"So, this is one of his?" I asked, still none the wiser about Mr Shitters or his dad or whatever.

Barney laughed, a sort of gurgling noise that turned into a cough. "No, boy, not one of his. Didn't Danny tell you? It's one of mine."

"Isn't it quite old, though?" I asked.

"I finished it last week." Barney chuckled. "I checked out the cartridge paper, which came from a batch I bought out of an old office supplier in the City. The watermark put it at nineteen-forty-something. The bus ticket is right, nineteen forty-seven, and the newspaper the same date. It would all check out, including the frame and the glass and the tape, as something made in the late forties."

"Genius," Tony said. He'd been quiet, probably not wanting to show his ignorance. He looked at the picture closely. "I still can't tell," he said. "It looks like a few bits of scrap paper to me."

"That's the great thing about Kurt Schwitters' work," Danny said. "You have to know a bit about it to know what it is, so it's not a mug punter's buy. Not like a piece of moody Chinese Staffordshire or a fake Picasso etching. Anyone who half knows their onions will get excited about a piece of work like this, because they know there's actually a chance of one being found on a market stall."

"So what would one of these be worth?" I asked.

"Well, an auction estimate could be anything from twenty-five to seventy-five grand for a collage," Danny told me.

Shit, I thought. Serious wedge.

"The earlier ones, made in Germany in the twenties, fetch as much as two hundred and fifty thousand," Barney pointed out. "But we need to make English-period work so the story looks good."

"One of Barney's got authenticated by Christie's a couple of years ago," Danny said. "We made sixty-five grand, which wasn't bad."

"Not for a week's work," Barney added. His big eyes twinkled behind the thick lenses and he picked a lump of oil paint from his beard.

"So, what's the deal if we take this one?" Tony asked. I couldn't help but feel that he was out of his depth here. After all, here he was doing business with a forger. It didn't sit right with him.

"OK," Danny said. "Here's the deal. We'll give Barney a few quid as a deposit. Then you put the picture out on the stall for as long as it takes to fetch a minimum agreed price, say two hundred, hopefully more. Then it's a fifty-fifty split."

"Why would you want two hundred for it?" I asked. "You said you could get sixty-five grand."

"We can't put another one into auction so soon," Danny explained. "Besides, Tony wants a bit of bait to put on the stall, so we've got to price it right. A loss-leader – knock this one out cheap and see where it ends up."

"Bait?" I questioned.

"A sprat to catch a mackerel," Tony said. "I don't know anything about art, but apparently people look out for this kind of gear. We'll put it out and see who bites."

THIRTY

Sophie was really pissed off with me. She told me I was stupid to drop out of college in the last year.

I told her I didn't have a choice, that my grades so far had been terrible and the college had "invited" me to leave. She said she didn't want to hang out with a loser. I was genuinely offended. I didn't like the fact that Sophie could think of me as a loser. But I could hardly tell her that I already had a proper job.

That I had been employed to spy on her, and her family.

So I told her about the market stall that I was setting up at Bermondsey Market from the following Friday. Said that I would prove to her that I wasn't any kind of flake and I could make a living flogging antiques.

"I admire your enterprise," she said coldly. "Good luck."

I decided to leave her alone for a few days while she got used to the idea. She would come round, I was sure.

Danny picked me up in his van at 3 a.m. on Friday morning and drove us to Bermondsey. We drove up along

181

Lynton Road, which Danny told me was one side of the Bermondsey Triangle, an area supposed to house the biggest concentration of villains in London.

At 3.30 a.m. the market was already cooking. It was still dark and traders were unloading their vans and Volvos by torchlight. Other dealers circled and dived into boxes and the backs of cars with their torches, looking for treasures that others might have missed. Danny explained to me that until quite recently, Bermondsey Market had traded under an ancient law that declared that the source of anything sold before sunrise was not questioned. This meant that the market had been a place to freely trade nicked goods for centuries. The law had changed about ten years ago, but the old habits of dealing in the middle of the night seemed hard to break. Personally, I could have waited till daylight.

We paid for a stall and unloaded the van. As I unpacked, the other traders glanced over what we had for sale. The stock looked as if I had been doing it for a lifetime. Danny explained to me what some of the gear was and how much I should be asking for it: a Turkish kelim rug, a Georgian silver candlestick, a Victorian moneybox, a ship's compass, a top hat and an African mask. I put Barney's collage at the front of the stall, stacked among a few cheap pictures of boats and a rusty enamel sign for Woodbine cigarettes.

Danny bought me a tea and a bacon roll, then went off in search of bargains, leaving me to mind the stall. The sun came up around 7 a.m. and a few more people started to fill the market. Some were obviously

American, wearing duvet jackets and baseball caps and talking loudly, but there were also Italians and Japanese, who spilled out of cabs that had brought them from their West End hotels.

I sold two metal toys to a Japanese woman for fifty quid. We had thirty pounds on each, so I did a deal for the two. Then I sold a walking stick with a carved dog's head to an old American man for sixty-five and began to feel that I was getting the hang of it. By the time Danny got back I had taken nearly two hundred. I'd also turned down a dodgy-looking gold Rolex offered to me for three hundred by a shifty bloke in a cheap suit.

"Good start," said Danny. "It's a nice day for it. Crisp, sunny. Any interest in the Schwitters?"

I shook my head. A couple of people had looked at it blankly and moved on. Then, as if on cue, a man in a smart tweed jacket knelt down and inspected Barney Lipman's picture. He picked it up and studied the back, the pencil inscription and the old tape that sealed it in. He took a magnifying glass from his pocket and looked closely at the front, reading the scraps of newsprint that had been used to make the collage. He looked up and waved the picture at us with a questioning look.

"I'm looking for three," Danny told him. "I don't know what it is, but it looks right."

The man went back to scrutinizing it. "Any idea where it's from?" he asked in a posh voice. I got the gist: he and Danny were playing a game of faking ignorance, each not letting the other know how much he knew about the picture.

"It came from a house clearance up in the Lake District," Danny said, providing the man with the kind of clue he was looking for.

The man licked his lips and put the picture back down again.

"Thanks," he said. "I'll think about it." And he went away.

"You watch," Danny said to me. "He'll walk round a couple of times and the picture will be eating away at him. He doesn't want to spend three hundred quid this morning, but he thinks he's on to something. He's not completely convinced yet, but he'll be going over it in his head until he is."

I watched the man in the tweed jacket walking along the next row of stalls, glancing over in our direction. My powers of observation were becoming pretty well tuned. I noticed his hesitant steps, his nervous glances.

"All about psychology, this game," Danny said. "Here he comes…"

The man in the tweed jacket was trying to look casual as he approached the stall again. "Will you take two hundred for the picture?" he asked. He looked nervous, chewing his lip. Danny shook his head.

"No, mate. Sorry." The man walked away and Danny grinned. "He'll be back."

"Didn't you want two hundred for it?" I asked. I remembered that had been the agreed bottom line.

"Not from him, I don't," Danny said. "I don't think he's going to be of use to us. He probably has an antique shop in the Cotswolds, or he's a bit academic and thinks he's found something special. Been watching too much *Antiques Roadshow*."

I sold a pair of nineteen-fifties kitchen chairs to a young couple for eighty quid. Five minutes later, I saw the man in the jacket circling again. He checked in his wallet and counted out some notes. I nudged Danny.

"Hooked." Danny smiled. "Watch this." He leant down, picked up Barney's picture and hid it behind the stall in a bag. The man approached our stall for the third time. He looked down to where the picture had been. Flicked through the frames, searching for what he clearly thought should still be there. He looked up, panicky.

"The picture?" he said. "The one I was looking at earlier?"

"The Kurt Schwitters? It's sold, mate," Danny said. "Should have been quicker."

The man was deflated. "But…" He was sure it couldn't have been sold because he'd been circling our stall all morning. But he knew he was beaten and shuffled away.

"Bit cruel," I said. Danny grinned.

"There's more juice in that picture yet. That bloke wouldn't have given us any leads. We'll keep fishing."

He glanced at his watch. It was nearly midday. I counted what we had taken. Three hundred and fifty pounds.

"Good day today," he said. "Let's start packing up and we'll grab a bit of lunch."

THIRTY-ONE

Sophie continued to give me the cold treatment.

I had texted her a couple of times, but she had been too busy to meet, she said. I guessed that the best thing was not to make too much of a fuss. Not to look needy and wet. If she could play hard to get, so could I.

Besides, Anna called me up a few days later to see how I was getting on. I told her fine and she suggested we meet up. I took the train up to town and met her in a bar in Soho not far from her office. We had a couple of drinks; she was easy company and always made me feel good about myself. The undivided attention of a woman as gorgeous as Anna was bound to make a bloke feel special. We talked generally, cracking jokes. I told her about my market stall. Then she changed tack.

"How are you getting on with Sophie?" she asked. I was a bit taken aback.

"Er, fine," I said. "Well, I'm not seeing much of her at the moment. She got the hump when I dropped out of college."

"Have you shagged her yet?" Anna asked directly. I blushed. Anna continued to stare at me. A smile curled at the corner of her mouth. "Well? Have you?"

"No," I said honestly. We had snogged and all that, but I hadn't actually slept with her. Something held me back. Fear of involvement, maybe.

Or maybe just fear.

"You need to get back on track," said Anna. "Don't let her cool off too much, will you?"

It suddenly dawned on me. "You've been reading my text messages, haven't you?"

Anna shrugged and raised her eyebrows. I realized she had been sent to check me out, to find out why there had been so little contact with Sophie Kelly for the past couple of weeks. They were watching my every move, every phone call, every text.

"Don't take it personally," Anna said. "It's the nature of the business. It's for your own protection."

"Do you know everything about me?"

Anna smiled. "*Almost* everything," she admitted. "But I'll try to find out a bit more if I can." She reached across the table and I felt her sharp fingernails dig into the back of my wrist. "Let's go eat," she said. "I'm hungry."

We ate at a conveyor-belt sushi place in Brewer Street, and drank hot sake and cold beer. Anna suggested that I soften Sophie up a little: send a couple of gooey texts and a bunch of flowers.

"I haven't done anything wrong," I said.

"It doesn't matter, just send some flowers. Get her back on message."

187

"Is that what it takes?" I asked.

"It won't do any harm," she said. "Women like men who look like they know what they're doing. Show her you do."

I ate raw pink salmon and creamy scallops. Anna wolfed down oysters, tuna and tempura prawns. We spilled out on to the street, my gut warm and contented from the food and the sake.

Anna hailed a cab. "Better head back," she said. A black taxi screeched up beside us and I got in. Anna followed and sat down beside me, her leg pressed against mine.

"Deptford Green," she said to the driver. He initially baulked at the idea of going south of the river, but then caught Anna's eye and became charm itself.

"You coming back with me?" I asked. I could feel her brushing against me.

"All the way," she said. I felt her nails again, this time on the top of my leg. "For coffee. Do you mind?"

I didn't mind. The cab pulled away and Anna leant across and kissed me. I didn't mind a bit.

The flowers worked a treat. I sent Sophie a couple of soppy messages and told her how well I was doing on the market. She called me later in the week and seemed a lot friendlier. She said she had a plan. Said we should meet up at the weekend … maybe I could go to her place for Sunday lunch – her dad was doing his roast beef. I said I'd speak to her after I'd done the market on Friday.

I'd been stalling out for a few weeks. Between times

I had been out and about with Danny, picking up odds and ends. We had been to a huge midweek antique fair near Gatwick and bought plenty of cheap stock. Danny had introduced me to some colourful characters: he knew pretty much everyone and they were all happy to do the new boy a deal.

I'd bought a couple of nice watches, one a big, military pilot's watch with a huge winder. I'd also got a few other bits from planes: an altimeter from a Hurricane, a clock made out of the end of a propeller and a bookshelf made from an old, riveted wing tip. I paid two hundred pounds for the lot. I quite fancied them myself – thought they'd look pretty smart in the flat. Danny quipped that I should probably have a go at flogging them first.

We set up the stall as usual, my fourth week at Bermondsey, but we had done a Sunday fair the weekend before, which had been a bit of a washout. I had plenty of stock. Most of it was new, but Barney Lipman's painting was having another outing. Danny told me that dealers can smell new stock. When something comes on to the market, they have an instinct for it, like fresh meat.

His theory seemed to hold true. We had a busy couple of hours early on and then it calmed down. Most of the dealers thought my new bits were too dear for them to make anything on. I didn't really mind, I was quite happy to hang on to them. Barney's Kurt Schwitters stayed in a stack on the ground at the front of the stall.

Around nine, a murmur went round among the dealers. Someone important had turned up. I looked past the tea van to a parking bay where two big cars had drawn up, a navy-blue Merc and a metallic-blue Bentley.

"Stand by your beds," Danny said.

A nearby stallholder, an old cockney with an impressive moustache, sidled up to us. "They reckon it's some big face come to pay a visit," he said.

I went cold immediately. Surely not…

"Ron says it's Tommy Kelly." My heart began to pound. Why the hell was Tommy here?

Danny tried to put me at ease, told me that the market had a tradition of visiting villains, especially in the old days when the ancient rules applied. It looked like a royal visit. I watched as Tommy Kelly, flanked by two giant minders in good suits, browsed the stalls. The blokes looked like heavies from a gangster movie, one massive with a face that looked like it'd been through the mill, the other just as large, with a less bashed-up boat race but an air of calm menace.

Tommy didn't look like a villain by comparison. He wore a long, charcoal-grey coat, a striped scarf, a baker-boy cap and shiny black boots. He looked more like someone who owned a chain of smart clothes shops – not flash, but quality. I watched from a distance as he walked up and down the rows, saw how the stallholders smiled in that ingratiating way people do when they meet film stars or the Queen. As he came closer to our stall, I noticed Danny becoming increasingly nervous.

"Do you know him, Danny?" I asked.

"Only by reputation," Danny said. "Here we go. This is the one we've been waiting for."

And then Tommy Kelly was approaching our stall.

"Hello, Eddie," he said. "Sophie told me you had a stall down here." His voice was light and friendly, just as it had been at the house. If anything I could detect a bit more South London in his accent, as if he adjusted it for the market. I struggled to say something.

"Yes, I've been doing it about a month," I said. "It's going well." The minders stood either side of him. The brutal-looking one frowned, the other had a glimmer of a smile, maybe because his boss was being friendly. Tommy Kelly looked at the bits and pieces on the stall. He picked up the propeller clock.

"You've got some nice stuff," he said. "Quality gear. How much is the clock?"

I didn't know what to say. I couldn't imagine taking money off him for anything.

"I was looking for one-twenty," I began. "But I'm sure I could—"

"What about the shelf?"

"Best would be one-fifty, but—"

"I'll take them both," he said. "You know I like old planes." He scanned the rest of the stall, then knelt down to look through the stack of pictures and frames in front. I could feel all the other stallholders staring at me. It was as if Bermondsey Market had suddenly frozen and I was held in the beam of a cold spotlight. Tommy stood up again. In his hands he held Barney Lipman's Kurt Schwitters collage.

"What's this?"

"It's supposed to be by some German artist, but—"

"I thought you didn't know anything about art," he said.

Tommy Kelly seemed to have a habit of cutting me off every time I tried to explain myself.

"I don't really, I—"

"Kurt Schwitters?" he asked.

"I think so."

"How much is it?" He turned it over and studied the back.

I glanced at Danny. His face was white. Like he didn't want to be passing fakes to the most notorious crime lord in South London.

"We were after three hundred," I said. "But really we're not sure if it's right or not."

"Of course it's not right," he said. "It's a good one, but it looks like a Barney Lipman job to me. Am I correct?"

I shrugged. Danny shrugged too, and looked guilty.

"I'll take the other stuff," he said, "and what about two-fifty for the fake? I know someone who will like it. I might even sell it to him for twenty grand." He laughed, showing white teeth, his eyes crinkling good-humouredly. One of the minders laughed with him, the other looked a gnat's less scary for a second, then went back to resembling a stone wall. Tommy Kelly took out a cigar and lit it. "Well?" he asked. I realized I hadn't given him an answer. I looked at Danny, who nodded nervously.

"Sure," I said. "If *you're* sure?"

"Course I am." He blew out a stream of fragrant smoke, then as an afterthought added, "Did Sophie say anything about lunch on Sunday?"

"She did mention something."

"Good. Come at half twelve for a drink. I'm doing my roast beef."

"Thanks."

Tommy grinned and nodded at Danny while the unfriendly minder gathered up the purchases.

"Pay the man, Dave," Tommy said to the other one and began to walk away, business done. The big man took a roll of cash from his pocket and peeled off eleven fifty-pound notes.

"That's too much," I called after Tommy.

"Buy yourself some breakfast," he called back. "I'll see you Sunday."

And as he walked away, the rest of the market traders looked at me, mouths hanging open, awestruck.

THIRTY-TWO

"I sold the picture," I said.

"I know," Tony replied, bursting my bubble. "Danny told me."

"So you know who bought it?" I asked.

"What are the chances?" Tony sounded like he wasn't at all surprised by the coincidence of Tommy Kelly buying the fake. "It's amazing the shit people will buy. I still don't get the appeal of that piece of crap, but it's now a piece of crap with a microchip in its frame in the hands of Tommy Kelly. Be interesting to see where it ends up."

"So does Barney Lipman work for us?" I asked. "I thought he was a proper forger, you know, criminal."

Tony chuckled down the phone.

"Barney works for whoever pays him. But no, Danny planted the chip, drilled a little hole in the frame and filled it afterwards."

"Oh, right," I said. "He didn't tell me." I was beginning to feel stitched up. After my evening with Anna, and talking to Tony now, it seemed like everyone knew what was going on except me. I was the one who had charmed Sophie Kelly and her old man, and I was the one they were keeping out of the loop. It felt like I was being set up by all of them, when it was me taking the major risks. I started to feel my temper rising.

"I'm going for lunch with them, Sunday," I said snippily. "But I expect you know that already?"

"Don't be like that. You're doing great."

"I won't need to let you know how it goes because you'll probably be listening in." I was getting quite shirty. "In fact you probably shoved a mic up my arse when my back was turned."

Tony didn't respond.

I remembered my night with Anna and thought that it might have been a real possibility.

On Sunday I took a train from Lewisham down towards Sevenoaks and got off at the station Sophie had told me to. I texted her five minutes before, but she was already there when I arrived.

I had put on a white button-down shirt with jeans and a navy-blue jacket, with white Converses so I didn't look overdressed – like I was trying too hard. It was bright, so I wore my black Wayfarers. I felt pretty sharp. I wanted to look good when Sophie saw me.

I hadn't seen her for a few weeks and I had almost forgotten how lovely she was. Tall, blonde. Denim jacket, skinny jeans and boots.

"I've missed you," she said, kissing me.

"Missed you too," I replied. I kissed her back and got

into the Mini. Sophie slipped into the driver's seat and I smelt her familiar perfume. It brought back all the good feelings I had about her. I leant over and we kissed again until she pulled away.

"Better get home. Heaven help us if we're late for his roast beef." She left the little station and drove fast down the country lane. I looked across at her. She was chewing her lip.

"Just thought I should warn you..." she said. "My brother's going to be there."

"OK."

"It's just he can be a bit awkward with people he doesn't know."

"Fine," I said. From everything I had heard about Jason Kelly, awkward didn't figure on the scale. By all accounts he was a right bastard.

First impressions didn't prove me wrong.

Cheryl was all over me with hugs, telling me I looked too thin, like mums do. The boss was in his office as the dinner was underway in the oven. Jason Kelly sat at the big kitchen table, drinking a beer, leafing through the "News of the Screws", and didn't look up when I came into the room. Rude. Starsky and Hutch paid me far more attention.

"Jason," said Sophie, "this is Eddie."

He looked up. He was dark, olive-skinned with black hair, and he had an earring. Nineteen, maybe twenty. He looked hung over and pudgy; a bit sweaty with dark rings round his eyes. He didn't hold eye contact for long. I took a step towards him, my hand held out.

"All right?" he said flatly, shaking it. His hand was big and damp, and he didn't return my firm grasp. I could smell strong aftershave on my own hand afterwards.

He perked up a bit when Tommy Kelly came in. Jumped to attention. Tommy came towards me and clapped me on the back.

"Hello, son," he said. "Glad you could come."

"Thank you for asking me," I replied.

"Doesn't smell too bad, does it?" He opened the oven to check. It did smell good. "Three ribs … organic, from a farm down the road. Knew the cow's name and everything," he said. "They always see me right."

I supposed they did.

"Shall we have a drink, Cheryl?" He opened the big steel fridge. Gold-foil tops poked out from the wine rack inside.

We drank two bottles of champagne before lunch and the atmosphere was full of loud laughter. Jason laughed at everything Tommy said but shut up abruptly if I joined in. Tommy made some gravy while I took hot dishes over to the table. Jason sat still, watching me.

Tommy was very proud of his Yorkshire puddings, which had risen impressively. I'd helped him by whisking them. "Two eggs and a splash of beer" was his secret, he told me.

"Great Yorkshires, Dad," Sophie flattered him. "Eddie must have given them a proper beating."

"He's got the touch," Tommy said, winking at me.

Jason sniffed and stabbed one with his fork, deflating it slightly before pinning it to his plate.

We wolfed down the beef, hungry after the bottles of bubbly. Jason helped himself to plenty more wine and Tommy topped up my glass.

After lunch, Tommy walked through to his office. Jason and I followed. He snipped the end off a cigar and lit it. Jason smoked one too, making smacking noises as he puffed, smoking it too fast and filling the room with clouds of smoke.

I guessed it must have been quite hard growing up as Tommy Kelly's son. But there was no denying that Jason was a complete arsehole.

"I bought a picture off Eddie," said Tommy. I began to feel nervous. Was this why we had been summoned to the inner sanctum? He gestured towards an easel with his cigar. My Barney Lipman-Schwitters was presented on it. Alongside the other paintings in the room, it certainly didn't look out of place.

Jason Kelly glanced at it and grunted. He clearly wouldn't have known the difference between a picture and a bar of soap.

"We didn't know Mr Savage was bent, did we?" Tommy said, laughing. I felt increasingly uncomfortable. He seemed to be trying to get a reaction from his son. And somehow trying to catch me out at the same time.

"Danny – the bloke I do the stall with – found it," I protested.

"Where does Danny fit in?" Tommy asked. I needed to be careful.

"He's an old mate of my dad's," I said, adopting the slightly sad tone of voice that I put on when I talked about my imaginary dead parents. "He took me under his wing."

Tommy nodded. "Don't know him. And I know most of them down at Bermondsey."

"He used to do Portobello until recently. He lives up that way," I bluffed. "He started Bermondsey because it was nearer to me."

Tommy appeared to accept my explanation. He looked at the picture again. "Thought it might be up Lexi Bashmakov's street," he said to Jason. "Bashi likes a bit of Dada. I might not tell him it's a moody one." Tommy grinned at his own subterfuge.

Jason shrugged. "Looks like an old bus ticket to me, Pa." He looked closely at the picture. "But you know best what the Russians like."

"My son's not a big fan of modern art, I'm afraid," Tommy said.

"To be honest," I said, attempting mateyness, "I didn't know what it was either, Jason."

Jason shot me an unsmiling glance that shut me up.

"More of a hands-on man, aren't you, Jase?" Tommy looked at his son, who was still puffing hard on the cigar. "You want to take it easy on the lardy stuff and the sauce if you're training."

Jason stubbed the cigar out in a big ashtray.

"Jason's got a big fight coming up," Tommy told me by way of explanation.

"I didn't know you were a boxer," I said. Another attempt at communication. Jason unconsciously made a fist and caught it in the palm of his other hand.

"I'm not, I'm a businessman," he said. "I do a bit of martial arts … kick-boxing, ju-jitsu and that. It's just a charity boxing match."

"It's not *just* a charity match," Tommy filled in. "It's a big event, next month, up in Woodford. A benefit in aid of the son of one of my colleagues, who's in a wheelchair."

"Good cause," I said. I didn't like to ask how the colleague's son had ended up in a wheelchair.

"Maybe you should come," Tommy suggested.

"I'd like to," I said.

I looked at Jason. He didn't seem so keen.

THIRTY-THREE

I couldn't believe it when Sophie showed me the invite. First I thought it was for the charity boxing match, but then I realized it was too posh for that: stiff, white card with gold edging:

> *The Proprietors of* OK! *magazine request the pleasure of your company at the marriage of Miss Natalie Holmes to Mr Liam Baldwin...*

Natalie Holmes was the girl of the moment: singer, model, TV presenter. Liam Baldwin was the Tottenham striker who had just changed hands for millions and was off to Barcelona. It was a marriage made in celebrity heaven.

"I didn't know you knew Liam Baldwin," I said to Sophie.

"I don't really." She was grinning from ear to ear: she clearly found my wide-eyed, star-struck amazement funny. But the only famous person I'd ever seen was some bloke off *X Factor* getting into a taxi at Charing Cross. "I was at boarding school with Natalie. Her old man does some business with mine."

It made sense that they knew each other. Natalie Holmes was similar to Sophie: they both had the same easy charm and classless accent that had made Natalie popular on TV. They were both drop-dead gorgeous.

I wondered what sort of business Natalie's dad was in. I guessed it wasn't double glazing. "I can't believe you never told me," I said.

"You never asked." Sophie laughed. "I'm not a name-dropper."

I looked at the stiff white card again. It was the first time I'd seen our names together: *Miss Sophie Kelly and Mr Eddie Savage.*

I liked the way they looked, written down. I was just about getting used to my new name, feeling like it belonged to me.

There was a list of conditions: no photos, no phones, no talking to rival publications...

"I'd better get myself a suit."

"We'll go on Saturday," Sophie said, kissing me. "I'll help you choose."

After Sophie had gone, I desperately wanted to tell someone. It was six weeks since I had first met her parents, and I was already being welcomed into the bosom of the family. I knew Tony Morris would be pleased with my progress.

I rang him from a callbox at Deptford DLR. I didn't want to use the mobile and have people listening in while I told him what a clever boy I'd been.

"Where are you calling from?" he asked. Always his first question.

"A payphone," I said. "In Deptford."

"Are you in trouble?" He sounded concerned.

"No. Nothing like that, Tony," I said, a bit disappointed by his anxiety. "It's good news. I've been invited to a wedding with Sophie Kelly."

"Where?" Tony asked.

"Down in Sussex somewhere. They're famous – it's Natalie Holmes and Liam Baldwin. You know, the footballer. Big posh do … *OK!* magazine are doing it."

Tony went quiet on the other end of the line. All I could hear was the rush-hour traffic rumbling behind me.

"Are you effing mad?" he said after a while.

"What?" My excitement began to drain away. "I thought it would be a good way of getting closer to the family."

"Yeah, and share it with half the bleeding country." Tony was beginning to raise his voice. "Imagine when the magazine is in every supermarket in the country and there's your face in it, prancing around with effing celebrities and the king of crime himself."

"I hadn't thought of it like that," I admitted.

"Have you told Ian?"

"No, it's only just happened. I'm sorry, Tony. I didn't deliberately get myself into it."

"All right. I'm sorry for shouting, mate. But listen, you're going to have to get yourself out of it."

We drove across Waterloo Bridge into the West End on Saturday morning. Sophie had borrowed her mum's convertible Beemer and we had the roof down. It was cold but sunny and the London skyline looked crisp and sharp in the bright light, like a backdrop to the opening credits of a film.

I hadn't said much on the drive up, but the wind rushing by and Mark Ronson's remixes had made conversation unnecessary. Sophie drove round the south side of Trafalgar Square, right by where Tony had taken me to meet Sandy Napier months back. She parked in a square somewhere off Haymarket and switched off the engine. The electric roof whirred back across, throwing us into shadow.

"What's up with you then?" she asked, not looking at me.

"Nothing," I replied.

"Good. So stop looking like a smacked arse and let's go shopping."

It was a phrase I could imagine her mum using and it made me smile.

"Sorry," I said, and squeezed her hand.

We walked along a street full of what you'd call gentlemen's clothes shops: hats, tweed jackets, smart shirts and suede shoes like Tommy Kelly wore. We looked in a window that displayed shoes of every shape and colour. I caught Sophie looking down at my scuffed Nikes.

"In you go." She grinned. "We'll make a gentleman of you yet."

The shop assistant sounded as posh as the Queen but treated us like *we* were royalty. Ten minutes later I walked out with a pair of highly polished, handmade black loafers, each in its own cotton bag stuffed with a wooden shoe tree.

"Three hundred quid?" I gasped. I didn't know shoes could cost that much.

"You get what you pay for," Sophie said.

"But I can't pay that," I pleaded. "I've got just about enough for a suit. I can't let you buy me shoes."

"I didn't," said Sophie. "They went on Dad's account. He told me to get you kitted out. He wants you to look right."

Two handmade shirts and a pair of cashmere socks later, we sat in an Italian café sipping lattes. I was still trying to figure how I was going to get out of this wedding, and it must have shown on my face.

"You're looking like a smacked arse again," Sophie said in a sing-song voice.

"I'm sorry, Soph. I just feel out of my depth with this wedding and being bought expensive clothes and everything. I don't think I should go."

Sophie's face dropped. "What do you mean?"

"I don't think I'd feel right there," I bluffed. "With a load of celebs and people I don't know, in clothes I don't own."

"Don't be stupid, Eddie." Sophie had her no-messing look on. "You'll be with me. They invited you."

I stared at the froth in the bottom of my cup. I was wriggling on the hook.

"Besides, Mum and Dad are really chuffed you've been invited." Sophie's tone softened a little. "They're fed up with taking me to places on my own like Nelly No-Mates, with every bloke frightened of even talking to me. You're the first one who's dared come home with me. They like you for it. *Dad* likes you."

I felt like I was being made an offer I couldn't refuse. I looked up at Sophie. She was smiling, but she knew she had me by the short and curlies.

"You wouldn't want to upset him," she said. "Would you?"

"No, I wouldn't."

"Right, well that's sorted." Sophie stood and collected up the shopping bags. "Let's go and buy this suit."

Tony Morris was quiet on the other end of the phone.

"I'm going," I told him. "I can't get out of it."

Silence.

"I promise I'll keep my nut down, Tony. You wanted me to get close to them, and now I really have."

Deep breath.

"It's just that I've got so far, they'll be suspicious if I don't go. I'll feel safer if I'm there with them rather than blowing them off. I can avoid the press."

Tony spoke at last, sounding resigned. "You'd better make sure you do. Or you're stuffed. *We're* stuffed."

"I promise," I said. "You won't be sorry."

"I'd better not be. One more thing, Eddie…"

"Yes?"

"You're an obstinate little bastard."

"Sorry, Tony."

"Like your brother."

THIRTY-FOUR

The village was one of those quiet, English picture-post-card places that normally would have been still and sleepy on a warm spring afternoon. But this Saturday it was like the circus had come to town. One or two old women, out walking their dogs or tending their roses, looked dis-approvingly at the queue of limos and large black cars that snaked through their village street. Four-by-fours were parked up on the kerb in front of the pub and curi-ous drinkers, smoking outside, craned their necks to see whether anyone famous was behind the tinted windows.

I got out of the Kelly Bentley, Tommy's everyday motor, and held the door open for Sophie, turning my face away from the couple of paparazzi who had turned up in the hope of catching a sneaky pic. Luckily for me, *OK!* maga-zine wasn't about to let anyone else in on the action and the moment we stepped from the car, a heavy from the mag came over to protect our privacy with a big black umbrella.

All the guests were escorted to the path that led up to the village church and the stately home beyond, where the reception was being held.

We queued while security men checked everyone's invitations and took away their mobile phones, which were named, bagged and put into a crate. Sophie handed over her iPhone. I gave in mine too, but kept my tiny emergency mobile tucked into my sock.

Just in case I needed my hotline to Tony or Ian Baylis.

In front of us, Tommy and Cheryl seemed to get stuck for a moment as a security guard at the church gate checked for his name on the list.

"You won't find it on there," Tommy said, smiling patiently.

The heavy began to flex his muscles beneath his suit. He was shaven-headed and stupid-looking. Dead behind the eyes.

"Sorry, sir," he said. "If your name's not on the list, you can't go through." He continued to look at Tommy, his mouth set in a tough-guy grimace, as if to say there would be no compromising. Whoever you were.

Tommy looked at Cheryl and smiled. "Sorry, darling," he said. "Looks like we'll have to go home, doesn't it?"

I could sense trouble and my guts began to feel watery. People in the line behind us were starting to mutter impatiently. Dave, Tommy's driver, had been standing by. He stepped up to the security guard.

"It's Mr Kelly," he said quietly. "I suggest you tell your boss."

The security guard looked at Dave, who was a good few centimetres taller than he was. He pulled out his walkie-talkie and muttered something into it. Within seconds, a worried-looking man ran across from the church, tripping over himself, the apologies tumbling from his open mouth.

"Do come through, Mr Kelly," he spluttered. "Very sorry for the misunderstanding…"

Tommy paused briefly to speak to the security guard, whose face had turned white, draining him of aggression and leaving him looking like the fat bully he was.

"You'll remember who I am next time, won't you?" Tommy's voice was calm and friendly.

"Yes, Mr Kelly. Sorry."

"And you might try smiling in future."

Tommy tucked something into the security guard's breast pocket and escorted Cheryl through the gate. The guard didn't even look at our invites, and Sophie and I followed her parents up the church path.

Coming out of the church it became clear just how many people had been invited as they spilled onto the lawn outside. The grass led up to a terrace in front of the main house, where waiters in white coats stood with trays of cold champagne. Sophie and I made our way up to the terrace, where she chatted with girls she knew. As she introduced me, they all gave me the same look: a once-over, wondering how I had dared get involved. As I saw the deference ninety per cent of the guests showed to Tommy Kelly, I wondered the same thing myself.

The terrace was crammed with A-, B- and C-list celebs. There was a world-famous singer wearing a white silk suit with medals, his boyfriend dressed in baby blue beside him. TV presenters from reality shows. An actor from *EastEnders*. There were representatives from most of the current girl bands, looking like their record companies had sent them as diplomatic envoys. They all seemed slightly smaller and better-looking than they did on TV. Then there were footballers, loads of them. Some faces I recognized, others I didn't know from Adam. Liam Baldwin was a popular boy.

The older generation was mostly represented by couples of Tommy and Cheryl's vintage: well-preserved, middle-aged types with all-year tans. The women with Botoxed expressions and the men all smoking cigars. Tommy Kelly's was the biggest.

I was relieved to see that the photographers were only interested in the celebrity faces, and they were all happy to pose for the cameras – another day's work. As Sophie was dragged to have a group shot taken with the bride and her posse of girlfriends, I sloped off to a shady corner, taking another cheeky glass of champagne from a waiter's tray on the way.

"Easy does it, sir," the waiter said. "Need to keep your wits about you."

I was about to say something clever, but then I recognized the man beneath the moustache. It was Oliver, the bloke I'd seen hanging around Baylis, always watching me.

"What?" I said.

"Just in case," he said. "Ignore me."

I did as I was told and sipped my drink, the taste of it dry on my already dry mouth, and went through to where the food was being served.

THIRTY-FIVE

The dinner was top of the range. For starters there was a cold soup that tasted of tomatoes and chilli, which sounds dodgy but tasted great. Then there was sort of thin spaghetti with lobster, followed by slices of roast beef with little Yorkshire puddings, then a fruit salad that tasted like cherry brandy, and chocolate profiteroles. All made by a famous chef who came out and took a bow. There was white wine, red wine and more champagne for the toasts and what have you, and although I only took a few sips of each, I was beginning to feel a bit pissed by the end of it.

The light was fading when everyone drifted away from their tables and out to the marquee. I began to feel a bit more relaxed now the lights were low. Music was playing already and a band was setting up on the stage above the wooden dance floor.

A TV presenter, a lads' mags regular who had been MC through the speeches, got up and introduced the band. The drummer counted in and the guitars came in with a familiar riff.

"Ladies and gentlemen," the MC shouted. "Please welcome to the stage … Mrs Liam Baldwin!"

Natalie, still in her wedding dress, took the mic and launched into the song that had been a hit for her the year before.

Everyone cheered and stamped the floor, and people started dancing. Halfway through the song, Natalie made an announcement. People applauded and whooped.

A tall, bearded figure strode on to the stage and picked up a guitar. He strapped it on as if it was a missing part of his body and played a blinding solo that must have lasted five minutes. Everyone in the tent went mad. I could see Tommy Kelly, cigar clamped between his teeth, beaming all over his face and nodding his head like he was approving every note. Sophie nudged me and rolled her eyes.

"He's his hero," she shouted into my ear. "Embarrassing, isn't it? Nat's dad paid fifty grand to his charity to get him to come and play, just to impress the old man."

Then I realized who the guitarist was. I remembered his face from the CD shelf at home. He was one of my brother's heroes too. "The man is a god," he used to say.

If he could see me now.

After a few more songs, the band took a break and a DJ took over with one of those floor-filling, wedding-party anthems. One that I hate.

I'm not overly keen on dancing, but Sophie grabbed me by the arm and pulled me on to the dance floor. I shuffled around a bit while Sophie strutted and shook her stuff; she loved dancing and she was good.

"Come on," she said, grinning. I clearly wasn't showing enough enthusiasm. I took another glug of wine from our table and began to dance.

"Come on, Eileen…"

Sophie took hold of my hand and spun me around towards her and, as she did so, I felt the mobile hidden in my sock slip out. I watched as it went skidding across the dance floor.

I let go of Sophie and scrabbled on my hands and knees between people's legs, desperately trying to grab it. It hit a chair leg on the edge of the dance floor and, spinning, finally came to rest.

Right at the feet of a waiting bouncer.

I reached out to pick it up, but before I could, the bouncer leant down and closed his meaty fist around it. "No phones and no photos," he said, shaking his head. "You were meant to hand this in. Who knows what you've been doing. Taking pictures? Phoning the papers?"

"I'm a diabetic," I said. "It's for emergencies."

He could tell I was lying. "I'm going to have to confiscate it. Might have to destroy it."

He wasn't going to budge. I hadn't taken any photos, of course, but my calls to Tony and Ian Baylis would be listed on there, along with their numbers and the hotline to Sandy Napier's department. My heart was thumping and I began to shake, not knowing what to do.

Suddenly the expression on the bouncer's face changed.

"I'll look after that," a familiar voice said from over my shoulder. It was light, almost high-pitched, but the threat was undeniable.

I turned to see Tommy Kelly holding out his hand for the phone. The bouncer nodded and put it into his hand. Then, instead of giving it back to me, Tommy slipped the phone into the pocket of his jacket.

"Bit silly, wasn't it, Eddie?" he said, and winked.

Then I knew I was as good as dead.

Donnie got the call early evening. He'd had a couple in the pub at lunchtime and nodded off in front of the football when his mobile rang.

The firm's one.

He gulped down a cup of black instant coffee, lit a fag, then climbed into the Merc. He pulled off the estate, where any car worth over fifty quid was done over every five minutes. But nobody ever touched Donnie Mulvaney's car.

When he got on to the motorway, he floored it. He picked up Jason on the way, stopping outside his flat to call him on the mobile.

"Mike Hunt," Donnie said when Jason finally picked up. "Mike Hunt's outside."

Jason sleepily acknowledged Donnie's usual joke and told him he'd be a couple of minutes.

Donnie read his paper while the lazy sod got out of bed as it began to get dark. He waited half an hour while he shit, shaved and showered and put on his best bib and tucker. Gucci suit and shoes. Gold Rolex. Hair gel.

The car filled with Jason's aftershave as he got in and slammed the door.

"All right, Jase?"

Jason nodded. "Bit caned," he said. "Heavy night last night. Completely mullered." He closed his eyes and sunk back into the seat.

Donnie tutted to himself. When he'd been nineteen, he'd have been training, road running at four in the morning, rain or shine, even when he'd had a skinful and blown his wages the night before.

"You'll be all right once you've had a drink," Donnie said. He passed the hip flask to his passenger and headed for the M25.

THIRTY-SIX

"Are you all right?" Sophie asked me. I'd gone outside to get some air and try and work out what to do next. My heart was going like a train and my legs felt weak. "You look like shit, babe," she said. Even in the half-light outside the tent she could see that I looked terrible.

"I think I've had a bit too much to drink," I said. "I'm not used to it."

"Lightweight." She smiled and put her arm around me, which made me feel even more trapped and I instinctively pulled away. I caught the look in her eye.

"Sorry, Soph," I said. "I think I need to go to the toilet. Back in a minute."

I turned away towards the main house, but Sophie caught my hand. "Eddie," she said. "Is there something you're not telling me?"

She fixed me with those blue eyes, normally warm and smiling. Now they were cold and hard, searching. I tried not to look away.

"Honestly, babe," I insisted, "I just feel a bit sick." I

hoped I didn't look as guilty as I felt. "I'll be better in a minute."

She let me go and I walked towards the main house, feeling her eyes on my back, watching me go.

To say that I felt sick was no lie. It was an understatement. I wasn't really drunk, but I felt sick to the bottom of my stomach. The fear that was chewing away in my guts made me want to throw up; when I found the toilet, I did.

I looked at my pale face in the mirror, wondering what to do, calling myself every name under the sun for my own stupidity. I'd been warned not to come, but I'd dug my heels in. And now Tommy Kelly had my phone with all my calls and contacts on it. Access to everything I knew, and to everyone who was on his case. My mistake could cost them all their lives. And mine.

And in a few hours I was supposed to be travelling home with him, his wife and his lovely daughter.

I rinsed out my mouth and splashed my face with cold water. Then I punched my own cheek for good measure, hating myself, ducked out of the toilet and into the corridor. I looked around and made my way towards the kitchen, where all the catering staff were coming and going in their white jackets.

The kitchen was still clattering with activity. Champagne on ice was still being sent out, along with trays of coffee, beer and more food. I looked for the waiter I recognized. He wasn't there. I panicked again, terrified that he had gone off duty. I pushed through the fire door that led out behind the house and found a group of waiters taking a break.

On the edge of the group was my man Oliver with the moustache. He was alert and had seen the fire door open. When he recognized me, he cocked his head, broke away and walked off into the darkness of the garden.

I followed and caught up with him by a pond. He threw his cigarette stub in and it hissed. "Well?" he asked.

"I've lost my phone," I confessed, feeling like a child.

"Which one?" He looked instantly concerned.

"The hotline," I said.

"You—" He called me a few four-letter names and then slid his own phone out from the back of his trousers and started to punch in a number.

"Get yourself back in there before they miss you," he snapped. "I'm going to have to try to get head office to override the PIN before anyone looks at it. But whatever you do, don't make any further contact with me. Got it?"

"Thanks," I said, pathetically grateful that he was taking charge. "But how will I know if you've managed to block it in time?"

"Because if I have, you'll still be alive tomorrow. Now sling your hook."

I was about to apologize, but his call connected, so I turned and ran across the wet grass towards the lights of the house, every bone in my body telling me to run in the opposite direction. And never stop.

The gravel crunched under the Merc's wheels as it purred up the drive. The house was completely lit up and music was throbbing from the huge marquee that spread out across the lawn. Disco lights and lasers lit up the night sky.

Donnie saw that his passenger had woken up and was swigging from one of the cold bottles of water that he always kept in the mini fridge in the back of the car. Jason sniffed loudly and Donnie took it as his cue to speak.

"I'll drop you off by the tent, Jase. Then I'll park up by the house. I've got a meeting. Someone I need to find."

"Nice one," Jason said. The car stopped a few metres from the marquee and he got out, ready to party. "Catch you later."

Donnie drove off and parked in front of the main house. A security man came out to meet him, to tell him that parking was forbidden there, then quickly changed his mind. Donnie shook his hand, asked a couple of questions and walked down towards the marquee.

Donnie stepped over the guy ropes and worked his way around to the back of the tent, looking for someone. It wouldn't take him long to find them. It never did. He had an instinct for it.

Behind the marquee was a smaller tent, a kind of gazebo, where the security boys hung out, keeping a low profile. Donnie pushed the tent flap aside and walked in. Three heavies were standing around, drinking cans of beer and talking tough. They looked at Donnie as he stepped in, checked out his light-grey suit and took him for a chauffeur.

"Got a pick-up at midnight," he said, confirming their assumption.

One of the heavies looked at his watch. "Bit early, aren't you?"

"A bit," Donnie said. "Thought I'd get here sharpish, check

out the crumpet and the famous faces, see if there's any deals to be done." Donnie winked at them and patted his pocket. "Been a good night, has it?"

The security men seemed to warm to him a little: he was one of them. Up to a bit of this and that on the side.

"Yeah, cracking," one of them said. He sounded Welsh to Donnie. "It's up to the tits with celebs in there." He nodded towards the tent. "Like the bloody Royal Variety Performance."

Donnie turned to the other two.

"What about villains?" he asked. "I heard there are a few in attendance."

"One or two big fish," the larger of the men said. "Can't tell you who for security reasons." He puffed himself up with pride: in the know, mixing with the big boys, keeping things to himself.

Donnie let out a slow whistle, apparently impressed.

The heavy warmed to his theme, keen to show his own uncompromising stance. "Yeah, had a bit of a run-in with one," he said. "The biggest. Soon sorted it out, though. He's a real gent once you know him."

Donnie looked impressed as the heavy lifted out a red banknote from his breast pocket. "Even gave me a nice drink to show there were no hard feelings." He tucked the fifty back into his pocket and Donnie Mulvaney knew he had his man.

"Got some very nice gear you might like to spend that on," Donnie told him. "Interested?"

He stepped outside the tent and the heavy followed him.

Donnie was looking up at the stars. "Lovely night," he said.

"What've you got then?" the heavy asked.

"Steady on, son," Donnie said. "What's your name?"

The heavy paused a second. He looked at Donnie with the permanent scowl he wore. His face had fixed into a hard-man grimace for so long that any other expression was almost impossible.

"Wayne," he answered, suspicious.

"Well, Wayne," Donnie continued, "I like to deal on a friendly basis, first-name terms and that. I like to observe the little niceties. Manners don't cost nothing – a little tip of the hat and a smile here and there, to show respect. That's what I was taught."

Wayne began to look confused and his scowl hardened. "What about this gear?" he asked.

"I'm getting to that," said Donnie. "But if you don't deal with people on a nice, friendly basis, they'll think you're just a thug…" Donnie pulled a monkey face and scratched his hands under his armpits like a gorilla.

Wayne didn't like it. "Are you taking the piss?" he said, his fists clenching automatically.

"Easy, tiger. Just having a chat." Donnie patted Wayne on the shoulder and pulled a pack of cigarettes from his pocket. "Fag?" he said.

Wayne took one and put it in his mouth while Donnie found a light. He sparked up the lighter and held it out with his left hand at chest level so that the heavy was forced to lean down to catch the flame, his mouth slack around the cigarette. Then, as the tip caught the flame, Donnie let go with his right hand: a punch so hard and fast that it broke the fat man's jaw in one fluid sweep.

A sucker punch.

Wayne flew backwards, two teeth flying from his mouth as

he fell and, before he knew where he was, Donnie was on him, his knee on his chest, squeezing the air out of him.

"Like I said," Donnie whispered, right up close, "a smile don't cost nothing."

The cut-throat razor was already open in his hand and he put it into Wayne's mouth, slicing left and then right, opening the cheeks almost to the ear, the blood spurting down his throat and across his chest.

Donnie stood up, wiped the razor on Wayne's jacket and put it away. He checked his own suit for blood, then kicked the security man in the bollocks, forcing his newly widened mouth to open in a red scream. Donnie leant down and took the fifty from Wayne's breast pocket, screwed it up and shoved it into his bloody mouth.

"Buy yourself some stitches, son," he said.

Donnie stood back and tugged at the front of his suit, readying himself to walk round to the front of the marquee for a much-needed drink. He swung a parting kick at Wayne's bloody head, rocking it like a punchball.

"And remember..." Donnie said. "Smile."

IV

Jason

THIRTY-SEVEN

"You'd better get up here straight away." Tony's voice was cold, sharp. I'd never heard him angry like this.

Monday morning.

I'd spent most of Sunday in bed, hiding under the duvet; glad of the sanctuary of my safe house, where no one, except Tony, Ian and Anna, knew where I was.

Saturday night I'd stayed at the Kelly house, not sleeping, shitting hot conkers, convinced I was about to be taken out and shot. The atmosphere in the car on the way back had been all right – for everyone else. It was just me.

I'd really messed up.

Tommy and Cheryl had clearly had a good night, though there had been some kind of ruck with a couple of the bouncers. We saw the aftermath on the way out. One of them had been in a fight and had got cut up. An ambulance had been called and as we left, Tommy had steered his wife and daughter away from the ugly scene.

Sophie was a bit off with me, probably because I'd behaved like a knob all evening. I blamed it on the drink, but that didn't make it any better in her eyes. She felt I'd let her down. Cheryl had given her sympathetic glances in the car on the way back, suggesting that I'd just got over-excited. Tommy had stared out of the Bentley's window. He didn't mention my phone.

When we got back, I'd been shown to a guest room with crisp, white sheets and deep pillows, where I'd tossed and turned until daylight.

Cheryl dished me up a full English, which I could hardly eat, then Sophie dropped me off at the station at around ten. I don't know if I was being paranoid, but everyone seemed a bit quiet. I was hoping it was down to hangovers. I still didn't have my phone, and it hadn't been mentioned when we got back either. I apologized to Sophie again, saying I hoped to see her in the week, and got back to the flat as quick as I could.

I remembered Oliver's parting words: that I would still be alive if they hadn't hacked into my phone. But it felt like I had a death sentence hanging over me.

I met Tony outside the pub off Trafalgar Square. Ten o'clock sharp. He looked like thunder. We ducked through the pub and out along the alleyway into the ministry building. The smell of overcooked cabbage made me feel more nauseous than I already was.

They were waiting for me. Both Sandy Napier and Ian Baylis were sitting behind a table in a sparse room, lit by a fluorescent strip. Hamish Campbell, the technical spod, was there too. Tony guided me to a chair and I sat down in front of them.

Sandy Napier cleared his throat. He looked as if he was about to bite someone. Me, probably.

"Well," he said. "Bit of a cock-up on Saturday night, we hear."

"Yes, sir," I said. "It was an accident."

"An accident that could have cost some of us our lives," Ian Baylis spat. It was as if he had been waiting for this moment since he'd first met me. "Were you pissed?"

"I'd had a glass of wine, but I wouldn't say I was drunk," I replied.

"Oliver said you were drinking," Baylis said.

"I'm afraid this incident gives me serious doubts about your suitability, Savage," said Napier. "What's your view, Hamish?"

"As far as we can see," said Hamish, flicking through several pages of printout, "no calls were made from the phone that evening. We managed to disable the SIM by 11.30 p.m."

"Good," Napier said.

"What we can't tell from this is whether the SIM has been copied or cloned." Hamish looked up at me from his sheets of paper.

"With respect," I said, "Tommy Kelly doesn't know the first thing about computers and technology."

"As far as you know," Baylis added sharply.

"No, he really doesn't. I'm sure of it. It's not how he works."

"I should keep your trap shut while we decide what to do about this," Napier said. I had been told. "He may not have done anything about it that evening, but he'll have people who can. As far as we know, he still has the phone and could be having it taken apart as we speak."

I had no argument. I had let the hotline phone slip into enemy hands.

"Well…" said Baylis after a moment, looking at Tony. "I think this justifies my objection to putting a child on the job."

Tony and I bristled. Tony went red.

"I think that's a bit rich, Ian," he said cautiously. "OK, he's made a serious slip, but he's done a hell of a lot of good work in a short time. He's got us closer than ever before to the heart of this organization."

"And blown it."

"Not necessarily," Tony continued. They were talking about me as if I wasn't there, but I was glad Tony was defending me, especially as I knew he was majorly pissed off.

"I think these arguments are irrelevant," Napier said, holding up his hand to silence both of them. "The immediate problem is what to do with Savage. If we take him off the case, we have to disappear him."

My stomach lurched. I didn't like the idea of being "disappeared", whatever that meant.

"It would mean sending him up to another safe house," Napier continued. "The Aberdeen one, perhaps – nice and remote. Another change of ID and so on."

I started to feel frightened.

"Or," suggested Tony, "we could put him back in the flat for a few days, lie low, see if anything occurs and then make a decision?"

They considered for a moment.

"OK, agreed – until the end of the week," Napier said. "By that time we'll know if there's any fallout. Everyone on Code Red."

Code Red was department speak for full alert.

They were probably all cursing me, but I breathed a sigh of relief. Hamish Campbell pushed another small phone across the desk towards me.

"Your new hotline," he said. "Don't lose it."

I was driven back by Tony in a silver car with darkened windows. They really weren't taking any risks. Tony said very little in the car. All I could feel was an overwhelming sense of his disappointment in me; that I had made such an elementary slip. He dropped me off at the flat in Deptford.

"Keep your nut down," he said. "Don't go out or make contact with anyone except me or Ian. You still have the iPhone, don't you?" I was about to joke that I'd lost that too, but it wasn't the moment. "Incoming calls only, got it?"

I nodded. "Sorry, Tony. I'll try and make it up to you."

He shrugged and got back into the car. "Await further instructions," he said.

I didn't have to wait long. I spent the afternoon watching a war film on DVD: *Saving Private Ryan*. Or "Shaving Ryan's Privates", as Steve had called it. It's a good film: tough, brave and full of brotherly love and loyalty. Just what I was missing. I wondered what Steve would have made of my complete balls-up. Then, around five, my iPhone rang. It was Sophie.

There *were* further instructions, but not from Baylis or Tony.

"Dad wants to see you," she announced. "Tomorrow morning."

I was white and shaking like a leaf, glad she couldn't see me. "OK," I said weakly.

"Dave will pick you up at nine."

THIRTY-EIGHT

"I know," Tony said down the phone. "Right now, even when you fart, I know about it."

"So what do I do?" I asked. To be honest, I was terrified.

"Same choices apply, really. I've spoken to Napier and Ian already. Ian's handed this bit over to me, what with you being my protégé and everything. Lucky me."

"I'm glad," I said. And meant it.

"Either we spirit you away, and Sophie and her old man wonder why the hell you've disappeared. If he's cracked the SIM, then by now he'll know why and he'll be after you wherever you've run to."

"Or?" I asked. The first option didn't sound great.

"Or you face the music and go down there."

I was silent. Option two sounded every bit as bad.

"We can keep a close eye on you, get someone to track you down there. Put a marksman in the grounds. But once you're in the house, you're pretty much on your own."

"I'm pretty certain nothing would happen in the

house," I said. "He likes his home life too much. It's really comfortable in there. His wife's lovely, the food's great, Sophie—"

"Yeah, all right," Tony stopped me. "Don't forget that your cuddly Uncle Tommy slices people up for ninepence."

"Right," I said. My situation came crashing back. "But I'm pretty sure I'd be taken elsewhere if they were going to…" I didn't like to think what he might do if he rumbled me. But it made my guts turn to water.

"So…" said Tony.

"So?" I asked.

"What do you want to do?"

I paused for a moment, summing up. But I already knew my decision.

"I'll face the music."

I spent the night in the flat off the high street so that Tommy's driver would know where to come, but I didn't feel safe there. It was shabby and rickety, not new and secure like the apartment down the road.

I hardly slept and was up at six, as soon as the light came through the curtains. I had a shower, gulped a Diet Coke and tried to listen to the radio, humming along to middle-of-the-road tunes to distract myself.

"I've had the time of my life, and I've never felt this way before…"

The cheap words made me feel worse, so I switched off the radio. I couldn't eat. I felt like a condemned man waiting for the hangman to arrive. I paced the flat. I almost wished I smoked, which I would have done to calm my nerves and pass the time. I chewed my nails instead.

At five to nine, I looked down at the street and saw a large car draw up outside. It looked like it was turning up for a funeral: I hoped it wasn't mine. A motorbike drew up on the other side of the street and the rider got off and went into the newsagent with his helmet still on.

I recognized the man who got out of the black, 7-Series Beemer. Dave Slaughter, Tommy's driver. He'd driven us to the wedding. Of the men that hung around Tommy, Dave was probably the nicest, relatively speaking. Although he must have been six foot three or four, he had a friendly-looking face – unmarked, smooth and lightly tanned as if he spent his time off on a golf course. He was the only one I'd seen whose nose was straight and hadn't been flattened across his face. His hair was short and always neatly combed, and his grey suit was immaculate. He almost looked kind.

Appearances can be deceptive.

Dave walked round the back and I heard the buzzer. With my heart banging like a steam-hammer, I picked up my jacket and went down the stairs.

"Morning," Dave said. He didn't sound unfriendly, or particularly friendly either. He opened the door to the back of the car. I climbed in.

We drove off towards Greenwich and I noticed that the biker who had gone into the newsagent was now following us. Dave noticed it too and I caught his eye in the rear-view mirror. He didn't say much as we drove, except to curse at the traffic and comment on the weather. He kept checking the bike behind and, as we headed towards the traffic lights in the Greenwich one-way system, he suddenly sped up, crashing the red.

"Oops," he said.

I didn't dare look behind, and Dave shot off fast, taking a dog-leg through some back streets.

"Short cut."

After a minute, I couldn't hear the bike any more. Unless someone was tracking us discreetly, I was pretty much on my own. Despite my nerves, I managed to plant a small magnetic tracker underneath the passenger seat while I was doing up my shoes. I was determined that *someone*, somewhere knew where I was.

Twenty minutes later we arrived at Kelly Towers. Sophie was at college and Cheryl must have been out with the dogs, because there was no barking as we crunched up the drive. The house no longer seemed pretty; it looked cold and foreboding, not helped by the grey morning light.

I felt sick.

Dave opened the door and ushered me into the house.

THIRTY-NINE

Tommy Kelly was sitting in his study as usual. I could smell the cigar smoke as soon as I entered the hall. What was sometimes a nice smell of Christmas and celebration now seemed harsh and aggressive, invading my lungs. Overpowering me.

"Come in, Eddie." His voice was no more threatening than usual. Not threatening at all. I stepped into the room and Dave stood behind me. "It's OK, Dave. I'll have a chat with Eddie, then call you in when I'm ready."

Dave nodded and stepped back out of the room. Tommy was sitting on the sofa looking at a new piece of art propped up on the easel. It was a picture of a man's head against a plain, dull-red background. The head was large and exaggerated. It looked like it had been through a mincer, as if the skin had been flayed and the flesh of the cheeks had been exposed. You could see all the teeth. The image was blurred. A bare light bulb hung over the head.

"Have a look," Tommy said. It was quite similar to the picture I'd seen in Barney Lipman's shed. "Looks like you can see his soul. Everything he feels. His pain. Bloody genius."

I searched my brain for the name Danny had said.

"What do you think?" Tommy asked. The name came to me.

"Bacon?"

Tommy looked at me, surprised.

"You have come a long way," he said. "Yes, Francis Bacon is exactly what I think we're looking at. Self-portrait." He got up from the sofa and beckoned me over to his desk, where he sat down behind a pile of art books and open catalogues. "It feels right, it smells right, but there's nothing in any of the books."

"Could you get someone to look at it?" I asked. I was relieved to be talking about paintings; I didn't want to ask where he had got it.

"I don't want some failed estate agent at Sotheby's turning his beak up at it and making it worthless just because it's been out of circulation. I've got to find it a bit of provenance. You know, who bought it, where it was exhibited, where it's been hiding for thirty years and all that." He laughed. "Or make it up."

I nodded, not sure what I was supposed to be contributing.

"Sit down," he said. I didn't argue. "Listen, I've been thinking. You've left college, right? You're doing a bit of ducking and diving on the market to keep your head above water. It's OK – a good way of learning the ropes. But it's not going to make you rich, is it?"

"No."

"You know, you remind me a bit of myself when I was your age. Finding your feet. I was a porter – used to stack crates of fish over at Billingsgate. I used to come home smelling like a kipper's knickers. Didn't pull many birds at that age." He puffed on his cigar, smiling to himself, enjoying his Big Daddy act.

I was still cacking myself about where all this was leading.

"So what I did was offer my services to more fishmongers than I could handle, so I had five or six jobs on the go. Then I recruited some boys from my neighbourhood, got *them* stacking the fish, collected the money, paid them, then took my cut." He looked at me. "You see?"

I thought I did.

"So I got paid and didn't smell of fish any more. QED." I guessed that was the end of the gospel according to the Reverend Kelly. "What do you think?" he asked.

"Nicely done," I said, trying to make it sound as if he was a genius. I felt the need to flatter him. "Clever."

"Exactly. Now, you're pretty quick on the uptake and you don't ask stupid questions."

"Thanks." I took it as a compliment.

"I just wondered if you wanted to do a bit of work for me?"

I nearly fell off my chair. "I, er…"

"Help me out a bit," he said. "You're enterprising. I think you've got an eye for pictures. You're good with computers – you could do a bit of research, couldn't you?"

"Doesn't your son – Jason – work for you?"

"Yeah, he does. But Jason's a bit of a law unto himself.

Pictures aren't really his thing. He's more involved in the hands-on end of the business. Most of the people who work for me are hands-on. That way I can be hands-off."

The question of what exactly the "business" involved hung heavy in the air. I felt myself slipping into deep, dark, muddy water. I looked at the floor. "I'm not sure what I'd be able to do for you," I said honestly.

"There's plenty to do in my firm," he said. "I run a nice, tight family outfit. There are all sorts of jobs. Let me be straight with you…"

Here we go, I thought.

"Some of my businesses skate on thin ice, if you know what I mean. We skirt around the law a bit. Do deals." He was the master of understatement. "But look at the City: the hedge-fund managers, the futures market, the stockbrokers, the insurers. Which of them isn't propping up tinpot dictatorships? Which of them isn't supporting drug cartels? Which of them isn't fleecing old bags of their savings to line their own trousers?" He shook his head at the injustice of it all. I supposed he had a point.

He wasn't finished. "It's just that they do it all under cover of the City, the old boy network. It's all about deals, putting people in touch with each other. I do the same, except I have my own rule book." He looked at me, waiting for a response.

Short of telling him I was working for the other side, I didn't have one.

"Well?" he said.

"I don't know enough about pictures," I said lamely. He chuckled.

"The pictures are my hobby, the icing on the cake. They're a bit of bunce that work as a calling card. My main activity is putting interested parties in touch with each other. I'm a broker, a consultant. If someone from Russia wants something and I know someone in America who has it, I bring them together. Whether it's a painting or a boat or a bit of hardware, I introduce them, take a fee. We hold a bit of stock here ourselves; you have to be diverse because markets shift and change all the time. Most of my clients like the high life and the paintings are a way of flattering them. It appeals to their vanity, makes them feel like they have good taste. Art's the new status symbol for most of my associates. It sweetens the deal. They've had it with diamonds and watches and helicopters. Art is what marks you out as a tycoon." He paused for a moment. "And most of them don't know what the fuck they're looking at." He laughed loudly, so I smiled.

I couldn't help feeling that I'd been given a pretty glossy version of what actually went on. I didn't know what he meant by "stock", but I guessed it wasn't shirts and knitwear.

"You can start straight away," he told me. I felt a rush of panic. "If you don't like the look of the business, we can talk again." I was being backed into a corner. "Cheryl likes you," he said. "She thinks I can trust you, and that's good enough for me."

I was about to protest, but then he opened his desk drawer. He took out my phone and pushed it across the desk to me.

"You forgot this the other day." He fixed me with a

cold, grey stare. I'd seen the same look in Sophie's eyes. "Be more careful next time," he said.

And I knew I had no choice.

FORTY

Donnie hated Monday mornings like these. He had a bit of a head. He'd drunk half a bottle of whisky when he'd got in from the pub the night before, which on top of six or seven pints hadn't given him any problem sleeping, but a whisky hangover always made him feel aggressive. More aggressive.

He'd picked up a few grand from a couple of clubs and dealers on his way. Some of it insurance money, some of it for goods. Everyone had paid up, which was a little disappointing, as he was in the mood to give someone a slap. Then he got Dave's call and felt even more like thumping someone.

"Don, get yourself back to HQ," Dave had said, his voice full of irony. "His Nibs wants to give the kid the SP. The basics."

Donnie seethed and muttered to himself all the way back round the South Circular. He didn't know what things were coming to.

Donnie had the ultimate respect for Tommy Kelly. Tommy hadn't had to touch the mucky end of the business for at least ten years now. He had accumulated enough from the firm's various enterprises to sit back and control everything from his *study. He didn't have to get his hands dirty – he paid others to do that for him. The genius scam he had pulled off, Donnie and Dave agreed, was franchising out the Kelly name to other firms. So if a smaller gang wanted to pull off a bigger job than they were capable of – a one-off armed blag or a quick-hit fraud – Tommy would hire them some muscle and administrative back-up, enabling them to put the fear of God into the underworld by claiming to work for the Kelly gang.*

Special K, they called it. A crime "brand".

All the small firms had to do was pay Tommy fifteen per cent of their haul, or a minimum £250 k for the use of the family name. Just like a multinational investing in start-up businesses. Genius.

And if they didn't pay, Donnie was there.

Tommy didn't have to get nasty because he paid others to get nasty for him. Donnie, Dave Slaughter and their associates: blokes like Johnny Reggae and Stav Georgiou, Engin Kurtoglu and Paul Dolan. Hard men, enforcers. Early on, Tommy had been careful to make allies within the Brixton Yardies and the Greek and Turkish gangs in North London. He'd also got in with the Irish Republicans. Tommy came over all Blarney Stone when he talked to the Irish – liked to think he was one of them. He'd bought The Harp in New Cross to keep up his links with the Paddies.

Tommy had shown them that cooperation with each other was the way ahead in business. He'd encouraged them to bury the deadly rivalries of the past and continue in a spirit of mutual support. The law was their enemy, not each other.

But Donnie had noticed a change in the boss in the last year or so. Like he was trying to kosher up; appear more straight, like a legit businessman, an art dealer or something. Which would be hard, seeing as all his gear was nicked or fake. Maybe it was his age, Donnie thought – Tommy must be fifty-five. Maybe Cheryl was behind it, or the girl.

Whatever was bugging him, Tommy was still well in charge of the discreet organization that kept them all in business, but sometimes Donnie questioned the guv'nor's wisdom.

Donnie and Dave both agreed that the son was getting bang out of order. He wasn't a chip off the old block at all; wasn't developing the business the way the old man wanted. He was more like Tommy's nut job brother Patsy, who was holed up in Fuengirola, drinking himself to death. Jason must have inherited some Irish pikey gene: he'd nick anything if it stood still long enough and he was a fair enough businessman as long as the deal involved porn, a fight, dancing girls and enough drugs up his hooter to stun a horse. Although Donnie wasn't a big fan of Jason Kelly, at least he knew what made the beast tick.

And now, as well as getting Jason more involved, the boss was welcoming in the kid who was hanging around with Princess Sophie. Stupid.

Donnie had seen the boy once or twice, but he didn't much like the smell of him. He seemed quite mature, well-built, but too straight. Probably good-looking if that was your thing. But no one knew him. Donnie had learnt that this business depended on knowing exactly who you were dealing with – someone's son or brother. Someone off your patch, with a pedigree. One of the tribe.

Bringing in outsiders had never worked, in Donnie's experience, and now and again he'd had to sort them out. This one came from nowhere, and for reasons best known to himself,

Tommy had taken a shine to him. Risky, Donnie thought. But orders were orders. No one questioned Tommy Kelly.

Donnie took a quick snort from the tiny bottle in his glove compartment and headed down the A20.

Dave took me out by the front door. A sleek, navy Mercedes had pulled up outside and I recognized it from when I first saw Sophie being dropped off outside college. I also vaguely recognized the scary bloke who drove it.

"Eddie, Donnie," Dave said as the big bear got out of the car. "Donnie, Eddie."

Donnie grunted at me and nodded his head. "Where we going?" he asked Dave. He didn't sound like he wanted to go anywhere.

"Erith," Dave said. "In your car." They got in the front and I got in the back and we headed for the M25 – in a car I hadn't bugged.

There wasn't much conversation, but what there was related to the "business".

"Mr Kelly wants us to show you part of the enterprise," Dave said. "We have various businesses around London, and one or two offshore. There are managers in most of them. Donnie and me tend to keep an eye on the south-east and we have colleagues in other parts of London and abroad." He made it sound as if they were involved in sales management.

The vast pillars of the Dartford Crossing came into view and we pulled off the M25 on to a slip road. I always shuddered when I went near the bridge, given what had happened to my brother. But I reminded myself of why I'd got into this thing in the first place; resolved that I was doing it for Steve. We drove down towards the river, the sweat sticking my shirt to the leather car seat. I still wasn't convinced about the real aim of this trip.

A sign on a roundabout directed us to Erith and Long Reach. The area was grey and bleak, with patches of rough, faded grass at the side of the road, scattered with car wrecks, gypsy ponies and junk. We turned off into an industrial estate and parked outside a unit at the far end. Barbed wire lined the fence beyond.

A board outside announced who the business premises belonged to:

LONG REACH SPECIALIST PAINT AND VARNISH CO.

The board was white and flaky – business didn't look too brisk. Dave pressed the intercom.

"Paul Trombone and Angus McCoatup," he announced. Donnie grunted a laugh. The door buzzed open and we went in.

In front of us was a trade desk with an old, brown computer. Behind, metal pots and plastic tubs of paint were piled from floor to ceiling. A nervous-looking bloke with a ratty face and an earring stood behind the counter. Tattoos crept up his neck beyond the line of his T-shirt. He was wearing a white coat.

"Specialist paints," Dave said to me with a wry smile.

"Invisible paint, tartan paint, polka-dot paint, striped paint in all colours. You name it."

The bloke behind the counter gave a sickly grin. He'd obviously heard Dave's jokes before, but I bet he smiled every time. He lifted up the counter hatch and gestured for me to walk through. Dave and Donnie followed, slamming the hatch down behind them.

"Right," said Dave. "Take the young man downstairs and we'll show him what makes us tick."

Without the tracker, I really hoped someone knew where I was.

FORTY-ONE

The man in the white coat took the lid off an apparently random tin of paint and reached inside. He appeared to have pressed a concealed button because I heard a mechanical clunk, like a lock opening. The man grabbed at one of the uprights on the metal shelving unit behind him and the whole thing swung away from the wall, paint pots and all. Behind the shelf was a staircase, concrete and industrial, leading down. The man began to descend and I followed him. Dave and Donnie brought up the rear, shutting the door behind them.

The staircase and the room at the bottom were lit with harsh halogen spots. Everything was painted white and there was a smell of damp and solvents. Four people were working down there, all in white coats. The space was huge, far bigger than you could ever imagine from the scruffy paint shop upstairs. There was equipment that looked like stuff from a school science lab: scales, centri-fuges, tubes and Bunsen burners. Dave introduced me to the bloke who seemed to be in charge. Sean, I think he said, who spoke with a thick, Northern Irish accent. He showed me what they were making. Mostly MDMA, he said: ecstasy. The market was still strong, but there was quite a demand for some of the other stuff, which they also synthesized here: speed, Valium, LSD and steroids. Uppers, downers, mind-benders and sporty stuff, he said. All areas covered. I didn't really know what most of them were, but I recognized the names – and the fact that they were all illegal and lucrative. He gave me a pot that contained samples of various pills so I could see what each of them looked like. The ecstasy was a pale-blue pill with a shamrock stamped into it. The various amphetamines – speed – were whiteish powders.

"Don't take them all at once," Dave said. "If you've got any sense, you won't take any at all. These are for the mug punters."

I nodded. I had no intention of taking anything. I had already nearly got myself killed by drinking too much and getting careless. I wasn't out of the woods yet, locked in this drugs factory with the Kelly thugs. I swore that if I got out and lived to fight another day, it was nothing stronger than Diet Coke for me from now on.

"If you're sent to pick up from here, I'll give you a pass name and an address to drop them off at. You'll speak to no one and pick up the goods in paint tins. You won't need to see down here again."

There was something I still didn't understand. "Why is Mr Kelly showing me all this?" I asked.

"Because once you've seen our work here, there's no going back," Dave explained. "Now you know some of what we do, Mr Kelly won't have to mention it to you himself. But you'll know what's what when you're sent on an errand, see?"

It seemed to me that going back and telling Tommy Kelly I didn't fancy it wasn't an option. I was in the firm because I had been let in on the secret.

I was in, and beyond the point of no return.

They dropped me off a few miles away at Bluewater, the big shopping centre off the motorway, where I was apparently meeting Tommy for a late lunch. I was still reeling with all the new information as I went into the Italian restaurant. It was part of a smart chain: big and airy, with shiny steel shelves and tables. The staff were all attractive and attentive, and a nice Italian girl showed me to the table. Tommy was sitting with his back to a window that looked on to the terrace.

To my surprise, Sophie was sitting next to him. They both looked great. A well-heeled, tanned father taking his gorgeous blonde daughter for lunch. Both dressed in pale-coloured cashmere, both with killer smiles. Sophie stood up and kissed me on the cheek before I sat down. People sitting near by stared.

"How did you get on, Eddie?" Tommy asked.

"Good." I couldn't think of anything else to say.

"Dad says you're going to do some work for him," Sophie said. "Great, isn't it?"

"Yeah." I forced a smile, feeling numb.

"What do you fancy?" Tommy asked, passing me the menu. I didn't fancy anything much; I still felt pretty sick from my long morning's initiation into the Kelly business. I chose minestrone soup and Sophie and Tommy both ordered the squid salad. Tommy offered me a glass of red but I put my hand over the glass and asked for fizzy water.

While Sophie went to wash her hands, Tommy took his chance to have a word.

"Everything OK?" he said. "Grasped the nature of the business?" I nodded. "We won't involve you in that end too much, but you need to know. You can work for me, looking up pictures on the computer and doing all the stuff I can't." He saw Sophie coming back to the table and held a finger to his lips. "Not a word to Her Ladyship."

"Sure."

"Bit of bad news this morning," Tommy said, changing the conversation as Sophie sat down. "Jason's opponent's dropped out of the charity match."

"Oh." I don't think Sophie cared, but she liked to make the right noises for the old man.

"Broke his thumb, training."

"When's it meant to be?" I asked.

"Next month. It'll be a hard job finding someone else at short notice."

"Is he good?" I don't know why I wanted to know. Something to talk about.

"Jason's got a very fast right hand," Tommy said. "His defence needs improving, but he's got a good punch. He's not stylish but he doesn't quit. If he didn't like his leisure activities quite so much, he could be really good."

I nodded, impressed.

"He'll be at Brands Hatch on Saturday morning for the Indy bike races, if you're coming?" Tommy said.

"Of course we are," Sophie replied for me. It was the first I'd heard of it, but it looked as if I was going.

Tommy left us after lunch and we spent the rest of the afternoon shopping. Sophie seemed pleased, as if me being recruited by her dad made everything good between us. Truthfully, it *was* good between us. I still fancied her and she still seemed pretty keen on me, leaning against me, squeezing my hand and kissing me every now and again as we rode up the escalators.

"I told you it would work out, didn't I?" she said. I couldn't remember her saying anything of the sort, but she had obviously played a part in getting me a job.

Clearly she had plans for me. She just didn't seem to know how much shit she was getting me into.

FORTY-TWO

"I'll be honest. We lost you." Down the line, Ian Baylis's tone was slightly apologetic. But fell short of saying sorry.

"The bike was a bit obvious," I said. "The Kelly driver knew straight away that it was following us."

"The bike wasn't ours," Baylis said. "We had a white van that was marking you all the way down to the Dartford bridge. You didn't see that, did you?"

"No," I admitted.

"The car you'd changed to pulled into the slip road at the very last minute and our vehicle was railroaded into the lane for the tunnel. He couldn't turn around."

"So I was in an underground drugs factory with two Kelly enforcers and no back-up?"

"About the size of it," Baylis said. "Although we lost the bug, we knew roughly where you were by the satellite track on your phone – but that all gets a bit unreliable once you go underground. You'll just have to get used to it."

I had given him details of the paint warehouse and what they were manufacturing. He took down everything

I said, including the stuff about Tommy Kelly's paintings but, as usual, gave little in the way of feedback.

"So, what are you going to do?" I asked. "Bust the place now I've found out where it is?"

"Not that simple," Baylis replied. "We'll keep a close eye on it, but we know it's not the only source of Kelly income. Shut that operation down and it will spring up somewhere else, then we'll have to find it all over again. We need to find out how the network operates. Who delivers the raw materials and where things go from there. We need the bigger picture, the connections – and that's where you will be able to help."

"Look," I said. "Tommy Kelly runs a drugs factory. Can't you just go in and arrest him? He's the hub. If you get him, it stops."

Baylis almost laughed. "Tommy Kelly is smart. There's no evidence to connect him with anything. He keeps himself remote from all the goings-on. There are companies and sub-companies, all of which keep him at a distance from the nitty-gritty. It won't just be the drugs. They are simply easy money. We think he has bigger plans. Organized crime is rarely about one area. As well as narcotics, it will be money laundering, arms ... anything that turns over big money. And with the big bucks comes the power. When you have that kind of money, you can buy people off: police, customs, organizations. And that's where we come in."

"The only thing he seems interested in are his paintings," I said. "He never mentions anything else."

"The forged and stolen paintings are just a sideline,

remember," Baylis said. "The idea seems to appeal to him as a man of taste, or some such bollocks. Bottom line is, he knows if he gets collared for forged pictures, he's facing a three- to five-year stretch at worst, and no one thinks too badly of a forger. They're almost gentleman villains, and he'd be treated like a king inside. Remember, Tommy's no gentleman villain: there are about twenty-three killings we're trying to pin on him. That's mass murder."

If I hadn't already felt way out of my depth, I did now. I barely knew what Baylis was talking about.

"So what do you expect me to do?" He was scaring me.

"All you have to do is go deeper undercover," he said. "Now you're in, you will live your life according to the Tommy Kelly rules. Find out what you can, we'll do the rest." He was making it sound easy. "We can't risk you being tagged all the time, but you will continue to plant devices wherever there's a possibility. In their bedroom would be particularly good."

This put a picture in my mind that I didn't want to see.

"We will need reports back, of course, but they will be less frequent. Keep coded notes in your books so you remember stuff for our meetings," Baylis continued. "We would prefer them face-to-face, up here at head office, rather than these friendly evening chats on the phone. And remember, we need to find something that links him directly with the big stuff."

"OK," I said. Now the job was getting really dangerous. They were leaving me in the capable hands of Tommy Kelly while actually reducing my back-up. It didn't make sense to me.

"You will also need to make less contact with Tony, and Anna," he added. "I will be your first point of contact in all circumstances."

"You're cutting my lifelines!" I protested.

"*I* am your lifeline," he said. "Now that you've been embraced by the Kelly firm, all contact with the outside is potentially dangerous. The more people you speak to, the more chance we have of being rumbled. You will need to use the high street flat as your base – the safe house will just be in case of emergency. From now on, you will also refer to me as Nimrod."

"What?" I said. *"Nimrod?"*

"Taken from Elgar's 'Enigma' Variations. All our codes on this case will be based on them."

I looked blank; I didn't know my Elgar from my elbow.

"Maybe you should ask your Mr Kelly," Baylis said. He sniggered, which was about as close as he ever came to a laugh. "He likes classical music, doesn't he?"

"Dunno," I replied. I felt like a sulky teenager. Which I was, I suppose.

"Keep up the good work, Eddie."

And that was about the size of it. I was on my own.

I rang Tony, of course, to have a moan. He was a bit more sympathetic but told me that from their point of view, I was doing great. They now had a man right on the inside, which had never been the case before. He told me to keep my nose to the grindstone and do whatever was asked of me, however illegal, as it would help with the case.

Nothing would be held against me.

He said that he would call round to the flat tonight, and we could maybe have a drink. I told him I didn't drink. The couple I'd had at the wedding had made me drop my guard and I hadn't touched alcohol since. I didn't want to get caught out again. Tony told me that I was doing fantastic work and rang off.

Personally, I felt I was having my bollocks yanked in all directions.

Tony dropped by at around seven. I was watching the widescreen, enjoying my remaining time in the apartment, and he quietly let himself in. Tony had a knack of just appearing out of nowhere.

I got him a beer from the fridge and a Diet Coke for myself. We didn't say much at first, he just kept looking at me. I think he had come to give me a pep talk.

"Listen," he said. "I just wanted to say, in person, how proud I am of you. You had a bit of a slip-up the other week but you had the guts to go in and play it to your advantage. That gamble has paid off and got us leaps ahead."

I thought back to when Tommy Kelly had returned my phone and told me to be careful. I was beginning to wonder if he didn't care more about me than Tony and his lot.

"I don't think it was brave," I said. "I don't think I had a choice – like everything else that's happened to me since Steve died. I've been manipulated."

"I'm sorry you see it like that, mate," Tony said. He took a glug of San Miguel. "We have to … arrange situations in this game. Line stuff up to create the best opportunities for intelligence to emerge."

"Move people around like puppets, you mean?"

"Your words."

"OK. Tell me you lot didn't line Anna up to hit on me."

"Well…" He scratched his chin. "There was perhaps an element of that. We wanted her to look after you. Keep you sweet."

"Keep me sweet?" I laughed. "Never heard it called that before."

He looked at me directly. "Not complaining, are you?"

I thought back and blushed. "Not really," I admitted. "I just feel such a prat, deluding myself that she might, just for a moment, have actually fancied a seventeen-year-old bloke."

"Eighteen next week," Tony reminded me. I had almost forgotten. My birthday seemed insignificant in the scheme of things.

My eighteenth.

"I spoke to your mum," Tony said. "She's worried about you, of course. I told her not to be." He pulled an envelope from his pocket. "She sent you this."

I took the envelope and put it on the glass table.

"Shall I give her a call?" I asked. Tony shrugged.

"You *could*," he said, the doubt clear in his voice. "But it might not be helpful right now. For either of you. You know, the tug of the old apron strings…"

I knew what he meant. To hear the old girl's concerned voice might have me in bits. I knew she would blub if I spoke to her. I picked up the envelope. "I'll save it for my birthday."

Tony continued to big me up for the next half an

257

hour. Told me that they had been trying to nail Tommy Kelly for nearly ten years, but the bloke was like Teflon. Tommy Teflon: everything they tried to pin on him didn't stick; every investigation hit a dead end. Every time they tried to convict an associate, no one would testify or give evidence. Tony and the others were sure that Kelly was paying people in Revenue and Customs, in the police … everywhere. Every time he was pulled in, they could find nothing directly against him. On the other hand, with almost every single piece of organized crime that cropped up, Tommy Kelly's name was mentioned somewhere. Tony told me just to keep my nose clean, do as I was told by Tommy, and report back to Baylis as and when. Then he said we wouldn't be seeing each other for a while.

I heard his voice crack as he hugged me and said goodbye.

When Tony had gone, I opened the envelope from my mum. There was a birthday card with 18 on the front and a racing car. It looked really babyish. I laughed. Inside was a soppy message, which made my eyes smart. She told me how proud she was of me and how I must take care of myself. I found myself missing her, resolving to spend more time with her when this job was all over.

She had enclosed a fifty-quid note that I wanted to give back, knowing that she couldn't afford it and I could. I hadn't had to think about money since I'd joined. There was an anonymous bank account, plus a brown envelope with three hundred quid cash from Baylis that was delivered once a week. The old girl had also sent a note and a gold signet ring, engraved with the initials *E.S.*

The note explained that the ring had belonged to my mum's dad, my granddad, the original Edward Savage. He'd died before I was born, so I'd never known him. But I knew he'd worked on the river, then gone into the Navy. That he'd been through the Second World War and survived a sinking in a torpedoed ship. What he had been through was worse than anything that had happened to me, I thought.

I was nearly eighteen. I made up my mind to stop whingeing, shape up and make men like my granddad and my brother proud of me.

I never knew Edward Savage, but I was glad to have the ring. I fixed it on a thong around my neck. For luck.

FORTY-THREE

I could hear the roar of the bikes long before we arrived at Brands Hatch. By the time Sophie parked up at the circuit, the scream of the engines was high-pitched and deafening, setting my teeth on edge and making me feel more anxious than I did already. For Sophie it was the opposite: she found the noise exciting, said that it got her revved up. Once we got out of the car, she squeezed me round the waist and kissed me.

She had dressed in a kind of biker style for the outing, which made me laugh because she was going nowhere near a bike. She wore a tight, white leather jacket, white jeans and biker boots. Her hair was scraped back and she wore red, wrap-around shades. She drew glances from the off-duty sponsorship girls smoking fags near the entrance. She drew glances from the stewards and race marshals. In fact she drew glances from everyone, because she looked hot. I felt proud that she was with me. It made me feel better.

We watched a couple of races from the trackside:

blokes throwing themselves around the tarmac at ninety miles an hour, their knees scraping the ground as they dropped the bikes on the corners. Sophie pointed out Jason's bike to me. He was driving like a nutter, weaving in and out of the other bikes. The sun was shining and the air was thick with the smell of burnt fuel and rubber. Around us there were pin-up girls in sponsors' T-shirts holding up numbers, and craggy-faced blokes waving flags and changing wheels. I had to admit, the atmosphere was as cool, sexy and exciting as an action movie.

"Let's go and get a drink," Sophie said. We walked away from the track up into the stands. Needless to say, Tommy Kelly had a private enclosure that looked down on to the circuit. Inside it was insulated from the roar of the bikes and was filled with the noise of loud laughter and chatter. There was a private bar and a buffet laid out with food. In the middle of it all was the man himself, nursing a gin and tonic, surrounded by other men who were hanging on his every word. It was Sunday, so there were no suits, but they all sported those kind of smart-casual clothes that golfers wear: sharply creased trousers, Italian shoes and disgusting jumpers in garish colours. The smell of aftershave was strong in the air and caught in my throat. Heads turned as Sophie walked in, and Tommy's associates, all flat noses and capped teeth, smiled nicely at her as we crossed to the bar. Whether they looked at me or not, I didn't notice. I looked straight ahead. Sophie got us Cokes and I picked up a couple of sausage rolls from the buffet. A late breakfast.

Tommy called us over. "Sophie you know…" he said

to the man he was chatting to. "And this is Eddie, who I was telling you about. Eddie's going to be helping me out with the pictures." The man held out his hand. His face was tanned and his features sharp.

"Saul Wynter."

"Saul's my accountant," Tommy explained. "Financial genius, keeps all the books straight."

The man laughed and appeared to think better of something he was about to say. I was searching my brain for a topic of conversation that I could have with the man who cooked Tommy Kelly's books without putting my foot in it, but I was saved by Jason coming in from the track. A smattering of applause went round the enclosure.

"Nice one, son," Tommy said. Jason's face was smeared with soot and people slapped him on the back of his leathers as he crossed the room to his father. Tommy hugged him with the arm that wasn't holding his gin.

"Did you win?" Sophie asked.

"Weren't you watching?" Jason looked at his sister and then at me.

"We were," Sophie protested, "but I don't understand who's winning and when. There are lots of numbers."

"Personal best," Jason said. He reeled off some times that made no sense to Sophie or me.

"Congratulations," I said. He ignored me. Someone handed him a cold beer, while others gathered round and joined in the backslapping. From what I had heard, Jason wasn't especially popular, but everyone present wanted a piece of him just to keep in with his old man.

"What's happened about the fight, Jase?" an old bruiser with short white hair and a nose like a mashed potato asked him.

"Still looking for someone. A suitable opponent has yet to be found," Jason said in a silly posh voice, sticking his fists up like a prize fighter.

"It's not easy," Tommy Kelly said, joining in. "All the good amateurs are matched up. And we're not going to put him against any old donkey. Or anyone too good, come to that."

"Thanks, Dad!" said Jason.

"No, I don't mean it like that, kid." Tommy put his arm around his son again. "It would be stupid to put you in with a pro. Dangerous. We just want a good fighter about your age and weight for a good exhibition bout."

Jason looked at me. "How old are you?"

"Eighteen." Sophie was about to protest. "Next week."

"Are you a scrapper?"

"Jason, I don't think—" Tommy began.

"I can look after myself," I said, feeling the hairs rise on the back of my neck. He gave me the pip.

"Why don't I fight him then?" Jason asked. He squared up in front of me. He was bulkier than me, but I had a couple of centimetres or more in height over him.

The voices around me faded into the background: Sophie telling her brother to leave me out of it, Tommy saying it wasn't a good idea, one or two others suggesting that perhaps it was – that I looked up to it. It was one of those decisions only I could make.

Fight or flight?

I could either pick up the gauntlet or run scared, but I needed to prove myself in front of these people.

"I'll fight you," I said.

FORTY-FOUR

I started training the following morning.

I'd had a bit of a row with Sophie the night before. She was dead against me fighting her brother. Said it would split her loyalties, put her in a difficult position. I argued that Jason had put *me* in a difficult position and that if I'd backed down, everyone would have thought I was a complete wuss. I needed their respect.

Tommy Kelly seemed to have come round to the idea by the evening, saying it would be a good bonding exercise. People gain respect for each other in the ring, he said. As long as neither of us beat the living daylights out of the other, it should be a good exhibition bout. He even went as far as booking me in for a few training sessions at a gym over in Canning Town. Jason had been training up at the Elephant and Castle for a while and Tommy didn't want anyone having an unfair advantage.

I got up at six on the Monday and started running, down to the waterfront and along to Greenwich. It was chilly and a mist rolled in from the river. I jogged across the wet cobbles on the old side of the river, past the burnt-out wreck of the *Cutty Sark*, then up towards the park. By the time I reached the statue at the top, my heart was pumping and my throat and lungs were on fire in the damp air. I wasn't as fit as I'd thought. I put my hands on my knees, panting, looking out across the river to the Dome and beyond. I thought how far I'd come since my first date with Sophie at this same spot.

It was a long way.

At ten I bought a ticket and got on the DLR at Deptford. The train went under the river, emerging among the skyscrapers I had seen from the other side a few hours before, then on into the badlands of the old docks. The people in business suits all got off at Heron Quays and Canary Wharf, and by the time I got out at Canning Town, the only people around were Indian women with kids and ratty-eyed blokes with Staffies.

The gym was down a side street. Outside it was a small bronze statue of a boxer: an eighteen-year-old boy who, according to the plaque underneath, had died of a brain haemorrhage in the ring. I didn't want to think about it. It was a shit statue anyway.

"I've been booked in by Mr Kelly," I told the girl on reception. "I'm training with Gary Cribb."

The Kelly name got me immediate attention. An energetic man with cropped grey hair and a Lonsdale sweatshirt was out to meet me in seconds.

"Eddie?" he said. "Gary." He shook my hand and clasped me on the shoulder. He was lean, his hands like steel and his accent pure East End. "Great to have you here. Have you done much boxing before?"

I told him that I'd done a bit at school … that I'd won a cup when I was fourteen and also had a brown belt in judo. He laughed at that.

"Not a complete novice then?" He winked and feinted a punch at me, which I instinctively defended. I didn't tell him that I had also done a five-day crash course in killing with a Welsh sadist.

He showed me to a changing room and threw me a pair of gloves. "We'll do a couple of rounds so I can see where we are."

I changed into a vest, track pants and boxing boots, then pulled on the big, elasticated sparring gloves and went out into the gym.

There were four rings in the space and a couple of blokes were sparring in one of them: a giant of a black bloke lumbered forwards slowly, throwing thudding jabs at his trainer's pads.

Elsewhere boxers pounded speedballs, the noise throbbing against the walls of the gym. Others worked at heavy bags that hung from girders across the ceiling. I walked past a sweaty, well-muscled bloke who was slamming hefty hooks into the bag. Every blow sounded like a cricket bat hitting a leather sofa, and I was glad it wasn't my ribs that were soaking up his punches.

Gary Cribb was waiting for me, stripped down to a vest. He must have been nearly fifty but he was in really good shape. Sculpted and hard. He helped me up into the ring.

"Have you been doing this long?" I asked.

"Training?" he said. "About twenty years. Long enough. I was pro before that, middleweight, and before that I was in the Marines."

It sounded like a pretty good pedigree to qualify as a hard bastard, I thought. "Why did you give up boxing?" I asked.

"It hurt too much." He pressed a finger on his broken nose, flattening it against his upper lip, and laughed. "Right, let's have a go."

I chased him around the ring, trying to catch the pads that he held high, at face level. He called out encouragement to me, telling me to watch his eyes, not the pads. You can anticipate an opponent's moves far better by looking at their eyes than their fists, he said. By the time you've looked at their fists, it's often too late and the thing's in your face, busting your nose. We did a round like that and he said I was pretty fast and accurate, but needed to get more strength behind my jabs, to come off the back foot more. The weight behind my punches needed to come all the way from my back heel.

We did another round with Gary wearing gloves too. He came at me, jabbing through my defence, showing me my weak spots. I led with a good left, which stopped him coming forward for a moment, but then, pleased with myself, dropped my right. Gary didn't waste a second and his left hook found the opening, swinging into the side of my head. We were only wearing big, 10 oz sparring gloves, but the blow stunned me and I staggered back. I'd hate to be hit by this bloke for real.

"You all right?" he asked. "You completely dropped

your guard. Fatal mistake."

We took a break and Gary asked what I knew about my opponent. I told him very little except that he wasn't much of a stylist and had a good punch. Gary nodded. He said he'd seen Jason Kelly fight at Repton Boys' Club in Bethnal Green a couple of years previously. I needed to try and dominate the centre of the ring, he told me, to keep him at bay with stiff jabs and to deflect his charges, like a bullfighter.

Gary showed me how he thought Jason Kelly might work, rushing me with combinations and wild flurries of punches. He showed me how to work the corner of the ring and the ropes, how to defend myself while my opponent wore his energy down trying to get at me. The Rope-a-Dope, he called it. Perfected by Muhammad Ali in the "Rumble in the Jungle" against George Foreman in 1974.

We boxed about eight sparring rounds, then Gary worked me on the heavy bag, trying to get weight and speed behind my hooks before finishing on the speed-ball.

He sat me down in the café area after and made a list while I necked a protein drink. I was cream-crackered but buzzing with the aggression I'd unloaded. Gary listed my training regime, which included running, sparring and weights. He said he thought that I was pretty good. That I should be ready to have a go in six weeks.

I told him I only had four.

"Has anyone mentioned anything about enhancing your performance?" he asked in a low voice.

I was confused for a minute. "You mean ster—?" He put a finger to his lips and nodded. "No," I said.

"It's your choice," he said. "I won't lie to you. Regulated boxing's generally as clean as a whistle, carefully policed. But there's plenty of that gear available around here. The place is funded by it and I expect you know where it comes from."

I began to make the connection in my head. "No, I don't want anything like that."

"Good man," he said. "Just remember, it's a charity event. For villains. The rules aren't quite so stringent. It's outside the board of control, so your opponent will probably be up to the gills in the stuff."

"Thanks for the tip," I said.

FORTY-FIVE

It was my eighteenth birthday and Sophie took me out for the evening. We went up to the West End and Sophie drove. The city looked surreal as we crossed Tower Bridge. The towers were lit up bright and the modern buildings beyond were glowing with blue neon. Further down the river someone was popping fireworks, which made the night sky flash red too. The Tower of London loomed on the left and it felt as if we were driving into a fairy tale.

One with no guarantee of a happy ending.

We had a drink just north of Covent Garden in a downstairs bar full of ultra-skinny art students and fashion people. I felt a bit square among the bohos. They had crazy haircuts and were all wearing vintage skinny jeans and pointed shoes. And half of them were outside smoking roll-ups on the steps. Sophie didn't seem to notice. They all looked at her anyway.

She gave me a present. It was a classic Omega watch, stainless steel and chunky. "Speedmaster Pro. First watch on the moon," she said. "Dad said Neil Armstrong wore one." It had a black dial with push buttons and a steel strap.

I was really chuffed. It was a great watch and must have cost her a few quid. It meant something, given because she liked me. She was pleased that I was happy with it.

We walked from the bar a couple of blocks to The Ivy. The booking had been made for us, otherwise I don't think they'd have let me in. The service was amazing – they treated us like film stars. In fact, sitting two tables away was an A-list American actress who was over here in a West End show. Sophie told me not to stare, and I tried not to, but she looked as if she had come from a different world altogether. Which I suppose she had.

I had shepherd's pie, which sounds boring, but it was fantastic. The mash on top had been grilled until it was crisp and the meat inside was melting and delicious. Sophie had grilled Dover sole and they gave us both a glass of champagne. I broke my rule and drank it. It was my eighteenth birthday after all. Sophie was all for going on to a club, but I cried off. I'd been up since five-thirty, running, and had to do the same again the next day. Gary had allowed me a lie-in, but only till six-thirty. Hardly a luxury.

We drove back across Waterloo Bridge with the lid down. The evening was cold but dry and the city still looked impressive from this angle: the London Eye sparkling white with its spiderweb cables. Big Ben's clock face lit up yellow, clanging out twelve.

I thanked Sophie for a fantastic evening and asked her if she wanted to stay at mine. She kissed me in the car outside the flat but said she needed to get back, and anyway didn't I have to get up at the crack of a sparrow's fart? I agreed that I did, and she touched me on the nose, said my birthday treat could wait. As she drove away, I felt a real sense of loss. I'd wanted her to stay with me.

I'd become more dependent on Sophie since I'd had less contact with Tony; since I'd lost my security blanket. I called and texted her more often and she seemed pleased, as if she liked me to need her a bit more. And why wouldn't I? She was lovely.

And I was falling…

I found it hard to sleep, but at half six I was back out on the road. The run to the top of Greenwich Park was getting easier and I was now on nodding terms with one or two early dog walkers. There was an old boy with a white pug who looked just like him. He asked me what I was training for and I told him. He said to work on the body: keep laying into the ribs and solar plexus until the head drops and then go for the nut.

Everyone had a piece of advice for me except the advice that I wanted – from the people who were supposed to be looking after me.

I had texted Ian Baylis the bare details of the fight arrangements and had heard nothing back. My only ally was my trainer.

Fortunately, Gary was very encouraging. Although I was tired after my night out, he was pleased with my progress. The speed of my combination punches was improving, my footwork was good and I was launching attacks off the back foot, making my leads and jabs twice as effective. A stiff jab poked regularly and hard into the opponent's face is a very tiring weapon, Gary advised.

He also worked on my ability to soak up punishment, by battering my ribs and dropping medicine balls on my stomach from a height. Plus I was doing sit-ups, stomach crunches and press-ups by the hundred. I could skip so fast, forward and backwards, that you couldn't see the rope, just hear the whip of it spinning and the crack as it hit the floor.

The third week Gary put me in the ring with sparring partners. One was a black guy, Gilbert, who was a good bit bigger than me with a much longer reach. He kept me at bay with a long, heavy jab, and swung slow hooks at my body. My job was to parry the jab and try to step inside his defence. Also to try and ride his shots, slipping back, so they didn't land on me with full force.

The other guy, Billy Cable, had a face that looked like it had been carved out of rock. He was fast. His hands were a blur and he caught me with flurries of punches, confusing me by coming from all angles. He cut my lip and raised a swelling over my right eye.

"And he hasn't even broken a sweat yet." Gary laughed. "But don't worry, you won't be up against anything as hard and fast as Billy."

"Great," I said through fat lips.

Billy danced high on his toes on the other side of the ring. He grinned through his gumshield, winked and

tapped his head with the red sparring gloves before pum-
melling me through another gruelling round of sparring.

By the end of the fourth week with Gary Cribb and his
boys, I felt ready to face anything. Or anyone.

FORTY-SIX

The tournament was up towards Woodford, beyond the East End, in a big hotel off the main road. It was a large, red-brick building, mostly used for conferences and business events.

The car park was rammed with Jags, Mercs and flashy motors of every other luxury brand you could name. I arrived with Gary Cribb in his beaten-up Mondeo. Training obviously didn't pay as much as some of the other trades in his circle.

Sophie had gone with Tommy and Cheryl. They had been careful not to show a great deal of favouritism towards Jason, which I appreciated. Reading between the lines, I think they were all a bit ashamed of him challenging me. They all had some sympathy for the underdog.

In the back of their minds, they probably knew that I was going to get mullered.

The place was already filling up as we arrived: men in black or camel overcoats, women in furs, the evening air tangy with the smell of their cologne and perfume. It was obviously a night to be seen. Tacked on to the back of the hotel was a hall, where the ring had been set up. I felt a flutter in my guts as we walked past it, spotlit from above. Rows and rows of chairs and tables ranked back from the ring. It was pretty cavernous and must have seated at least five hundred.

All of them soon to be baying for my blood, I imagined. Unknown, unconnected.

There were twelve fights on the card and not much in the way of dressing rooms, so Gary and I were given a section of the ladies' shower room and toilets attached to the hotel's leisure centre. Our opponents were in the men's. I tried not to take it personally that I was in the ladies' bogs. There were five other fighters sharing the area, all trying to find their personal space so they could get into the zone.

It stank of feet, piss and underarm sweat.

The tournament would start with a couple of juniors, just over sixteen, and work its way up to a pair of well-seasoned heavyweights, the main draw of the evening. My fight was about halfway up the card, so I had a while to wait.

I could hear the crowd getting louder as it swelled in the hall. I heard the roar of anticipation as the MC got on the mic and made his announcements about the charity the evening was in aid of.

I didn't give a shit. For me, it was personal.

The first lad went out. Callum Furey. He must have been sixteen and wore a green Repton Club vest. His face was fixed and he stared straight ahead as he entered the hall.

Another roar.

"Popular boy," Gary said. "He's a very useful boxer. He's going to be good. Mind you, his brother was very handy too. But he's the charity case in the wheelchair."

"What happened?" I asked. "Car crash?"

Gary laughed. "Yes, some of them call it that. One of them car crashes where you get shot in the knees and get your head caved in with a bat. He can still smile and wave, but beyond that, the kid's a cabbage."

"Who did it?" I asked.

"Not really the best place to talk about it," said Gary. "People round here like to blame it on an Asian gang from Commercial Road. But the Fureys are one of the big families in this neck of the woods. They like to throw their weight around."

"So?"

Gary lowered his voice to whisper. "So, a lot of people reckon the kid getting hit was a warning to them to quieten down."

"From who?" I said. I was beginning to get the picture.

"Various names have been mentioned. Including your guv'nor's, though no one would dare say that out loud. Of course here it's all backslapping and kisses, but the tensions are still there, underneath."

We heard applause from the hall. The announcement that Callum Furey had won inside three rounds. A popular decision.

The next guy got ready to go out, bobbing and weaving. The rest of us weren't wearing head guards or vests, being outside the board of control rules. He thumped light punches into his own face, preparing his body for the punishment it was about to receive. I patted him on the back, felt the sweat already soaking him. A fanfare blared from the hall and I heard the cheers as he went in. By now my heart was pumping and my guts were runny, and I was still a good three fights away from my beating.

Gary taped my hands up tight until they felt rock-hard, put my gloves on and laced them up. Old-school, 8 oz leather cherry-reds with laces rather than Velcro. They were padded with horsehair and felt hard. As nails. My opponent would be wearing the same.

I lay down on the bench and Gary massaged my shoulders and legs, getting the blood flowing. He karate-chopped my back and I felt the vibrations go through me, every muscle and sinew beginning to sing.

I rested on my back, covered in towels, and shut my eyes as the noise faded into the background. I had almost drifted off to a nicer place when I heard a roar and Gary Cribb's steely fingers shook my shoulder.

"You're on, son. Here we go."

FORTY-SEVEN

A spotlight hit me the moment I entered the hall. A roar
went up and the theme from *Rocky* pumped through the
sound system. I almost smiled, because it was so naff and
showbiz, but it made the adrenalin surge even more.

I jogged on my toes towards the ring, bright and white
in the middle of the hall, focusing on Gary's shoulders
ahead of me.

Gary jumped up and held the ropes open while I
ducked through, onto the canvas surface of the ring. The
MC stood in the centre, announcing my arrival: "In the
blue corner, fighting out of New Cross, South London,
and weighing in at sixty-seven kilos, Ed–eeee Savage!"

Gary whipped the towel from around my neck and I
raised my hands in the air. Not so much in expected vic-
tory, but more so they could see who I was. There was a
mixture of mild applause and booing. I looked out into
the crowds, but the lights were so dazzling that anything
beyond the first three rows was just a dark mass. I saw the
kid who the night was in aid of. He was in a wheelchair at

the ringside, a baseball cap perched on his damaged head, clapping, his movements jerky and spasmodic.

I briefly caught a glimpse of Sophie with her mum and dad in the second row, and she blew me a kiss. Before I could acknowledge it, the MC's voice boomed in again and a massive cheer rang through the hall. The theme from *Rocky* had been replaced by an old hip-hop track, each whump of the bass blasting through the cheering like a blow to my stomach. Jason had chosen his own fanfare, and it was working on me:

"Pack it up, pack it in,
Let me begin,
I came to win.
Battle me that's a sin,
I won't tear the sack up,
Punk you'd better back up…"

I remembered the name of the band: House of Pain. He'd got that right, for sure.

The cheering continued as Jason slipped into the ring. "Ladies an' gen'men… In the red corner and fighting out of Bexley, and weighing seventy-five kilos … Ja–son Kell–eeeey!"

Either he was very popular, or the whole crowd was sucking up to his old man. He was wearing a white silk dressing gown with "Kelly" and a shamrock embroidered in green on the back. Donnie slipped the dressing gown off his shoulders and Jason waved at the crowd. His body was brown and sleek, not over-muscular, and covered in

Japanese and Celtic tattoos. I remembered that Gary had told me too much muscle was bad for boxers: could make you too stiff. Jason threw punches, jogging and shadow-boxing fluidly while Dave stood in the corner, geeing him up. Donnie came over to our corner.

"All right, Cribby?" he said to Gary. "All right, son?"

I nodded. While Gary rubbed my neck and put in my gumshield, Donnie leant into my ear. His huge paw patted my cheek as if wishing me luck. "Try not to win," he growled. "If you know what's good for you." He patted my cheek again, harder, slapped Gary Cribb on the back and returned to Jason's corner.

The referee called us to the centre of the ring, his voice a blur as he outlined the rules. I found myself caught in Jason's stare as he eyeballed me, his eyes black and unreadable. He stood so close that our noses almost touched and I could smell his breath.

We touched gloves, the bell rang and Jason was straight on me. Before I'd even thought about squaring up, he swung a right up from his waist and caught me hard on the side of the head with the laced inside of the glove.

The crowd gasped.

Tommy had been correct, Jason's right hand was fast and hard but unstylish. He used it more like a baseball bat, and as I tried to recover from the first blow, he clubbed his left hand hard into my face then brought the right swinging round again, this time catching my jaw and twisting my neck. Something like an electric shock shot down my back and my legs went weak.

The crowd bellowed as one, like a hungry animal; they

obviously sensed blood early in this fight and the favourite was about to dish them up some carnage.

My tactics had been all wrong. I had expected to come out on the bell with my gloves up in defence before putting out a few range-finding jabs and doing some boxing. Wrong, really wrong.

This was a real scrap and now, inside of fifteen seconds, I was on my last legs. I went down on one knee.

The referee piled in, preventing Jason from raining more heavy blows down to finish it, to see off the interloper in good style. So that I couldn't hold my head up in front of his parents or his sister, ever again.

He wanted to destroy me, and I couldn't let him.

I took a count of eight. As my blurred vision cleared I could see Gary Cribb's worried face in my corner, screaming at me. "Defend yourself!" he yelled. "Get back on the ropes, remember! Recover yourself then open up…" His face was a picture of anguish, like he knew all his hard work had been in vain.

Another person I was letting down.

I got up on seven and the ref had to hold Jason off as I wiped my gloves, ready to carry on. I held my fists high so that they'd take the worst of Jason's swinging blows. As he piled into me, I did as I was told and reversed into the ropes towards my corner. I felt them burn across my back as I slid and rode Jason's punches, keeping my fists tight to my head and my elbows tucked into my body while he battered me, trying to break me down. I gradually felt the strength return to my legs and I took about ten or twelve hard shots to my sides before the steam seemed to go out of his punches a little. I heard Gary Cribb scream, "Fifteen seconds!"

I pushed Jason off with my arms and tried to meet his eyes. They were still glazed over in a frenzy of violence. I dodged a left and then parried a right and, for the first time, I was able to land a blow on him. It was a good right cross and it caught him on the chin, taking him by surprise and making him reel a bit.

This was my opportunity to step off the ropes and get on him. I followed him, throwing another right, unbalancing him, then bringing a short left hook up to the other side of his head. He looked stunned, as if he had expected to get through three rounds without being touched. The expression on his face gave me confidence and I got on my toes, dancing and throwing fast jabs and hooks, attacking from the back foot until the bell went for the end of the round.

His round. No contest.

With my arms burning from the effort, I followed the wave of applause back to my corner.

FORTY-EIGHT

I felt I had lived a lifetime in the first three minutes, and in no time at all the bell went for the second round.

Gary had worked fast on me. He had rubbed Vaseline around my eyes, which were beginning to swell already. Three rounds wasn't long in boxing terms, but it meant that all the aggression and action had to be packed into less than fifteen minutes. And Jason was determined to go hell for leather, to get this one finished inside the distance.

He started the second as he had the first, coming like a bull from his corner and swinging wild blows at my head. He caught me with a glancing one, but I was more prepared this time, riding the punches and stepping back. I caught him on the way in with a hard jab that landed square on his nose, and I swear I felt it crunch under my fist. Blood soon started flowing down across his lip and over his gumshield. This seemed to make Jason angrier and we went toe-to-toe for a minute, with him swinging heavy hooks and me countering with blocks and short hooks to his head. I tried to keep my jab working on his nose, smearing the blood across his face and down over the tattoos on his chest.

As we traded punches I could feel his blood, wet and sticky on my gloves. I remembered my training and broke through Jason's defence, taking the inside position so that I could work on his body. I drummed punches into his ribs and up into his stomach, but I didn't seem to be having much effect. His fists were beating around my kidneys and drubbing into the back of my head. I palmed him off, pushing up under his nose, and ducked on to my back foot, bringing an uppercut hard into his solar plexus. I heard him grunt in pain and I knew I had hurt him.

His eyes seemed to focus and his face went pale. He swore at me, shouting insults into my ear as we went into a clinch. Our elbows became locked together. The ref came to pull us apart, but Jason wrestled me around into the neutral corner away from the referee's eyeline, then brought his head down hard on my eyebrow. It felt like a hammer.

As the referee pulled us apart I could see that Jason's chest and white shorts were soaked with blood. I looked down and realized that I was covered in blood too.

My own.

The crowd were baying for more as the bell went to end the second round. I looked to the ringside but there were spaces where Sophie and Cheryl had been. Tommy was talking heatedly to an ex-champion and didn't glance up at either Jason or me.

My eyebrow had split open like a ripe peach and Gary worked hard to staunch the flow of blood. He ironed it out with a freezing ice pack and swabbed it with Adrenalin on a cotton bud. Then he slathered it with Vaseline, and by the time he had sponged me off, I must have looked only half dead. I could hardly see Jason's corner, but they were all over him, screaming advice, patching up his busted nose.

The bell went again, and with Gary's advice to keep defending myself ringing in my ears, I went out for the final round.

There was no friendly touch of gloves this time and Jason rushed me once again. I tried to sidestep to take the centre of the ring, but he cut me off wherever I went, letting go with big, sweeping punches designed to club me to death, catching me with the backstroke, trying to open more cuts with the rough laces on the inside of the gloves. He foiled every attempt I made to outbox him, grabbing on to my arms, getting into clinches where he would start the dirty work: pushing me back against the corner post, rubbing his head into the cut over my eye.

His body was stinking and slick with sweat as he mauled me. He lifted his leg and grated the heel of his boot down my shin, making me yell with pain, all the while thumping at my ribs, wearing me down, punching low, his shots concealed by his own body.

I could taste blood and defeat in my mouth and in my aching bollocks. I pushed him away with both hands, blinking away gore and sweat, and put out a couple of feeble jabs, trying to keep him at bay. But he kept coming forwards. He threw a right cross, which I didn't see coming through my swollen eyelid, and rammed his thumb

287

hard into my good eye. The pain was unbearable. I was momentarily blinded as he lay into my head with more punches.

The noise of the crowd faded into the background, as did the screams of Gary Cribb, urging me to cover up and survive the remaining sixty seconds. I held on as best I could, shielding my head with my gloves, leaning on the corner post while he used my skull as target practice. Groggy, I slid on some blood and fell between the ropes.

The referee started a count but realized that it was a slip and waited for me to get to my feet. I could see the concern in his eyes as he checked my bloodied and battered face, and held fingers up for me to count. I could just see three. From somewhere deep in the distance, his voice asked if I was all right to continue. Through sheer animal instinct, I nodded that I was. Determined not to fall. Determined to die on my feet rather than live on my knees in front of these people.

I was ready to lose, but proud enough to want to be standing while I did it.

The referee waved for us to continue. Jason advanced on me, probing with his left, right hand hovering, waiting to plant his killer punch. My arms were trembling and weak, but I held my fists up in a show of defence. We circled one another while he looked for an opening. I saw Gary Cribb in the corner, ready to leap up and throw in the towel, ending my torture. Beside him I saw Sophie, tears streaming down her face, shouting out to me.

"Go, Eddie!"

She was out of Jason's eyeline, but seeing my glance to

the corner, he took it as my wanting to quit and stepped in close.

"Had enough?" he spat through his gumshield. He was panting heavily, as tired as I was, his hands dropped to waist level. "You fight like a girl." He let go with a left, underpowered and slow from exhaustion, missing its target.

And from nowhere, my own left hand found its mark. A surge of anger flowed through me, like new energy, and brought my left fist up and into Jason Kelly's slack jaw. The shock registered on his face for a millisecond: a millisecond in which I stepped back and followed through with a right that came all the way from the floor. Jason fell to the canvas heavily. His legs had gone.

I stood over him as the referee counted. His corner men and mine were in the ring already. Then, when the count had only reached eight, the bell to end the final round rang out. The roar in the hall was deafening, and there was pandemonium in the ring. The favourite had been beaten but had been saved by the bell.

As Gary Cribb held my arm up in the air, the contest – being outside the normal jurisdiction, which had scrapped the saved by the bell rule years before – was declared a draw.

There would have been an outcry if the fight had been on telly, but this was underworld rules. A few quid in a few pockets could sway any decision. Donnie watched as Gary helped me from the ring. The honour – if you can call it that – of the Kelly family had been saved, but I had been robbed.

*　　*　　*

I lay in the spare bedroom back at Kelly Towers in the dark, propped up on soft, feather pillows. It was nearly 2 a.m. and I couldn't sleep – from the pain and the adrenalin buzz that was gradually seeping out of my system.

For reasons best known to herself, Sophie had insisted that I went back there. I didn't want to, but after she had got me out of A&E with six stitches in my eyebrow, a burst blood vessel in the other eye, a cracked rib and various other cuts and bruises, I was too weak to argue.

"You should have seen the other bloke," I'd joked feebly to the nurse who was stitching me up. She'd spent too many nights in Hackney sewing up knife wounds to find me amusing.

In a way, it was true. Jason had taken a while to come round and was suffering from dehydration. Probably because he was pumped full of speed, Gary had said. He'd been taken away to spend the night under observation in a private hospital in Blackheath.

I had seen nothing of Tommy or Cheryl since the fight. I understood from Sophie that Cheryl had been unhappy about it all and had left before the end, and that Tommy was ashamed by the outcome and had slipped off without speaking to anyone.

Including his son.

Their bedroom door was firmly shut across the hall and all was silent. Until my bedroom door opened.

"Are you awake?" It was Sophie. I could just make out her hair in the half-light. She leant over me and the thin fabric of her nightdress brushed against my hyper-sensitive skin. She kissed me lightly and I could taste salty tears on her cheek. "I'm sorry, Eddie," she whispered.

"It's OK." My voice came out small, weak and cracked.

I felt her weight as she edged onto the mattress beside me. Even in my frail state, I couldn't help but worry about her old man, just a couple of doors away.

She planted small kisses all over my battered face and I felt her fingers trace across my belly, under the duvet, and tug at the waist of my boxers. A small sigh escaped from my throat. She must have thought she'd hurt me. She hadn't.

"Sorry," she whispered again.

I shuddered as she lifted her arms up and pulled off her nightdress. I remembered something about a birthday treat. Her fingers found the button on my shorts and undid it.

And as she slid down the bed beside me, I felt my pain begin to disappear.

V

Elgar

FORTY-NINE

I lay back on the deck, looking up at the blue sky above the mountains and thinking that life could be a lot worse.

Croatia was much prettier than I'd imagined. I'd thought it would be all grey buildings and nothing to eat except gherkins and garlic sausage, but I'd only just arrived and we'd had a top lunch outside a pink, quayside restaurant: noodle soup, crayfish risotto and some crisp, cold white wine.

OK, so I'd broken my pledge, but lounging on a massive yacht living the high life in the summer sun had made it impossible to resist. To tell the truth, since I'd begun to relax into my new role in the firm, I'd slipped off the wagon quite a bit.

I had been working for Tommy Kelly for a few months now, and he'd been pretty true to his word. I'd worked mainly on the paintings: making lists, Googling images on the computer. I would research auction prices for work and invent histories for pictures that had been "missing" or that had never existed until they had been "discovered" by Barney Lipman or one of a network of other artists that Tommy used.

He would often sit and watch me, still protesting that he couldn't work a computer. I didn't think that it was because he couldn't, it was more that he didn't want to. He didn't want to send his fingerprints into cyberspace, or leave evidence logged on a hard disk or server, ready to come back and bite him on the arse sometime in the future. Tommy never even used a phone: he spoke to Dave Slaughter and Dave used one. Tommy never laid his hands on anything more incriminating than a kitchen whisk.

Early on, I made sure that I installed the software that enabled the traffic to and from Tommy Kelly's computer to be monitored. If I'd been one of the spooks up at Beaconsfield reporting to Baylis or Tony, I would have been pretty disappointed with the results. It was all just Google searches and downloaded auction catalogues. All the emails were businesslike: questions and answers, sent and received by me at savagearts.co.uk. I'd set up the website myself.

There was never an email from Tommy, copied to a load of villains, reading, *The blag's going down at 11.15 p.m., Bank of England, Threadneedle Street, EC1. Be there or be square... TK.* As if.

Of course as well as the computer, I had bugged pretty much every room in the Kelly house by now and had got used to the idea that almost everything *I* said or did was also being listened to by someone. It was weird how I'd become accustomed to this. I had free rein to carry on with whatever was necessary to work for Tommy, but this must have made frustrating listening as well. Tommy never said anything incriminating. Sure, he would talk to me about paintings, which were his passion, but otherwise he never spoke about anything apart from food, cars, the dogs or his family. With the exception of Jason.

Tommy had never spoken to me about the fight, or mentioned Jason to me again. In fact Jason Kelly seemed to have made himself pretty scarce for the last few months. I didn't know what he was up to, and I didn't like to ask.

Every now and then I'd wake up in a sweat of paranoia, worried that Tommy might have uncovered a tracking device or that Cheryl had found a bug in the Hoover, but it hadn't happened so far. Up to a point, I don't think Tommy was particularly worried or suspicious about that stuff. He was so discreet at home; he never said anything that could nail him.

He was apparently untouchable.

Tommy had travelled to Croatia ahead of me, flying to Dubrovnik with British Airways. He went to pick up the boat and make some connections, he said.

I'd followed a couple of days later with EasyJet to Split. The early-morning flight was pretty much a holiday charter and I had been told to travel as an art student, so I'd dressed in tatty, skinny jeans and some old trainers. I wore a faded lumberjack shirt and felt a bit scuzzy. I didn't fancy the Kurt Cobain look: I'd got used to dressing a lot sharper. I took a portfolio of life drawings and flat canvasses with me. To the untrained eye, it all looked like a pile of shit. In a cardboard tube I had a Francis Bacon rolled up inside another, abstract painting: to the untrained eye, that looked like a pile of shit too. When I went to the desk, no one took a second look at any of it. I checked it all in with my holdall.

I had a momentary panic at Split airport when my bag came out of baggage reclaim by itself, but the portfolio and the tube appeared on the carousel soon after and I walked straight through customs without anyone batting an eyelid. Outside the airport I picked up a people carrier that had been booked in advance and it took me the few miles to the harbour at Trogir.

The town itself looked like it was straight out of a Disney movie, with castles and buildings with flags flying from little turrets. The harbour was across a cobbled bridge, part of an island right in the centre of Trogir. It was rammed with charter yachts and motor cruisers, their crews gearing up for the summer season.

It wasn't hard to spot Tommy's boat, a Sunseeker Predator 92. A ninety-two-foot arrow of white fibreglass, steel and teak. It really was an awesome machine, tied up to a berth of its own at the end of the pontoon. I spotted a couple of Croatian crew tidying up the ropes and polishing the metalwork on deck.

"Mr Kelly here?" I asked. "I'm Eddie Savage."

They helped me climb on board the yacht. It had an afterdeck with a gangplank and a separate launch that was stowed in the body of the boat. I found Tommy sunbathing on the upper deck, smoking a cigar and drinking gin, out of view of the people who cruised the pontoons, gawping at the boats. There was some serious money in the harbour.

Tommy welcomed me aboard and introduced me to the Croatian blokes who were crewing for him. There was room for four crew and eight guests on the boat, he said. Saul Wynter was with us, down below, taking a nap. Tommy also had a couple of hard men who were looking after him: he pointed down to the foredeck where they were sunbathing. One was black, wearing baggy Hawaiian surfing shorts, the other olive-skinned, in Speedos, his body covered all over with thick, black hair.

"Johnny and Stav will be looking after us," he told me.

"No Dave or Donnie?" I asked.

"Dave will be joining. Donnie's not much of a sailor." He laughed. "Drink?"

FIFTY

After lunch we motored north out of Trogir and headed up the coast. The crew knew what they were doing, and once we were out to sea they opened up the motor and the Predator raised its nose. We carved through the crystal water, ploughing a great wake of white froth. I sat up on deck behind the wheel. Darko, the skipper, let me take the controls for a bit and I felt a million dollars. Which is probably what a tank of fuel cost to run the beast.

Being on the water took me back to that one and only family holiday on the Isle of Wight, and I thought how distant it now seemed. I remembered how stupidly excited I'd been on that holiday, puttering around Ventnor Bay in a dinghy with an outboard motor. My memory of the colours had faded and, up to a point, so had my memories of Steve. I didn't want to bring him back to mind right now. To do so would have reminded me why I was really there on Tommy Kelly's yacht, and as it was I was enjoying myself.

It was a real buzz for me, watching the Dalmatian

coast zip by mile after mile as we outran the sailing boats and fishermen that pottered along closer to the shore. A few miles further on, Darko took the wheel again and we turned in towards the coast and into the mouth of a river that went inland.

As we slowed down and headed on up the river, Tommy and Saul joined us on deck, fresh from their nap. Tommy introduced me to the muscle: the hairy one was Stavros Georgiou, and the black guy they all called Johnny Reggae. They were a scary pair, sitting with their shirts off, cracking endless cans of Export lager and smoking fags, but they were friendly enough to me. The boss's bitch.

Johnny got out his iPod and hooked it up to the boat's sound system. I soon realized where he got his name as we cruised up the river. He played a ska version of "Guns of Navarone", which thumped out across the water. Johnny danced around the deck, making a *choom-chicka boom, chicka-chicka, choom-chicka* rhythm with his mouth in time to the music and grinning from ear to ear.

Even Tommy got into the groove, tapping his bare feet and laughing with Saul and the crew. He put his arm around my shoulder like a matey father who's had a couple. And for the first time I put my arm around his. We kicked our feet out in a nutty dance and everyone clapped. Tommy laughed like a drain, and when the track stopped he ruffled my hair, coughing, getting his breath back.

"Shame Sophie's not here to see this, isn't it?" he said. I nodded, grinning. "Mind you, sometimes the girls spoil the fun." He waggled his hand in front of his mouth in a drinking gesture, which Stavros took as a cue, cracking open a lager and handing it to Tommy. It was like we were all on a jolly summer lads' holiday together.

Tommy pointed out some caves carved into the cliffs on either side of the river at water level. "U-boat outposts," he said. We were in deep water, he explained, and the river had been an important hideaway for the German navy in the Second World War. The deep, dark holes in the rock suddenly looked more sinister in the afternoon sun. "Mad to think that fifteen years ago the natives were still chopping each other up in these hills. It's always been a war zone."

Tommy liked to know the history of places and, I supposed, his place in the big scheme of things. I hadn't realized that the Croatians had been fighting the neighbouring Serbs until so recently and suddenly I felt like I was a long way from home, remote and out of reach.

Somewhere where anything might happen.

We crossed a vast, inland lake and chugged into the harbour at Skradin a couple of hours later. The place was picture-postcard perfect, with houses perched up a hill, not so different from the place we'd just left, except that the harbour was small, with a dozen or so sailing boats moored up.

Anchored in the bay was a vast, silver motor yacht with tinted windows. It looked a good third bigger than ours, which must have made it about a 120-footer.

"Looks like Bashi's tub," Tommy said, examining it through a pair of binoculars. "We're in the right place, at least."

We showered while the crew launched the tender, and we – Tommy, Saul and I – motored ashore. Saul made a call on his BlackBerry and we headed for a bar along the quayside. The place was full, mostly Italians and Russians. You could tell the difference, and not just by the language. The Italians swanned around looking relaxed in expensive sunglasses and Gucci shoes. The Russians, though they clearly had money, looked as if they had just bought everything yesterday and had left the coat hangers in their clothes.

It was easy to find the party we were looking for: a table of serious-looking men glugging litres of beer and talking loudly on mobiles. As we approached the table, the man at the centre of the group stood up and smiled, flashing gold teeth.

"Tomasovitch!" he shouted and grabbed Tommy in a hug, kissing him on both cheeks. He was no taller than Tommy, but wide, with a large, shaved head. I thought he looked like a baked potato: brown, pockmarked and a bit flabby. Tommy looked momentarily flustered but introduced me and Saul.

"Saul, Eddie," he said. "Alexei Bashmakov."

"Eddie? Your son?" The Potato shook my hand and patted me on the shoulder.

"My assistant," Tommy corrected. "Jason's taking care of business while I'm abroad."

I caught Saul Wynter's eye and he looked away.

We had a couple of beers, Karlovačko. The Russians insisted on Tuborg. While Tommy and Bashmakov chatted about this and that, Saul and I nodded, smiled and clinked glasses with his mates. Mostly they kept talking on their phones and lighting up Marlboros.

"Alexei's kindly invited us for a glass of champagne on his yacht," Tommy said after a while. "Eddie, I need you to go back on board and pick up the artwork. And don't drop it in the drink." He laughed and the Russians laughed too.

I walked along the quayside to where the tender had been tied up, past a few smart little clothes shops selling striped sailing shirts and flip-flops. There was another large Russian yacht tied up at the mooring. Girls in bikinis were laughing drunkenly on the deck, and fat men stood on the quayside watching, wishing they were invited.

Opposite the boat, separated by a wide, cobbled path, was another café. People sat at tables outside, enjoying the view, watching the world go by. Sitting alone at one table was a sexy, dark-haired girl drinking coffee and smoking. She wore big, black sunglasses and a baggy white shirt over tiny shorts. I could have sworn she caught my eye from behind the shades. I looked at her for a moment, then I was sure. Anna.

I took a step forwards but she shook her head. I stopped. She stubbed out her cigarette and left money on the table. I pretended to join the men watching the yacht while she stood up and left the café. She turned up the next street of gift shops and bars, and I followed a few seconds later. I saw her stop at a newsagent's. There were postcards on a browser outside and European news-papers on a stand. She rifled through the postcards as if she was looking for something to send to her mum. I stopped and looked at the papers, trying to find something in English.

"What are you doing here?" I asked quietly.

"Same as you," she said. "'Working." I swear there was a hint of irony in her voice. "We need to talk. Meet me here tomorrow morning, if you can get away. Before twelve."

"I don't know what we'll be doing," I said.

"If you can't make it, I'll leave a card here for you, in this rack." She didn't look at me, but from the corner of my eye I saw her point at the third stack of cards down, in the middle of the stand. "Make an excuse. A present for Sophie, anything."

She picked out a card, a picture of a local waterfall, and went inside to pay for it. I waited for her, but she didn't look at me when she came out. She just continued to walk up the street. I watched her long, brown legs for a moment, and then realized that the man from the shop was doing the same.

I turned and walked in the opposite direction, back to the boat, shaken.

FIFTY-ONE

By the time Darko had taken me across from our boat on the motor launch, the champagne was in full flow on Bashmakov's yacht. Its lights shimmered on the still water and it was sparkling, not so much like a Christmas tree but more like a floating nightclub.

There were three decks, and the uniformed steward, who spoke no English, ushered me through the boat.

The lower deck was dark and full of girls and heavy-looking Russian blokes either lounging on banquettes or shuffling around to Euro disco music. They were all drinking and didn't look at me. The steward led me up a shiny, steel staircase to the upper saloon.

The atmosphere was more rarefied up top. It was deceptively large and I wondered how they managed to create such a space inside a boat. If I hadn't known better, I would have guessed we were in a posh bar in some international hotel. The floor was polished wood, as were all the fittings, and everything else was either gleaming chrome or cream leather.

Although there was laughter, and a couple of the best-looking girls in tow, Tommy, Saul and Bashi, as they called him, were having businesslike discussions. As if they were at a cocktail party.

Saul clocked me and called me over.

"Here's the man," said Tommy, and kissed me on the cheek. He'd had a few by now. "Show the dog the rabbit." Bashi laughed and we went over to the big chart table in the centre of the saloon.

I heaved up the portfolio and unzipped it. Tommy flicked through the plastic sleeves and pulled out my Schwitters.

"Here we go," he said. "My gift to you. Kurt Schwitters. English period. Up your street, I think?" He handed it to Bashmakov, who immediately flipped it over and studied the back. He put on his glasses to read the inscription, turned it back over and looked at the front, studying the corners of the frame and then finally the collage itself.

"It's good?" he asked.

Tommy held his hands up, mimicking an East End trader. "Of course it is," he said. "I nicked it myself!"

They all fell about laughing at that one, and Tommy's bravado seemed to be enough to convince Bashmakov of its authenticity. Perhaps he didn't care.

Tommy removed other paintings and drawings from the sleeves: other stuff I'd bought at auctions online, on his say-so. They were pretty ordinary, and I now realized that they were there just to pad out the collection.

"Piece of crap ... piece of crap," Tommy said, turning them over one by one until he came to another drawing on thick watercolour paper. I hadn't seen it before. "Here we go."

It was a pencil drawing of a Gypsy girl, with high cheekbones and flashing eyes. I was getting better at this. I quite liked it myself. It had a date of '07, which I guessed was 1907, but it looked really modern. Maybe it was.

"Augustus John," Tommy said. "Classic piece, 1907."

Bashi nodded approvingly. "I have the two oil portraits already. This I like." He put it to one side and I assumed the deal was done.

"You have good taste, Mr Bashmakov," Tommy said. "Show him our *pièce de résistance*, Eddie."

I uncapped the tube and eased out the rolled canvas from inside. Tommy peeled away the cheap painting that was protecting the good one and unrolled the Bacon on the chart table. It was pretty similar to the one I'd seen in Barney Lipman's studio months before, but I wasn't going to say so.

"The last one of these to come on the open market sold for twenty-five mil," Tommy said. "It's a study for *Figures at the Base of the Crucifixion*, which is in the Tate Gallery in London."

He poured Bashmakov another glass of Krug, then one for himself. He didn't appear hurried or eager to sell. It was more like he was showing off something from his own collection. I guess that was the trick. Bashmakov looked closely at the Francis Bacon, examining the edges of the canvas. There were nail holes where it had once been attached to a stretcher.

"It's 1944," Tommy continued. "All the critics agree

that this was the real starting point of Bacon's career. He destroyed almost everything he'd done before that. Which is what people assumed had happened to this one. It's as rare as rocking-horse shit."

Bashmakov sipped his champagne and lit a fag. He was beginning to look serious, like he was being seduced by Tommy's words – which, I admit, were pretty convincing.

"So where does this one come from?" asked Bashmakov.

"It's been out of circulation since the sixties," Tommy told him. "Everyone assumed it had been binned. But through an associate we found it in the home of an old poof in Bayswater. He'd been one of Bacon's boyfriends and had nicked the picture when they fell out."

The story sounded good to me. I believed it, and I was the one who'd made it up. I'd put in the research. Francis Bacon was well known for hanging out with villains in Soho. One of his boyfriends had been a burglar, Tommy had told me. Back then, being gay was as illegal as armed robbery. You could get banged up for receiving swollen goods, Tommy had joked.

"So it's stolen?" Bashi sounded unconcerned.

Tommy shrugged. "Apparently Bacon didn't notice it was missing. The old fruit was so pissed most of the time, he couldn't remember what he had or hadn't destroyed. But, strictly speaking, it was acquired illegally, so it can't go on to the open market."

"How much?" Bashmakov asked. He'd heard enough and Tommy's story stacked up.

"Like I say, Damien Hirst paid twenty-five for another

one like this. You'd have a painting that most of the museums in Europe would give their cobbler's for."

"Just tell me straight." Bashmakov laughed and put his arm round Tommy's shoulders. "Just give it to me without all the romancing. I'm not a lady." He squeezed Tommy and made a kissy noise.

"As you like it," Tommy said. "Five."

Bashmakov pursed his lips. "Euros? You're not shafting me, are you, Kelly?"

"Hand on heart," Tommy said.

"Three."

"Four and a half and you've got a deal."

Bashmakov grinned and they shook hands. Four point five million euros. Just like that.

One of Bashmakov's sidekicks came into the saloon and spoke to him in Russian.

"Sounds like the rest of the stuff's arrived, Tommy," Bashmakov said.

We peered out of the window and saw a yacht motoring up alongside us in the dark. I followed Tommy and Bashmakov out on to the deck and saw that there was a crew of four on board, Dave Slaughter among them.

"All right, Dave?" Tommy shouted down. Dave saluted in a naval fashion. They tied the yacht by the side of Bashmakov's and a couple of his staff went aboard and started unloading crates from the lockers. They were cases of what looked like champagne, taped up with polythene to protect them from the damp.

Dave hopped aboard. He looked as if he was bringing his own bottle of champagne to the party. He handed it directly to Bashmakov, who looked at the label and nodded approvingly, then took out a folding knife from his pocket and sliced clean through the top of the bottle as if it was butter. It was made of wax.

He then tapped the severed cap out into the palm of his hand and crumbs of lumpy white powder fell out. Bashmakov tipped the lumps on to the white fibreglass of the hull and crushed them into a powder with the side of his knife, chopping it into a line the size of half a pencil. One of his men handed him a rolled-up note and Bashamkov leant over and snorted the powder up his nose. He sniffed it back and then wiped his finger in the remaining dust, testing it on his tongue and rubbing it over his gums.

"Good," he said after a few seconds. "Pure. We'll keep this one for ourselves." He handed the bottle to his man and signalled his approval to the boat alongside. "We'll have a party."

It was true that they could make the finest vodka and synthesize their own pills, but for the newly affluent Russians the Bolivian marching powder was the drug of choice. And it needed to be brought in from further afield. By people with the right connections.

In the distance I could hear the buzz of another motor, an outboard coming from the far side of the lake. I broke into a sweat when Bashmakov's men muttered to one another and tried to find it with their night-vision binoculars. A sigh of relief went up when a flashlight signalled from the approaching boat. It was the one they were expecting.

The smaller boat came into view and moored alongside

the yacht Dave had arrived on. It was like a fishing fleet had come in. The men passed the crates from one boat to the other, where they were stashed below, and the second boat was loaded and away within about five minutes.

Stav Georgiou took Dave's place on the other boat and it left several minutes later. Bashmakov and Tommy watched them go, shaking hands on a deal smoothly done. Tommy's trick, it seemed, was to make sure of the delivery. Do the deal, but never be on the same boat as the goods. Once he'd checked it, he was offski. And once we were back on our boat, there would be nothing to see except a few bottles of duty-free gin.

I strolled along the rear deck, where I found Tommy debriefing Dave, waiting for our tender. He wanted to get gone. My deck shoes were silent on the teak, and I realized that they hadn't heard or seen me approach. I was hidden under the shade of the upper deck. To take another step would look like I was creeping up on them; to turn around would look like I was sneaking away. I pushed myself back against the bulkhead, caught between a rock and a hard place.

"Nice job, Dave," I heard Tommy say. "Good trip from Brindisi?" He was on form. The deal on the picture was done and the cocaine had been delivered safely.

"Yeah, not bad." Dave sounded like he was holding something back.

"What then?" Tommy asked.

"Just a bit of grief at home," Dave said. "Nothing to get worried about."

"Let me be the judge of that."

Dave's voice dropped to a whisper and I heard him mumble, sounding apologetic, not wanting to upset the boss.

Tommy let out a stream of four-letter words that made my eyes water. His voice was rasping and harsh.

"Get back to Donnie. Tell him to damage him. Open him up like a bag of crisps."

I shivered at the image the phrase conjured up. The light from our approaching tender cast a beam across the deck, and as Tommy turned, he saw me. I took a step, trying to look as if I was out for a stroll on deck.

"Eddie?" he said. "What's your game?"

FIFTY-TWO

Tommy's mood had changed overnight.

I'd been shitting myself, unable to sleep. I realized that I'd got too comfortable with all this and that I was in danger of slipping up. Tommy's words the night before had reminded me sharply of who he was and what he did for a living.

He wasn't nasty to me the next morning, just cold and withdrawn. Then he locked himself in the forward cabin with Saul and Dave. I could hear him shouting.

I'd never heard Tommy Kelly shout before.

When they came out, he told me they had a bit more business to tie up with Bashmakov and would be a couple of hours. I clearly wasn't invited. Saul winked at me, like it was nothing for me to worry about. I felt relieved. Whenever anything went wrong around Tommy, I immediately felt like I was to blame, in case any of the information I had leaked had come back to bite him.

And was about to come back and bite me.

"I wondered if it'd be OK to go ashore for a bit?" I said.

"Why not?" Tommy's mood seemed to lighten. "Maybe pick up a present or two for the girls."

"That's what I was thinking," I said.

Tommy smiled for the first time that morning and tapped his nose. "Good thinking, that man." As if buying souvenirs for Cheryl and Sophie was more important than the business he had to do. "We'll drop you on the quay when we go over to Bashi's yacht."

It was a bright, sunny day, so I walked around the cafés and bars on the quayside wearing my Ray-Bans, looking here, there and everywhere for Anna.

For a moment I was tempted to just run, I didn't know where. My emotions were mixed. Tommy's show of teeth had rattled me, but somehow I felt safer going back into the fold with him than taking my chances on the run in the big wide world.

The Kelly world was full of shady dealing and uncertainty, but it included Cheryl and Sophie, who in many ways felt like family to me now. Sure, I'd been doing collections and pick-ups for a few months whenever Dave had told me to. I'd seen one or two punters persuaded with a slap or three. But I didn't feel the need to report back *everything* I saw. My life also included family dinners at Kelly Towers, weekends away, the best seats in restaurants and shows in the West End. It was a cushy number, all the time Tommy was happy.

On the other hand, the legit world of Tony Morris, Baylis and Anna felt like a cold, hard place: manipulative and, bottom line, one that didn't have any real concern for my comfort or well-being. I didn't know which way to turn.

I'd put on shorts and a black Lacoste polo shirt so I didn't stick out like a bacon sarnie at a Bar Mitzvah. When I found her, I saw she had done the same: black vest, denim skirt. She had been hard to spot because of the colour of her clothes, but her attractiveness alerted another radar altogether and I quickly homed in – as had half a dozen other blokes, who were hovering around furtively. She was reading a paper outside the same shop as before.

As soon as she had noticed me, I walked on ahead, up a cobbled side street towards a small square with a church. In the middle was a fountain, so I sat down on its stone surround. There were a couple of nuns and a few of those old women dressed in black that always hang around churches in foreign countries. Old, black widows. Anna and I seemed to be following their dress code.

Other than the women, the square was empty. When Anna arrived, she studiously ignored me. She looked up at the carved architecture of the church. The bell in the church tower clanked the half-hour like someone bashing a saucepan with a spoon. Anna took a shawl out of her bag, wrapped it round her shoulders and entered the church.

I waited a moment, looked around, and followed her in.

The air was cool and musty inside, with that joss-stick smell you get in old churches. I walked down the aisle towards a gruesome-looking, life-sized Crucifixion. It must have been carved from wood and painted: the nails through Jesus' hands looked for real and the hole in his side was like a recent stab wound, oozing blood. His glass eyes had rolled upwards and even his tongue had been carved lolling out between his teeth. It looked more like a scene of crime reconstruction than a religious carving.

To the side was a small chapel with a black-and-white tiled floor. A rack full of melting candles burned at the entrance, and inside was an altar covered with old lace. Anna was sitting, rather than kneeling, on a bench in front of the altar. Praying wasn't exactly her style.

I slid into the bench behind her. "Hi," I whispered.

"What kept you?"

"It's not that easy to get off a yacht out at anchor. I can't just park it up on the quay."

"I know, playboy," she said. "I've seen it. Impressive."

She sounded pissed off, like I was pulling a fast one, which I thought was a bit much.

"Listen," I said, "I know you were set up to keep me sweet."

"Don't be wet, Eddie." She looked back over her shoulder. "I like you. You know I do. But grow up, it's part of the job."

"Where are you staying?"

"Best you don't know," she said. "Listen, Nimrod is getting anxious. He thinks you're not feeding back often enough."

"Is that why you're here?" I asked. "To keep an eye on me for Baylis?" I'd almost forgotten his stupid code name. Anna winced when I forgot to use it.

"Ssh! Yes, of course that's why I'm here. To see how the land lies."

"I'm deep cover," I said. "I shouldn't have to report back until something happens."

"And hasn't it?" she asked. "Why are you here?"

"Paintings," I said.

"And?"

In the past months I had got so used to parcels of this and that being delivered, I had almost forgotten about the cocaine-filled champagne bottles. The shipment of drugs hardly came as a surprise. Perhaps there was part of me that wanted to turn a blind eye to it. So as not to upset the apple cart.

"Dunno," I said. "They're out there now, discussing something or other. I'm not privy to all the information, as you can see. I'm here."

Anna looked at me through narrowed eyes, like she didn't believe me. "No mention of guns or arms?" she asked. "Nimrod thinks they're cooking up something bigger."

"Haven't heard anything like that," I said. It was true, I hadn't.

"You seem to be enjoying yourself, Eddie." She raised her eyebrows. "Have you been seduced by all the money and glamour?"

I shook my head, but I felt myself go red. Maybe I had.

"Nimrod wonders if you've gone native," she said. "I hope you still know where your moral compass is pointing, Eddie."

"That's rich coming from you," I said. Suddenly I felt

like a sulky boy. I dropped the bravado as my fear bubbled to the surface. "Listen, Anna," I whispered. "I'm shitting myself. This is scary out here. I'm beginning to worry he suspects me of something. If I wanted to, what are my chances of jumping ship?"

"None," Anna said. "Sit tight, get back home and report in. Try to remember which side you're on."

There was clearly no messing. At that moment I felt I just wanted to get into a taxi with her and run for the nearest airport.

"Listen, we've been here long enough, I've got to go," she said. She stood up. "Remember to pick up the postcard. I left it in case you couldn't come."

"Sure."

We left the church. The day looked supernaturally bright once we stepped back outside. My eyes adjusted to the light as we walked into the square. I could see the blurred image of a man coming towards me and Anna, and as I blinked the image came into focus and my mouth went dry.

"Eddie." It was Saul Wynter. He was carrying a briefcase.

"Hey," I said, flustered, still adjusting to the light, fiddling with my sunglasses. Anna walked away.

"*Merci,*" she said to me over her shoulder. "*Sank* you." Her accent was faultless franglais. Saul watched her walk off across the square.

"Bloody hell," he said. "Leave you five minutes and you're picking up foreign birds in churches. Catholic girls are always the worst." He winked at me.

"She was lost," I said. "French." My knees were shaking.

"Bet she was," Saul said. "Did you show her the way?"

We both laughed.

"What goes on tour stays on tour," Saul said as her long, brown legs disappeared across the square. "But you'll have to be nice to me on the way back so I don't tell Sophie."

Or Tommy, I thought. Saul looked at me for longer than was comfortable. And I was already wriggling inside, as uncomfortable as it was possible to be without having fish hooks stuck in my eyes. He punched me on the arm, as if to say in a manly way that my secret was safe with him. I wasn't sure if I'd got away with it. *Really* not sure.

"We're shipping out," he told me. "I came to find you."

We made our way back down the street, past the shops.

"I'll just get a couple of presents for Sophie," I said.

"What have you been doing with your time?" Saul asked. I shrugged.

"I've got to nip to the bank," he said, slapping his briefcase. He stopped outside the Credit Kuna, or whatever it was called, and looked back down the street. "Nice bird," he said. "Sure you didn't know her?"

"No!" I protested. It must have looked bad.

"Look, Eddie." Saul continued to glance down the street. "If you see anything ... unusual, you'll tell me, won't you?"

"Sure," I said. "Like what?"

"I dunno. Things you wouldn't want to mention to

Tommy. Anything you don't like the smell of. People poking about, stuff you might see Jason getting up to... We can help each other."

I began to get his drift. At least, I think I did.

"Mum's the word," he said. He squeezed my arm. "Meet you for a quick one in the bar on the corner before we go back."

Saul went into the bank and I went into the shops, confused. I wasn't one hundred per cent sure what all that had been about. I bought a sailor-striped vest for Sophie and a couple of soaps and bits for her mum. It didn't even cross my mind to get anything for my own. But it did strike me that God-knows-what was being traded just offshore, illicit euros were being paid into the bank and here I was buying soap. I went by the newsagent and searched through the postcard rack for Anna's drop.

It wasn't there.

I searched every row of postcards in the rack. Nothing. I felt sick. I hoped Anna had been smart and doubled back to pick it up when she saw who I was with.

I went down to the café, where Saul was already gulping the last of his beer. Mine was on the table. I sat down and took a long glug.

"Get everything?" Saul asked.

"I think so," I said. "Bits and bobs." I held up the carrier bag to show him.

"It's the thought that counts." He pulled a roll of cash from his pocket and gave it to me. It was a good grand's worth in euros. "Remember what I said."

I refused the money and he put his arm around my shoulder, like a generous uncle, pushing the wedge into my pocket. "You did good on the pictures," he said.

"Not that good," I said, trying to force the money back into his top pocket.

"It's nothing." He gave it back again. "Got to keep everyone sweet."

FIFTY-THREE

Donnie was sweating like a pig. He'd had a bastard couple
of weeks, being employed exclusively to try and mop up after
Jason. And now he was on the road again, at midnight, to clear
up some more of his shit.

The kid had gone mad. There had been a big family row with
Tommy and Cheryl the day after the fight, both of them scream-
ing blue murder about how he'd shown them up. How they
weren't proud of his performance. Tommy had hurt him, telling
Jason that he was no son of his. Donnie and Dave had shuffled
around uncomfortably while it all went off. It was rare for the
family to wash their dirty linen in front of them. Donnie saw it
as another sign that the old man was losing his grip. The boss
looked ready to pack it all in.

They'd never seen Tommy Kelly have to deal with a prob-
lem like this before, but then he'd never had a twenty-year-old
son locking horns with him. Flesh and blood flexing its mus-
cles. Jason had been a kid until now, but for the last year or
so he'd been trying to establish himself in the firm. And the
old man didn't like it. Jason seemed to think he was going to

inherit the business; Tommy didn't.

Neither did Cheryl or anyone else, it seemed. Donnie could see she didn't want her kids to have anything to do with the business. There was no need. Tommy had enough stashed away to keep them comfortable for the rest of. All invested and tied up, carefully laundered by Saul Wynter.

Donnie would be the first to admit, they were all getting a bit long in the tooth for this game. Tommy was mid-fifties, Saul Wynter late forties. He and Dave were getting creaky and lived in hope that their retirement plan involved a few hundred £k in cash and a bar in Palma Nova. If no one muffed up.

Donnie's mind drifted back to the summer he'd spent in Majorca after they'd got Patsy Kelly, Tommy's brother, sorted out in southern Spain. Donnie had salted away his earnings over there, carefully paid in through various channels set up for him by Saul. Donnie and Dave agreed that the guy was a genius with money. Normally Donnie would have stuffed the mattress with it. He dreamt of a cold litre of San Miguel and a plate of calamawhatsit – squid – sitting on the beach, lapping waves, a nice Spanish bird…

The splash of rain on the greasy South London streets brought Donnie back sharply from the beach. In the meantime, there was work to be done. Some mess to be tidied up. Tommy had said it was time to put their shop in order. Donnie hit the brakes as he approached the speed camera towards Lee Green. Speeding tickets and photo evidence were one of Tommy's big no-nos. He took a swerve at the Lewisham roundabout, down to New Cross to pick up Paulie Dolan from The Harp before they went to work.

*　　*　　*

Tommy had told me to take a couple of days off after our trip. I sensed that there was some business to sort out. Something that didn't involve me.

Once I was back on home turf, relieved that I had made it back in one piece without being rumbled, I realized that I'd almost enjoyed it. It had been a break. One that involved forged paintings, cocaine smuggling and international criminals, that was all. I remembered what Anna had said about my moral compass, but to be honest, I didn't feel all that bad. No one had been hurt, it was nice to be on flash boats in the sun and we'd actually had a few laughs. What's not to like?

Anna's words had sunk in, though. So in the afternoon I went back to the safe house and called Baylis.

"Hello, Nimrod. Elgar here." Elgar was my code name – Edward Elgar: Eddie. They really thought about this stuff. Personally, I thought it was a bit naff, like something the Boy Scouts would make up. If that was their best, it was no wonder the crims ran rings around them.

I didn't mention that to Baylis, naturally.

"Hello, Elgar," Baylis said in his reedy voice. He always sounded as if he was taking the piss. "Better late than never."

I told him that I'd made contact with Ysobel – Anna – in Skradin. He already knew.

"Where is Ysobel now?" he asked.

I didn't know. I told him I'd last seen her in Skradin.

"What about the drop?" I told him it wasn't there. He was silent for a moment. "What else?"

I told him about the paintings. The Schwitters had been

microchipped, the Augustus John I thought was kosher. I knew Tommy Kelly had lined up something good to make the others look better. But the Francis Bacon...? Although I had made up and researched the background for it, Tommy had never explicitly told me whether it was real or something that Barney Lipman had knocked up.

"Did you tag it?" Baylis asked. I hadn't. I'd never had the chance. "We think it's right."

"Right?"

"We think it might be a real one."

"So you know about it?" I said. It hadn't occurred to me that they might have already known.

"How much did he get for it?" asked Baylis.

I told him, and said that some money had probably been paid into a local bank in Skradin. There can't have been more than a couple of banks in a town that size. I told him that I thought some cocaine had been traded, disguised as champagne bottles.

"You might have mentioned that first," he said. "Did you know about it beforehand?"

"No," I said honestly.

"If you had, we could have nailed him for it," Baylis said. "We could have been there."

"I didn't know anything about it," I assured him. "They don't mention that stuff to me. And we were in the middle of the sea somewhere in Eastern Europe." I realized that I didn't actually know where Croatia was on the map. Stupid.

"Listen to me," Baylis said in his most serious voice. "We have ten years of evidence stacking up against Kelly.

Businesses, transactions, killings, all with his name on. Sadly, none of them can be directly pinned on him."

"I understand," I said, trying to take on his serious tone.

"Now we have good surveillance and recordings, thanks in some part to you ... when you're not being a complete retard."

Coming from Baylis, it was almost a compliment.

"What we need now is a slip-up. Some direct involvement. *Anything* with his fingerprints on. It could be shoplifting from Sainsbury's. Don't care, as long as we catch him with the Chicken Kiev in his hands. Get him to mug an old lady. Anything, and the rest will fall into place."

"I take your point," I said. "But Kelly never gets directly involved with the dealings. He makes himself scarce. It's like nailing a fart to a wall – he's elusive."

"Bit like you." I realized that was true. "Keep in touch," said Baylis. "More." He rang off without thanking me.

I'd taken a beating from Jason Kelly on their behalf. I'd stuck myself in the middle of the sea with people who could have chucked me to the sharks at any moment. And there wasn't a word of encouragement from the man.

I thought he was a wanker.

I walked back to the high street flat. Sophie was going to call round early evening to welcome me back.

She arrived at eight. I had ordered a takeaway curry, which was keeping warm. We had a couple of beers and ate saag aloo and prawn korma watching the telly. She asked me about the trip, asked if her dad had said anything about what was going on. I said that I really didn't know, other than he'd been a bit stressed out before we'd left. I tried to get more out of her. She thought it had something to do with Jason but wouldn't be drawn further. She acted really pleased with the vest I'd bought her.

After we'd eaten, we kissed and whatever on the sofa. I dragged her by the hand through to the bedroom. I was really pleased to see her and she seemed quite glad to see me. We messed around on the bed for a bit, and at around eleven she looked at her watch and said she had to go.

I walked her downstairs and on to the street where the Mini was parked. It was raining, so we hurried over to the car. I was just about to kiss her goodnight when a drunk lurched towards us out of the shadows.

"Son," he slurred. "Buy your old dad a cuppa tea."

Sophie pulled away from me and we looked at the bedraggled figure swaying in the streetlight in front of us. Sophie turned to me, confused.

"Not going to introduce me?" he said. He waved a grubby finger towards Sophie. I took her by the waist and opened the door, helping her in.

"You get off," I told her. I helped her into the driver's seat. "I'll be fine."

"It's my son!" he shouted. "Don't you remember me?"

I was beginning to panic. I went over to him, pulled a twenty out of my back pocket and stuffed it into his hand. "Eff off and buy yourself a drink," I hissed into his ear, pushing him away. He slowly registered the note and staggered backwards. I walked back to Sophie's window.

"Local nutter," I said. "Won't leave me alone." I patted the roof as she wound up the window. "Night, babe."

Sophie waved at me through the closed window and drove away. I watched the Mini disappear down the street, then turned to watch my drunken old man weave along the wet pavement.

In my experience, his turning up was never a good sign.

FIFTY-FOUR

Paul Dolan was waiting for Donnie outside The Harp. He was wet and Donnie could sense his mood as soon as he got into the Mercedes. There was always a buzz of uncontained energy about Irish Paul, like he was permanently wired. Dangerous, but a good man to have on your side in a row. And he'd been in a few.

"So what's the score?" Dolan asked. He lit a cigarette and offered one to Donnie, who took it.

"It's a right bleeding mess," said Donnie. He pulled away into the stream of traffic. "Young Mr Kelly is trying to carve out his own pitch. He's taken over the Chilli Peppa like it's his own. And now that he's got used to having Jason around, Tyrone Brown or whatever he's called – the twat that used to run the gaff – likes the idea of being in the firm."

"He's not, is he?" asked Dolan.

"Not a bleeding chance," Donnie said. "He hasn't realized he's only breathing fresh air because we let him. He's just the mug who runs it for us. The one who'll be getting the grief if it goes tits up."

"So what's the problem?"

"Jason's drawing attention to the place. There've been fights … the place is swimming in charlie. There's been half a dozen visits from the filth in the last week. They're beginning to take an unhealthy interest in the comings and goings."

"Just shut it down," Dolan said.

"We will," Donnie told him. "But this tit Brown, the manager, has been poncing himself from Peckham to Brixton saying he's Special K. That he's doing our deals and is protected by us."

"Cheeky." Dolan shook his head.

"Too right. He's all cocky dick, talking about Kelly this and Tommy that, like they were mates, and all the time he's knocking out weed and trips – and our Es – and trousering a slice of the proceeds. Unsanctioned."

Dolan tutted.

"It's only a matter of time before the place is busted or Brown's collared," Donnie said. He turned left, over Telegraph Hill. "And when he is, he'll squeal like a stuck pig."

"So he needs shutting up," said Dolan.

Donnie nodded. "But the guv'nor doesn't want Jason in the same city when it's sorted."

"Kneecaps?" Dolan asked, as if it was an item on a shopping list. Donnie knew that Irish Paul could kneecap in a number of different ways, depending on the level of damage that was required. It was his area of expertise.

"He's had fair warning," Donnie said. "I think it's gone beyond that." Donnie thought about the samurai sword he'd put in the boot earlier and drove across Hilly Fields, down towards Catford and the Chilli Peppa.

They pulled up outside the club. Jason's Audi TT was

parked there, as it had been most nights in the past few weeks. Next to Hyrone Brown's black SUV. A few people were leaving. It was a quiet weeknight and the place was generally empty by one. Donnie checked his watch: five to. He told Dolan to go in and make sure any stragglers were out, then get Jason off the premises and back to his flat. Paul seemed a little disappointed he wasn't going to be around for the action.

Donnie waited and watched as Dolan went in and the last few punters left. He took a good snort from the bottle in the glove compartment, turned on the wipers and watched as Dolan came out with Jason Kelly. Jason was glassy-eyed and staggering. Off his tits. He wouldn't think anything of a Kelly driver coming to pick him up. It was a regular occurrence. Dolan took Jason's keys from him and the remote on the Audi squeaked and the hazard lights flashed. Unnoticed by Jason, Paul nodded to Donnie before getting into the Audi and driving Jason away.

Donnie took out his mobile and speed-dialled a cab firm. He ordered a car from Deptford to Catford in an hour's time. "Use the kid," Dave had said. "Tommy wants him involved." Donnie got out of the Mercedes and opened the boot. He held the sword close to his leg as he approached the club. It made him walk a little stiffly across the wet gravel. A couple of the club's barmen were loitering just inside the doorway.

"Fuck off," Donnie said. They took one look at him and did.

Hyrone Brown was in the back office as usual. He was watching a music channel on a flatscreen TV and had his feet up on the desk, a spliff in one hand and a drink in the other. Donnie stood in the doorway and saw Brown's watery eyes widen and his mangled fingers tighten on the glass when he caught sight of him.

"Evening," Donnie said.

Hyrone swung his feet off the desk and stood up. "Jason's gone," he said. "Someone else picked him up."

"I know." Donnie smiled. "I told them to. It's you I've come for. Your good friend Mr Kelly asked me to call on you. Apparently you've been dropping his name around. I thought you'd had the rules explained clearly." Donnie looked at the man's maimed hand.

"No, no, no…" Hyrone Brown shook his head.

"Oh, and selling our gear without anyone's say-so."

"I can explain. Jason said…" He couldn't find the words.

"You don't work for Jason."

"Have a drink." Brown pushed a bottle of vodka across the desk towards Donnie. "We can talk."

"No, thank you," Donnie said politely. "I need to keep a clear head while I'm working. Driving, aren't I?"

"Where are we going?" Hyrone Brown's voice trembled.

"Nowhere," Donnie said. "Not just yet, anyway."

Brown took a swig from the vodka bottle and then threw it hard at Donnie's head. It missed, and he ran for the door. Donnie stopped him with his bulk and a punch to the stomach that had Brown on his knees.

"Open him up like a bag of crisps" had been the order. Donnie kicked the door shut behind him and pulled the long, curved sword from its scabbard. Then he did as he'd been told.

My phone went at two. I switched on the light and looked at the number. It was blocked. I answered the call. There was a pause and at first I didn't recognize the deep growl.

"Eddie? Donnie Mulvaney. I've got a bit of a job on. The guv'nor said you'd help me if I needed you."

I searched my brain. I couldn't remember Tommy saying anything about helping Donnie out, but then I couldn't exactly call him up to check at two in the morning.

"Sure," I said sleepily. "But I don't know what I'm supposed to be doing tomorrow."

"It's not tomorrow," Donnie grumbled. "It's now. There's a cab outside. Get in it and come down to Catford. It will drop you at the end of Honley Road. Walk up and meet me at the Chilli Peppa club. Don't hang about." He cut off the call.

I jumped out of bed and pulled the curtain back. A minicab was waiting downstairs, engine running. Shit. I pulled on a pair of jeans and some trainers, grabbed a hoodie and ran downstairs.

Things were beginning to unravel, I could feel it in my bones. First, the old man turning up, now this call. Plus I was still feeling paranoid about the trip and what Tommy Kelly might or might not have twigged. I felt sure I was walking into a trap. But I couldn't say no.

FIFTY-FIVE

The cab dropped me in Lewisham High Street. The road was wet and empty. It was nearly two-thirty. A police car sped past, throwing up spray, its siren wailing. I found myself wishing it had been for me. I would have been relieved.

I turned into Honley Road as I had been told. The place was just off the junction. It looked like a run-down bingo club. There was a wire fence to one side and I saw Donnie's Mercedes in the parking area. Another car was next to it, a black Mazda or something, a four-by-four. The entrance to the club was shut, and the neon Chilli Peppa sign was turned off. I could see a light round the back, so I let myself in through an open side door. The place was still warm and smelt of sweat and alcohol. A violet UV strip light still shone over the stage and sent a creepy glow over the dance floor. Beyond, I could see a door ajar and a chink of light coming from it.

"Donnie?" I called weakly. I walked towards the door and pushed it open. It was the office.

At first I thought it was joke, like someone had been in

and splashed red paint everywhere. Then I saw the body on the floor, its white shirt soaked in blood. Donnie was standing over it, his sleeves rolled up as if he had been doing housework.

"Don't just stand there," he said. "We need to move him. Find some bin bags or something."

I couldn't move or speak. Then, as if I was on automatic pilot, some practical instinct kicked in. I went back into the dance room and began to pull at the red velvet curtains behind the stage. The first one came down and I took it back into the office.

Donnie rolled it out on the floor, grunting and breathing heavily. "Help me, will you?" he said.

I took the dead man's arm. It was still warm and I could smell him as well as the sickly odour of blood and death. His black trousers were even blacker, with blood and piss. I tried to roll him over, and as I did my hand slipped into the gash that cut through his shirt, under his ribs and across his belly. He was almost cut in half. I felt bone, then the raw flesh, hot and juicy with bright blood. I quickly pulled my hand away, covered in it. Pushing out from the hole in his side, I could see twisted muscle and gut, purple and swollen. I threw up.

"Behave," Donnie said. He lay a bloodstained samurai sword on top of the body and threw the rest of the velvet across him. I saw the dead man's open eyes stare glassily at me as Donnie tucked the fabric around the head. Saw the rough, red knife cuts to the dark skin of his forehead, pink flesh showing through. It looked like the letter K. "Get the other one," Donnie ordered.

In a trance, I went through and pulled down the other velvet curtain. Ten minutes later we had something that looked like a roll of red carpet. Donnie picked up some keys from the desk and went outside. I stood, trembling, staring at the roll of dead body as Donnie reversed the Mazda up to the back door. I took the foot end and Donnie heaved the body into the back of the car, pulling the parcel shelf down and slamming the tailgate. I watched, as if in a dream, washing my hands in a muddy pool as he emptied a jerrycan of petrol into the bloodstained office.

He threw me the keys to the Mazda. "You're driving," he said. "Follow me. Don't stop. Don't look at anyone. Keep to a steady forty." I must have looked blank. "You can drive, can't you?"

I nodded. It wasn't the time to tell him that I hadn't had much practice. Donnie shook his head and hissed a few effs.

"Go on then."

I did as I was told and started the engine while Donnie put on his jacket, cool as you like, and lit a petrol-soaked rag. The flame glared orange as he threw it in through the door. Then he walked to the Merc and started it up, and we drove out on to Lewisham High Street back through Catford. I followed his tail lights, my hands shaking on the wheel, until we hit the roundabout on to the dual carriageway.

I put the radio on for distraction. A late-night station was playing middle-of-the-road rock for lorry drivers. A smoky-voiced, crap DJ announced, "It's three a.m. One for all you drivers out there… Mr Chris Rea."

"She said, 'Son, this is the road to hell…'"

I hate Chris Rea. He always sounds like he's singing on the toilet, groaning with the effort of curling out a tom-tit. My brother used to have his album. I switched the radio off.

I stuck strictly to the forty limit, following the Mercedes at about three cars' distance. The road was pretty empty until just past Eltham, when a police patrol car pulled out from a side road and sat on my tail. I stared straight ahead, trying to keep my nerve. I wondered for a second what would happen if I flagged them down and turned myself in. I imagined the scenario: Donnie would shoot off like a rat up a drainpipe and I'd be left on the hard shoulder with a samurai sword and a carved-up body. And traces of its blood on my hands.

I realized why I was doing the driving. If there was going to be a fall guy, it would be me.

The police car pulled alongside me. The Mazda's stupid personalized plate had probably given them enough cause for suspicion. There were two coppers. I checked them out of the corner of my eye. The nearest one was looking across at me: an eighteen-year-old, driving an expensive four-wheel drive at three in the morning.

On the other hand, I was sober and driving like I was doing the test.

He was probably weighing up what they might pull me in for. I began to sweat heavily. Could hardly feel my foot on the pedal. The blue light went on and I got ready to pull over, but suddenly the squad car sped away, shooting up to about eighty, passing Donnie in the Merc and disappearing within seconds.

Another call, something more pressing. A fight in a kebab shop or a drunken girl in a gutter.

If only they'd known.

Twenty minutes later Donnie signalled off the main road and turned off for Dartford. I followed as he headed down towards the industrial area near the bridge. I didn't recognize much in the dark, but I guessed we were somewhere near the "paint factory".

We drove along a new road, lit with orange streetlights. Warehouses and industrial units dotted the fields on either side. At a roundabout, Donnie took the smallest exit, which looked like a dead end. We drove past a boarded-up caravan that advertised tea and snacks, then turned down a smaller lane, potholed and rough. My headlights picked out a run-down farm building, with bales of straw and rusty machinery. Whatever was being farmed down here on the marshes must have been thin pickings. The land looked hard and sparse.

We drove on for another mile across the black marshes, electric pylons straddling the fields and the road. In the distance I could see the river, defined by the lights of a slow boat inching its way towards London. Donnie stopped, got out and, in the headlights, opened a steel gate on to another track. He climbed back in and we continued winding down the path towards the river.

When we reached the sea wall, Donnie stopped again and signalled me to stop. He opened my driver's door and moved me over to the passenger seat while he switched off the headlights. He put the Mazda back into gear and drove it up the steep grass bank that ran up to the sea wall. At the top he opened the tailgate and wrestled the body out, telling me to grab the feet. A pair of flashy Nikes were sticking out of the end of the roll. Almost as a mark of respect, I wrapped the velvet curtain back around them and picked up my end.

The rain had stopped, but a chill wind blew across the river. I could hear the tide lapping some distance away and I felt the sweat on my forehead evaporating in the night air. We heaved the body down, across the gravel and washed-up plastic bottles at the river's edge, and swung it out into the mud, where it landed with a wet slap.

"Tide'll take it downriver," Donnie said.

"It'll be found." I had imagined that Donnie was going to bury the body or "disappear" it in a vat of wet cement somewhere.

"Yeah," Donnie said. "It'll be a warning."

I looked at the roll of red-velvet curtain, darkened in the mud. I could still see a trainer sticking out and an arm had come loose and lay, thrown back from the body, fingers curled in the air.

All I could see was my brother, Steve.

FIFTY-SIX

I tried to sleep, but I couldn't. My hands were still shaking; the sights and sounds were burnt into my mind.

I felt vulnerable and paranoid, as if someone was going to knock on the door at any moment and take me away. The police, or one of the Kelly lot. The bogeyman. I didn't know.

I *didn't* know. Except I knew the bogeyman was real.

A warning, Donnie had said. A warning to whom? To others muscling in on Kelly business? I wondered why Tommy had insisted that I helped Donnie. Was he trying to warn *me*? Or was he trying to get me involved to a point where there could definitely be no turning back? Implicating me in a murder? I kept looking out at the street from behind the curtains, chewing my nails down till they bled. I decided that I'd feel better at the safe house, so I let myself out and ducked through the back streets down towards the river.

I didn't feel much better once I was inside. I sat and stared out of the window, across the river to where people were going about their normal lives, in proper jobs in conventional offices. I wished I was one of them, making an honest crust, having a nice ordinary life where I could sleep at night. If I could get out of this, I might be poor with no girlfriend, but at least I'd be back in normal society, *honest* and poor with no girlfriend. Doing normal stuff blokes of my age do.

But now I was beyond the point of no return.

I thought of calling Tony, or even Baylis, but in my state of shock I didn't know how I could begin to explain what I'd got myself into. I felt that I had been stained by the night's events to a level where I was beyond their help or understanding.

I went and found my notebook, hoping that if I wrote some of it down it would calm my nerves. Would help explain how I'd been involved in the disposing of another body at Long Reach.

When the sun came up, I finally got off. I slept all day and most of the following night, my body and mind drained by the trauma. When I woke at four in the morning, the horror hit me again and I started getting antsy. I had left my laptop at the other flat in my hurry to get back here. Not safe. I didn't want to go out, but I needed my computer, so when it got light, I slipped on some trackies, pulled a beanie over my head and jogged up the road to Deptford High Street.

The market was just waking up and life carried on pretty much as usual, but I felt like someone was going to jump me at any moment. I unlocked the flat and pushed back the door. It caught on a large, brown envelope, which was unusual. I never got post. I picked it up and shoved it into my bag with my laptop and jogged straight back to the apartment.

I felt a little better for the exercise and made myself some tea and opened up the envelope. It gave me a bit of a shock: inside was a postcard from Croatia, just like the one I was meant to pick up. I turned it over. On the back was written: *Check your compass. Wish you were still here?* My mind spooled through the possibilities. Anna, it had to be.

I took the other, folded sheets from the envelope. They looked official. I unfolded them and began to read:

POST–MORTEM REPORT, GREENWICH MORTUARY

Name: Palmer, Stephen Christopher
Age: 30 years

I sat down on the sofa.

External examination: Well-nourished, evidence of proper care and attention, height 5 feet 11 inches.

I scanned the columns, which detailed every inch of my own flesh and blood.

Internal Examination:

Skull: Compression fracture to frontal

lobe, commensurate with fall or impact from blunt instrument. Fracture to occipital bone, fracture of cervical vertebrae C1, C2, C3.

Brain: Contusion to medulla oblongata, intraparenchymal bleed to cerebellum.

From what I could understand, it sounded as if Steve had broken his neck, which had caused a brain haemorrhage. I looked further down the list.

Stomach: Evidence of curry meal, partially digested.

That made sense.

Pericardium, heart, blood vessels: Small food residue, odour of alcohol. High alcohol level in blood. Evidence of cocaine, cannabis, MDMA.

I was shocked. Steve had been chock full of drugs when he'd died.

Cause of death: Injuries to brain and central nervous system commensurate with fall or impact from blunt instrument, exacerbated by high level of toxins.

So he hadn't drowned. He'd been pissed and off his head, and had then hit himself – or been hit – round the head. Hard enough to bust his skull.

Then I found the detail that answered all my remaining questions:

```
Other remarks: Incised wounds to der-
mis of forehead, possibly knife wounds
in the form "I<" or letter "K".
```

I now knew exactly how he'd died and who had killed him.

FIFTY-SEVEN

Anna's desk was empty. I charged straight into Tony Morris's office. I hadn't seen him for a couple of months and he was surprised to see me.

"Hello, stranger," he said.

"Why didn't you tell me?"

He knew what I was talking about. "You're a big boy now, Eddie. Look how far you've come this year. You don't need spoon-feeding any more."

"You never told me," I spat.

"You never asked," he said. He had been expecting this day. He scratched his head and sat down heavily. He looked tired.

"You told me he jumped," I said. "I know – *you* know – that he was killed."

"That was the official line," he said. "We didn't want it to get about that we knew it was a killing. It would have made it worse for you and your mum. And it would have made *them* feel like they'd made their point. They left him there so we'd find him."

"He was using as well, wasn't he?" I remembered Steve coming back to Mum's and sleeping all day, mumbling excuses about a nightshift working as security in this or that nightclub. Remembered the smell of fags and booze that he gave off when he came home, and the remains of the takeaway curry he would hand over to me to finish. Some people remember their mum's Sunday roast or the smell of the log fire their dad used to make. Takeaway curries always reminded me of Steve and I loved him for it.

Tony brought me back to reality. "Drugs were part of the problem. Steve was never a stranger to narcotics," he admitted. "That's why he was so useful. But that's also why he was high-risk. He knew how to make them, who was selling them, who was buying. We couldn't *pay* for that kind of information. But he was under a lot of pressure and I think he cracked."

I felt I was about to crack myself. "And you thought now was the time to send me his death certificate, so I'd begin to join the dots?"

Tony looked blank. "I never sent you a death certificate," he said flatly. "But I'd like to know who did. I'll look into it."

I remembered the postcard from Croatia and realized who it was that was trying to open my eyes. Who it was that was trying to keep me on track.

"I thought you'd sussed it by now, mate," Tony said. "I thought you'd joined the dots already."

I hadn't. Probably because I didn't want to.

"So how come he got mixed up with Special K in the first place?" I asked.

"Our Irish connection put him in touch with Kelly through The Harp," Tony explained. "Tommy Kelly owns The Harp Club. He launders money through it and some of it gets back to the old country. The Real IRA and all those murderers he thinks he's related to. It's not about Catholics and Protestants any more, they're just part of the bigger, organized crime game. Like I said, it's all connected."

"What was he doing for them then?"

"Steve set up their first little E factory down in Dartford," Tony said.

"And you let him?"

"We wanted to control it, wanted to be able to trace it. It was Steve's idea to brand it with a shamrock." Tony rubbed his face. "And we wanted Tommy Kelly to get caught up to his elbows in it."

"So what happened?" I asked.

"Truth? Kelly outsmarted us at every move. He left the running of it to Steve and the Irish guys. The distribution was through health clubs and courier companies and sub-companies, a really well-run op. We couldn't keep up with it, and Kelly was five steps removed. But Steve got a bit unreliable. He started making mistakes and we couldn't help him. He slipped up and they rumbled him."

"Who?" I demanded. "*Who* rumbled him? I'll kill them." I thought I knew who. And it would take an atomic bomb to do it.

Tony shook his head. "It doesn't matter who," he said. "It's not personal. As soon as Tommy Kelly found out he had a cuckoo in the nest, Steve's number was up."

Tony was spelling it out for me, the part I wanted to deny. That my other mentor for the past year, the man who'd shown me the high life and had also trusted me with his daughter, his most precious possession, had killed my brother.

And there was a second home truth: that my brother, my boyhood hero, had feet of clay. He'd failed. I felt the emotion rise in my chest.

"There's another one," I blurted out. "Another body. I was there. I *helped*." I suddenly felt a huge relief letting it out. Able to tell someone what I had seen.

"Hyrone Brown," Tony said. "Club owner. We know about him. That may be why you were sent the report."

Tears sprung to my eyes involuntarily and my body heaved with sobs. Tony stood up and rubbed my back awkwardly. He took a bottle of whisky from his shelf and poured a slug into one of his disgusting mugs. I drank it gratefully and began to spill out the events of two nights before. Tony stood behind me and massaged my shoulders.

"I know, son," he said. "I know."

He picked up the phone and took it over to the window. I couldn't hear what he was saying. He was good at that. He came back off the phone.

"Do you want to sort things out?" he said.

Twenty minutes later we had done one of Tony's usual weaves through the back streets of Soho. We crossed the grey snail trail of Oxford Street, dodging through tourists and people holding placards for golf sales. By the time we had ducked behind a bus, danced around a few taxis and passed through the back of a clothes shop, I had pulled myself together.

Eventually we came out into Charlotte Street. Ian Baylis was already sitting at a table in the Greek restaurant.

"Good to have you back on board," he said as I sat down. "If you *are* on board?" He looked at me and raised his eyebrows questioningly.

I nodded. The last few days had frightened me.

Tony patted me on the back. "We thought we'd lost you," he said.

They scoffed hummus, lamb stew and stuffed vine leaves while I picked at olives, pitta bread and taramasalata. They talked about cars and Baylis's favourite wine. Nothing official – we were out in public – but one thing nagged away at me.

"Where's Anna?" I asked. "Sorry, Ysobel."

Tony and Baylis exchanged glances.

"No word as yet," Baylis said. Subject closed. I didn't mention that I thought I'd had contact.

Just as coffee arrived, I got a text. From Sophie:

R U in town? x

I texted back:

Yes. Where U? x

She came back:

Can you meet @ Tate Modern 3rd floor 4.30?

I showed the messages to Tony and Baylis.

"Go," Tony said.

I replied straight away:

I'll be there xx

I shook both their hands as I got up to leave. Ian Baylis actually smiled at me.

"Be lucky," Tony said.

I took the Tube to London Bridge and walked along the river to the Tate. The wind was cold and people had scarves wrapped around their faces so I could only see their eyes.

I went into the Turbine Hall at the entrance to the gallery. A black, steel sculpture that looked like a giant spider loomed over me, ready to bite. I crossed the hall and took the escalator to the third floor. Sophie was sitting on one of the sofas at the top. She was with her mum.

And her old man.

Sophie and Cheryl both kissed me. Pleased to see me, but looking drawn and edgy. Tommy shook hands and gave me a hug, relaxed as usual. He was wearing a soft, black overcoat with a grey scarf. He could have been an Irish priest with good taste.

"Why don't you girls get a cup of coffee," he said. "I just want to show Eddie some pictures."

Sophie squeezed my arm. "I'll get you a latte," she said. "See you in a minute."

They went up to the coffee bar and Tommy guided me through the galleries. Old paintings hung next to some of the modern ones. For comparison, I suppose. There was a German nineteenth-century snow scene hanging next to a Peter Doig of some tiny skaters on a massive, icy lake. In the snow scene was a cluster of tall pine trees and, in the middle, a man, dressed in black with his back turned, staring into the snow. It could have been Tommy Kelly.

"*Caspar David Friedrich*," Tommy read off the label. "Ahead of his time."

We went through to the next gallery. I recognized the paintings instantly. Massive, burgundy-and-black abstracts like the one Tommy had in his study. The room was empty except for us.

"Rothko," I said.

"The guv'nor," Tommy confirmed. "I always come to this room when I want to think."

We circled the room in opposite directions, saying nothing. As I tried to concentrate on the pictures, the colours began to push and pull against each other and create a kind of buzz. A feeling. Deep misery seemed to pulse from them.

"You know, I look at these again and again," Tommy went on. He came up and stood beside me. "But the more I look, the less I think I understand. I look and look again, and it's still a mystery to me."

I nodded. "They're sad" was all I could find to say.

"Rothko must have thought so," Tommy agreed. "He topped himself after doing these."

It made sense.

"What's this?" Tommy asked suddenly. Still looking at the paintings, he pulled his hand from his coat pocket and held something out in his open palm.

One of my magnetic bugging devices. I stared at it blankly.

"I don't know," I said.

"The cleaner found it under my desk."

"Looks like a microphone," I chanced. He glanced at it and nodded.

"Someone," he said. "Someone is trying to listen to me. I want you to take this away and think very hard about who, in my firm, that might be. Any suspicion, anything you might have picked up. Sometimes it takes a bit of an outside eye to notice these things. Look into it. I need a result, fast."

He folded the bug into my hand. Looked at me straight. "Let's go and get a cup of coffee."

I followed him out of the gallery, my palm sweating around the bug. He was right, I would have to work fast.

FIFTY-EIGHT

In my recent experience, there was one person, apart from me, guaranteed to bugger things up.

Jason Kelly.

It didn't take long for him to raise his ugly head again.

Sophie was round at mine, the Friday night after Tommy had found the bug. It was the weekend, but I was more jumpy and paranoid than usual. There was a short list of names of who might have planted the device. I needed something to happen before the only one left on the list was mine.

"What is it, Eddie?" Sophie asked.

"Nothing. Bit stressed." I knew things were tense for her at home too. The discovery of the bug had really cranked up Tommy's need to clean up his firm. Dave and the rest had been working overtime "persuading" Hyrone Brown's contacts that they were better off not being affiliated with Special K. Mr Brown himself was an example.

Sophie stroked my hair. "You've changed, babe."

She was right. I'd already changed a lot over the last

six months, but my whole attitude had shifted again in the past week. I looked at her. She was still every bit as beautiful, but when she stared back at me, I saw Tommy Kelly's eyes staring back at me and I had to look away. It was not conducive to romance, and I realized there would be very few more dates like this. It was coming to an end.

We were supposed to be going to a club in Bromley with some of Sophie's college friends, but it was getting late and neither of us really fancied it. We weren't in the mood. We hummed and hawed until about eleven-thirty and thought we might just go for an hour. I was getting a clean shirt when Sophie's phone rang.

"Naz…" she silently mouthed to me. Then her expression changed. "Oh my God," she said. "Oh. My. God." She sat down on the sofa. I could hear the voice of her friend almost screaming at the other end of the phone. Sophie's face was white and she chewed her lip.

"When?" she asked. "How? Where?"

Finally Naz rang off.

"What is it?" I asked, desperate to know.

"Do you remember Benjy French, from college?" Her face was pale. "He's been stabbed."

"Shit," I said. "Is he OK?"

"They don't know. The ambulance is still there." Sophie took out a tissue and wiped the tears that had sprung to her eyes. "Naz was calling from there. Apparently they were all in the car together going to the thing in Bromley. It was some kind of road-rage thing. Benjy got out of the car and was stabbed in the chest."

I could just imagine Benjy French with a couple of

pints of cider under his belt, having a go in a road-rage incident.

She clutched the tissue in her fist, chewing the knuckle of her thumb. Then she looked up at me.

"What?" I said. She was holding something back. I had a bad feeling.

"Naz said it was Jason who did it." She burst into tears. "Jason stabbed him." She stared blankly at the wall for a minute, then grabbed her things together. "I've got to go home." I didn't try to stop her. If what she said was true, all sorts of shit would be flying about and I didn't want to get caught in it. I would need to get in touch with Baylis.

Then her phone rang. A different voice gabbled at the other end.

"I'm at Eddie's," she said. She was sniffing and her voice was cracking in near hysteria. "Don't muck about, Jason. You can't."

Jason's voice was ranting wildly, shouting on the other end.

"Calm down, Jason." Sophie put her hand over the phone. "Can he come here?" she asked. I debated for a second or two, then nodded.

"OK," she told him. She cut the call. "He'll be here in five minutes. I don't know what to do, Eddie." She was crying again.

"We'll think of something," I said. "Put the kettle on."

This would be a new one, I thought. Jason paying me a visit. While Sophie was in the kitchen, I went over to the desk and lifted up the lid of my laptop. I switched on the webcam and set it to record, then clicked on the screen-saver. A picture of Sophie came up.

Then the buzzer sounded.

Sophie opened the door. Jason looked behind him before lumbering in. He was sweaty, damp from the rain and wired. His eyes were out on stalks and his mouth was dry as he talked.

"Listen," he said, pacing the room. "I'm sorry. I know we're not the best of mates, but there's been a right fuck-up. I didn't know where to go."

"I'll take you home," Sophie told him. "Dad will know what to do."

"We can't tell the old man. He'll kill me."

And save someone else the bother, I thought. "Listen, Soph," I said, "You can't stay here. It's too much of a risk. You get back home while I sort something out. I'll try and get hold of Dave."

Sophie looked relieved to be let off the hook. She hugged me and got her things together for the second time. "Call me," she said, and went out into the night.

I closed the door behind her and turned back to Jason, who was searching his pockets frantically. He finally found the wrap he was looking for.

"It's OK, Jason," I said. "Calm down and talk to me. We'll figure something out."

"You got a beer?" he asked. "Feel like my throat's been cut."

I went to the fridge and got him a cold one, and one for myself. He stayed put and began chopping himself a line of cocaine with a credit card, which he snorted through a ready-rolled note. I guessed it wasn't his first of the night. I came back in with the beers. He had cut out two lines and gestured to the remaining one. I shook my head, so he did that as well, then glugged back the beer and lit a fag. He shook his head, swearing under his breath.

"So what's up?" I asked.

"I've cocked up, is what's up," he said. "It's a fuckin' mess."

"Tell me," I said. He sat down on the sofa, facing the desk.

"You can't tell the old man, OK?" He looked up, almost pleading.

"I'll call Dave," I said.

"No. Not Dave. He'll dob me straight in when he knows what's happened."

"What *has* happened?"

"I'm down near Lee Green, right? And this piece of shit pulls out in front of me, a poxy Honda or something doing twenty. So I flash it and follow it down the High Road."

I could imagine Jason, coked up, sitting on the car's tail, flashing and hooting and shouting through the windscreen.

"So they speed up and I follow them up to the lights, but I don't see the lights change and go into the back of them. Smash the headlights on the Audi. I'm pretty cranked up."

"So then what?" I asked.

"I'm trying to reverse out of it to throw a U-ey, but then this kid gets out of the passenger seat holding a kebab and chucks it at my windscreen. Which pisses me off. So I get out to wipe it off, ready for a row, and he comes up and tells me he wants my insurance details and all that. He's pretty cocky, like he's had a beer or two. So I say OK, I'll go and get it out of the car. Then I go back and get out the knife that I keep under the seat for emergencies, and I stick it up my sleeve."

"Did he see it?"

"No. I go back and tell him I haven't got the stuff, but if he gives me his mobile and that, I'll call him with the details. Then he gets stroppy and tells me he knows who I am and that no doubt the police will be interested in sorting it out. So I go to scare him off and he grabs my arm."

I tried hard to imagine Benjy French getting into a stand-off with the drugged-up, psycho-butthole sitting on my sofa. I did my best to adopt a sympathetic tone.

"Shit, Jase. What happened then?"

"The Honda's full of girls and they're screaming at him to get back in the car. I try to leave, but he's got hold of my sleeve and won't let go. So I go to push him off and the knife goes in."

"Where?" I asked.

"In his chest."

A knife doesn't just slip into someone's chest, I thought.

"I mean, it's self-defence, isn't it? I just didn't know where to go." He reached into his pocket for cigarettes. The pack was empty. "You got any fags?" he asked. I didn't.

"Listen," I said. "You're fine here for a bit, while we

work out what's best to do. You can sleep on my couch tonight. I'll just nip out to the late shop for a few more beers, and I can get you some fags too if you like?"

Jason's jaw was clenched from all the cocaine and whatever else he had taken. He wasn't going to sleep any time soon.

"Good man. Good idea. Get a bottle of vodka, will you?" He pulled some crumpled notes from his pocket, which I refused. "Don't be long."

"I won't." I watched him sitting there, his knees bouncing as his feet trembled on the floor. His eyes were staring at me, wide open.

"I underestimated you, Eddie," he said. "Mate."

FIFTY-NINE

I stepped out into the rain and speed-dialled Ian Baylis's number. At last I had something that might please him.

"Nimrod? Elgar," I said, doing my best with the protocols.

"What?" Baylis snapped.

"I have JK in my flat. He's stabbed someone. I think I have plenty of evidence. He's drugged up and very jumpy."

"Keep him there. Lock him in if necessary. Even lock yourself in another room, if you have to. There will be a text on this phone when we're ready to come in. Keep your head down. It might get nasty. Go." He hung up, wasting no time.

I ducked into the late shop and paid for forty Marlboros, vodka and beer with shaking fingers. I couldn't return empty-handed.

I ran up the back stairs two at a time, trying not to make a noise with the chinking bottles. I got out my key and put it in the lock. The door was already open.

I walked in.

"Jason?" I called. Nothing. I went through into the sitting room. No one: just the smell of cigarette smoke. I checked the bedroom. Then I took out my phone and texted Ian Baylis:

He's gone. Sorry.

I felt ashamed. Stupid mistake, leaving him alone.

An hour later I was sitting in the flat while Baylis and Tony Morris drank what was left of the beer. There were four armed officers, dressed in black bulletproofs and prickling with automatic weapons. They searched the flat and outside, up on the roof and along all the backs, but found nothing.

A forensics guy asked me what stuff was mine. He emptied the ashtray of all Jason's stubs. He looked at the glass top of the desk and found smear marks and granules and the last of a wrap of cocaine. "Yours?"

I shook my head. The forensics man picked up the remaining dust on a strip of sellotape and put it in a plastic bag with the wrap.

We wound through what had been caught on the webcam. It was pretty good. The sound was a bit muffled and Jason was talking nineteen to the dozen, but it was all there. What it hadn't picked up would have been recorded by whatever else the flat was wired up with.

"Top stuff," said Tony. He didn't seem all that bothered that Jason had gone. He was confident they could find him. "He'll lead us somewhere else. If we put him inside tonight, the trail goes a bit dead. It's a case of watch and wait."

Baylis was on the phone to the Met, trying to track down CCTV footage from the traffic lights on the Lee Green High Road. Footage that could show just how accidental Benjy French's stabbing actually was. Tony swigged the last of his beer. There was something else nagging away at me.

"Tony?" I spoke quietly while Baylis was talking on the blower. Seeing Tony here in Deptford had jogged my memory.

"Yes, son?"

"My old man's turned up a couple of times," I said. "Sophie saw him."

Tony frowned. "Who did you say he was?"

"Just a drunken nutter,"

"That's about right," Tony said with a grim chuckle.

I felt relieved that he didn't think it was a major security gaffe. He looked at me squarely. "That waster's no threat. He's not connected. He's no father to you."

"Ain't that the truth," I said.

Tony told me to get myself to my safe house. We needed everyone out in case anyone tried to come back tonight, looking for me. It had to appear as if Jason had made a clean escape.

We were about to leave when the forensics guy pulled out something from under my sofa. It was a hunting knife. The first three or four inches of its vicious, curved blade were covered in blood.

"Looks like he left you a present."

Once they were on the motorway, Donnie sped away and relaxed a little. He hadn't liked the smell of it. One of those jobs that felt wrong.

Deptford was always waist-deep in the filth at that time on a Friday night. The whole area from Lewisham to Peckham was crawling with them, especially when one or two "incidents" had gone off and they were looking for clues. Like eager little Boy Scouts in their bulletproof vests and Noddy cars.

What had really bothered him were the blue lights that were already on their way up Deptford Church Street as he was pulling away from the kid's flat.

He cruised up to eighty past Gravesend. His fare was lying on the back seat wrapped in a blanket, shivering despite the gusts of hot air pumping out of the car's climate control.

Donnie hadn't hung around to find out where the blue lights were headed. But if it was the same address as his pick-up, then how would they have known? It niggled him. In an hour he would be able to relax. Sit out in the cool night air with a bottle of Scotch and a packet of fags and have a good old think about that…

It was getting light by the time I got into the safe house. It smelt clean and new. Fresh after the cigarette smoke and takeaway smell of my dive on Deptford High Street. I never wanted to go back there. I had a hot shower and lay down on the bed, taking deep breaths. My head was pounding. Of course, I couldn't sleep; it was becoming a habit.

I stared at the ceiling and thought about Benjy French.

He was the only one who had bothered to be nice to me when I'd started at the college. He was a bit of an oddball, sure, but clever and funny. Probably ready to go on to university by now and live the rest of his life. I thought about the hunting knife, covered in his blood. Thought about his nice, middle-class parents up in Blackheath, being woken with the news that their son had been stabbed.

I realized that, in the drama of the night's activities, no one had spared much thought for Benjy French.

I looked at my watch. Six-thirty. I got up again, picked up my phone, dialled 118 and asked for Lewisham Hospital, A&E.

"I'm enquiring about Benjamin French," I said. "He came in last night after an accident?"

A voice told me to hold for a moment and then I heard others, mumbling and whispering at the other end. The hush of a hospital ward early on a Saturday morning.

"Are you family?" the first voice asked.

"I'm a friend from college."

More whispers, then another voice came on the line.

"I'm afraid Mr French passed away at four this morning."

My stomach lurched. Poor Benjy French had been breathing his last while I had been drinking beer with Tony Morris a few hours before.

Watching his murderer on my webcam.

"Do you need counselling?" the voice asked.

"Yes, I do," I said, and put down the phone.

*   *   *

I left the flat and walked along the river, trying to get my head together. I felt dizzy with lack of sleep, but my brain was racing. I turned up towards the high street. I could go to one of the caffs on the market and get a tea and a bacon sandwich. Not that I felt much like it, but I needed to eat. I stopped to get a paper. Maybe I could take my mind off things by reading what was going on in the rest of the world. Famine, drought, flooding, war, global warming – cheery stuff like that. I came out of the newsagent's and turned up towards the high street flat.

Dave Slaughter's Beemer was outside. He opened the door and got out. I could see Johnny Reggae in the passenger seat.

"Where the—?" Dave let out a string of effs and called me a couple of C words as he interrogated me about my whereabouts. He wasn't happy. "We've been looking for you for hours, you—" More effs and a C.

"Jogging," I said, though my clothes didn't back up my words. I looked at Johnny Reggae. My experience of him to date had all been big grins and homeboy handshakes. Now he looked about as serious as a dose of clap.

"Get in," Dave said.

There was nowhere to run, nowhere to hide. I got in.

SIXTY

Donnie quietly closed the door of the caravan behind him and stepped out into the mist that came up off the sea. It was a nicer day in some ways. At least the rain had stopped. In other ways it was worse. He had a thumping whisky headache for a start.

He took a sip of tea from a plastic mug and lit a fag. Jason was sleeping it off inside at last, and Donnie could allow himself a few hours' P & Q before it all kicked off again. He could quite happily waste some time like this, he thought.

The caravan was a static job, on the edge of a holiday camp in the Isle of Thanet, down from the fashionable town of Whitstable but not as far as the chav-magnet of Margate. That hole drew all the illegals and druggies and kept the filth busy. No one ever came here, especially off-season. It had been a useful bolt-hole for the firm for some years – Donnie himself had cooled his boots here on a couple of occasions. He sat on a bench and looked out across the estuary. A couple of slow tankers and cargo ships floated up towards the oil refineries and wharves on the Isle of Grain.

He could kill Jason.

It was just an expression, but at the moment, disposing of the little shitbag didn't seem like a bad idea. Saul would be pleased, for one. As a purely mental exercise, Donnie went through the various ways he could make it happen. Sinking him in one of the many inland canals near here would do. Otherwise, Donnie knew plenty of building contractors who were pouring tons of liquid cement into motorway supports on a regular basis. The idea of Jason's body propping up a new motorway bridge appealed, and Donnie smiled to himself.

Then there was the other one. Jason shouldn't have run to him. Nothing had gone right since he'd appeared. What was it with all these small boys throwing their weight about? In his day, the business had been done by hard men of few words. Men who nailed other men's hands to tables. Men who rarely saw daylight outside private drinking clubs – unless they had stockings over their faces.

The idea of both little shits holding up a motorway bridge appealed even more. One at each end. Donnie warmed himself with the thought as he waited for the call.

The great and the not-so-good had been called to Kelly Towers.

I felt almost relieved when I saw four or five cars already parked on the gravel. Unless it was a kangaroo court for me, of course.

Cheryl was bustling about in the kitchen with the cleaner, making pots of coffee. She hugged me and gave me one of those down-in-the-mouth smiles, like I'd just turned up after the cat had been run over. That was the great thing about Cheryl: whatever was going on around her, she always acted like a prosperous builder's wife whose old man was doing no more than fixing a few loose roof tiles. She said she was off to Bluewater to meet Sophie. Shopping. I wished I was going too.

I went through to the dining room, where they were all gathered. The room had fancy curtains tied up with silk ropes and a massive dining table covered in a white cloth; it was not often used by the family. The occasion could have been a family funeral or a golf-club AGM, except that half the men there were built like cage fighters.

I knew a few of them: Johnny Reggae, Stav and Engin Kurtoglu, the Turkish guy who ran the casino in Bromley. He introduced me to a quiet, intense Irish bloke with cropped black hair and stubble.

"Paul Dolan," he said. The man crushed my hand, looking into my face with angry eyes. The name rang a bell, but I didn't know why. No Donnie, though.

They stood awkwardly, sipping coffee with three sugars from dainty cups. A couple of them were smoking on the terrace outside the French windows. Every time I moved, I felt like one of them was looking at me. Tommy came through from his room and sat down at the head of the table. He looked freshly scrubbed and suited in pinstripes, like a captain of industry. The cigarettes were swiftly put out under size twelves and everyone sat down.

"We have a situation," Tommy announced. Almost all of them looked down at the tablecloth in front of them. Tommy waited until a few of them raised their eyes to meet his. "As some of you will know, Jason's been involved in an incident. We need to get him clear, otherwise there'll be all sorts of bad press flying about."

It sounded like one of those situations where someone in the government has been caught with his pants down and doesn't want it all over the papers. I guessed that in those circumstances all the yes-men came up with ideas about how to bury the bad news. Here, nobody said anything. You could almost smell the lack of support for Jason Kelly.

"No one got anything to say?" Tommy looked from one to another. There were coughs and shifty glances. Some of them suddenly found the pattern on the ceiling very interesting. "Saul?" he said. "What about you?"

Saul Wynter rolled a pen between his fingers, trying to keep his hands occupied. Tommy's stare forced him to speak.

"Jason's … predicament is not connected," he said finally.

"Not connected? Come again?" Tommy said.

"I mean," Saul continued cautiously, "this business with Jason doesn't link up with any of our work. It's separate."

There was a rustle of pressed suits, shifting in their chairs as if in agreement. Tommy's fierce look silenced it.

"So what are you saying?"

Saul took a deep breath. He had unwillingly become the spokesman for everyone else.

"I mean that if Jason takes the rap, he maybe gets five for manslaughter. You know we can get around the witness statements, evidence and that, with our contacts. He does three and gets out before he's twenty-four. Then we carry on. Business as usual."

"So I let my son do time?"

"If we get him out of the country now, and get our collars felt in the process, then we're accessories," Saul said. He licked parched lips. "If Jason turns himself in, then it's not connected with firm."

"*Not connected?* How d'you work that out? This is my son we're talking about." Tommy slapped his hand on the table.

"If the firm becomes involved over something like this," Saul continued, "we put the whole organization at risk."

"Sorry, I forgot I was running a risk-free charity for old lags," Tommy said sharply. "We're always at risk. Now let's talk about *how* we do it, not *if*."

Paul Dolan spoke up. He seemed eager to please. "If we can get him down to Portsmouth, I can pick up the boat and go via the Isle of Wight or the Channel Islands, then sit it out in Ireland or northern Spain until we find a solution. I have contacts in both places."

"Thanks, Paul," Tommy said. "Now we're getting somewhere."

"They'll be watching all the ports," Saul pointed out. "They've been sniffing around the boat already." He seemed to be accepting his role as doom-monger.

"How is it you know what everyone will be doing and thinking?" Tommy looked at Saul. "And what's this?" He took something from his pocket and rolled it on the table in front of Saul Wynter.

It was another bug. My stomach shifted through several gears before I forced it back to neutral. Saul looked at it and his eyes widened.

"A listening device. Found in my office," Tommy said. "We've got them all over the shop, like woodworm. Someone put them there. Who?" He cast his eyes around the table. Saul shook his head in disbelief. No one looked at anyone else. I kept my eyes to the table. The list of who might have planted the bug was shortening fast.

And I was heading to the top.

"I suggest we take a fag break, then come back with some more positive suggestions." He picked up the bug. Saul looked like he'd been caught out.

Tommy stood up and left the room.

SIXTY-ONE

Half the people at the table stepped outside and lit up.

Saul Wynter stayed sitting at the table, looking like he'd just been slapped. Paul Dolan stared at him. No one wanted to say anything. No one wanted to take a position for fear of getting involved.

Tommy called Dave through to his study. Dave returned five minutes later and told Paul Dolan to go through. Dolan came back soon after and said that Tommy wanted to see me. My stomach lurched, but I think I felt marginally better than Saul Wynter. He looked increasingly uncomfortable at not being summoned to the inner sanctum.

Tommy was smoking a cigar and looking at the Rothko on his wall, thinking.

"What d'you reckon, Ed?"

I didn't know what to say. "I think they're nervous," I chanced.

"Of course they're bleeding nervous," he snapped. "They're worried their pensions are under threat. But if they think I'm going to feed Jason to the lions, they've got another thing coming. They need to remember who pays their wages. Without me they're just a bunch of barrow boys and thugs. Nothing. They do as they're told. I'm not having a friggin' mutiny. I won't have it." He puffed on his cigar, opened his mouth as if he was about to say something, then closed it again. He looked around as if the walls had ears. I wasn't sure that they did any more.

"What do you think about Solly Wynter?" he asked quietly. "Do you reckon he'd turn me over?"

I hesitated for a moment. Remembered Saul taking me aside in Croatia. I hesitated too long. My look told him something.

"Thank you, Eddie," he said. "Your silence speaks volumes."

"So. Where were we?" Tommy said.

Everyone was back at the table. They had all been talking outside and there was a new mood.

A dangerous one.

As I had come out of Tommy's study, all eyes had been turned on me. I had suddenly seen myself as they saw me. A rookie kid who had the boss's ear. An upstart who had somehow slipped past Tommy's guard and was shagging his lovely daughter into the bargain. And they didn't like it.

"I have a plan," Tommy said. "But first we need to clear up this business." He put the bug back on the table in front of him, as if looking at it long enough would reveal its secret. He was playing it like a game of poker, hoping someone would eventually buckle and show his hand, unable to bear the tension any longer.

It was Johnny Reggae who buckled.

"What about him?" he said, pointing a big, black finger across the table at me. The fact that someone had spoken released the pressure. There were several mumbles of agreement around the table.

I felt my legs go weak and the blood drain from my face.

"You know, everything's gone tits up since he's been around," said Johnny. "He's here all the time, he comes and goes to our offices and clubs when he wants, acting like he's the boss of us, innit. On the boat, he was creeping about, watching you, poking around."

I glanced around the table. There wasn't much sympathy for me.

"Eddie?" Tommy said.

I could feel mob rule gathering momentum. They needed a scapegoat and I was it. They were right, I supposed. It *was* me.

I felt moments away from a lynching. I had to do something radical. I had only one weapon, so I used it. Jumping up, I launched myself at Saul Wynter, dragging him from his chair by his shirt collar, holding him up so he was half strangled.

"You want a rat?" I shouted, shaking. "Here's your rat."

Tommy continued to study me calmly as I spat out the words. I felt like I was acting out a big scene, carried along by first-night nerves. Saul struggled against my grip, gasping, his face reddening. He wasn't a big man: I was too strong and he couldn't speak. I felt like a bully.

"If I was snooping about on the boat, it was because I was finding out what *he* was up to. Then he approached me with money for information." I turned to Tommy. "Stuff about Jason, things he didn't want you to find out about."

Tommy shrugged and nodded. I dropped Saul back into his chair. It had been a long shot, but it was all I had.

"I was trying…" Saul began. He tried to loosen his collar but couldn't speak.

Paul Dolan saved him the trouble. He had been silent until now, but for some reason he backed me up.

"I didn't want to mention this," he said. He pulled a sheaf of papers from his jacket. "But Saul's offered my guys in Belfast money as well. To feed information straight to him, bypassing you, Tommy."

"Think I've lost my touch, Saul?" Tommy said sadly.

"I'm trying to stop Jason from wrecking the firm," Saul croaked. "It's taken fifteen years to make this outfit watertight. I've made us rich and I don't want to see Jason piss it up the wall. He's a loose cannon. There, I've said it." He held his hands up in surrender.

I knew there were others around the table who agreed with him. But if they did, they weren't going to say so.

"OK, Saul," Tommy said quietly. "Fair enough. I hear you. I think you and I need to discuss that in private. See if we can work something out."

Tommy got up and brushed cigar ash from his suit. He looked miserable.

"Thank you, gentlemen," he said. "You'll receive instructions later today. We'll be on the move tomorrow. Saul?"

Saul stood up, rubbing his neck, and followed Tommy through to the study without looking at me. Dave followed.

The others shuffled away from the table in silence. They started to leave, back to their cars. Johnny Reggae planted a huge hand heavily on my back.

"Sorry, man," he said. He bumped fists with my trembling hand and left the room. Paul Dolan came across to me.

"I didn't want to do that," he said. "Saul's got a point."

He left and I found myself alone in the room. I felt like a small, frightened child. My legs were trembling and I needed air.

I pushed out through the French windows into the garden, where everyone had been smoking. I breathed in deeply and watched as Tommy, Saul and Dave walked across the garden, down towards the duck pond. They were clearly still talking business. I felt guilty. I hadn't wanted to land Saul in it. He was actually quite a nice bloke – he'd done me no harm and hated Jason as much as the rest of us. I'd used him to save my bacon; to deflect attention and buy myself a bit of time.

It was a peaceful scene. They looked like three businessmen, strolling across the wet grass in their suits and smart shoes. Hopefully, I thought, they would sort something out, like old friends.

But some instinct kept me watching. I took out my

iPhone and set the video camera rolling, up on the patio.

Then they did sort it out.

Saul offered no resistance. He knelt down on the wet grass and Dave grabbed both his hands from behind, pulled his arms backwards and planted a foot in the middle of his back, pushing his head down.

Then Tommy Kelly pulled out a gun and shot him in the head.

I staggered back behind the vines that tumbled down the wall of the house, my camera still rolling. I saw the blood spurt from Saul's skull as he lurched forwards, limp in Dave's grip. Saw the terrified ducks take to the air, squawking as Saul died.

I threw up violently into a plant pot: coffee, biscuits … my disgust.

For Tommy, clearly this one had been personal. But as sure as if I'd held the gun myself, I'd killed Saul Wynter.

SIXTY-TWO

I got back to Deptford early afternoon.

I was numb with the shock and horror of everything that had happened in the last twenty-four hours. I walked around like a zombie for a while, feeling light-headed, then realized I was starving. I couldn't remember the last time I'd eaten. I went into a café but walked straight out again. Couldn't stand the noise or the laughter of the hairy-arsed workmen who seemed to be able to eat gigantic fry-ups at all times of the day. I walked around, looking at the pavement, not wanting to meet anyone's eye. I was traumatized, I suppose. I bought some fried chicken from a takeaway and ate it on a bench by the river.

I didn't taste a thing. Just fuelled myself, watching the river flowing by, cold and metallic, like the taste in my mouth. Foggy and grey, like the feeling in my head. I went back to the safe house and slept for a couple of hours.

My phone rang about half four. It was Paul Dolan. I didn't feel like talking to him.

"You all right?" he asked.

"Yeah," I said.

"Don't blame yourself. He had it coming."

He gave me my orders. I was to be at the house the following afternoon. I would be going with Tommy. Paul filled me in on the movement details, ending up at Biggin Hill airport, the little airfield that the Battle of Britain pilots had flown from. He asked me again if I was OK. Said I sounded groggy.

"I've just had a kip," I said. "I'm cream-crackered."

He made me repeat the details back to him. "Can't afford any more cock-ups," he said.

I put the phone down and lay back on the bed, exhausted. An hour later it rang again. It was Sophie. She sounded stressed. Said she needed to see me. I told her I was too tired to do anything tonight. She agreed, said she had things to do. We arranged to walk the dogs in Greenwich Park the following morning.

I dragged myself to the kitchen and made strong, black coffee. I wanted out of all this, but I would have to get to work first. I sat at the computer for an hour, then called Baylis.

"Nimrod, Elgar," I said. "RV is at 8 pip emma tomorrow off A233, Jewels Wood, near Biggin Hill. TK will meet JK with at least two associates: DS, DM and PD tbc."

I had Google-satellite-mapped the area where Tommy had said we would be meeting and worked out in advance what to say to Baylis, writing it down in ministry jargon so I wouldn't make any mistakes. I was trying hard to get it right. I had stopped thinking about the personalities involved and was now trying to think clearly, coldly and professionally about tomorrow's schedule. Like they were all chess pieces. I wanted to toe the line and then get out. Quick.

"Good work, Elgar," Baylis said. "Will you be in attendance?"

"Yes." Tommy wanted me with him.

"Plan of action?" Baylis demanded.

"JK will be moved from RV to Biggin Hill, where light aircraft tbc will transport to Bembridge airport, Isle of Wight."

"Got that, Elgar. Anything else?" I had the feeling Baylis was enjoying himself. In his element.

"Second RV: fishing boat in Bembridge Harbour, where a second boat will pick up at the Nab Tower in the Solent for onward journey to Brittany. Then by sea or overland to Santiago de Compostela, Spain."

I was saving my trump card.

"Tommy Kelly's got his hands dirty," I said.

"What?"

"He killed Saul Wynter." I corrected myself. "TK has killed SW. I have video evidence."

I heard Baylis swear on the end of the line.

"You're joking." In his shock he forgot his professional tone. "Mail it to me." I heard him muffle the phone and say something to someone before recovering his composure. "Any indication that TK is travelling?" he asked.

"No," I said. "But I doubt it. He will try to keep clear. He'll be with me."

"We'll cover all bases, Elgar," Baylis said. "I suspect we'll have to strike while the iron is hot. At Biggin Hill.

For Christ's sake, act surprised when you're arrested too, Elgar."

I hadn't thought about that. Of course I'd be bloody surprised.

"I won't need to act, Nimrod."

"Good luck, Elgar."

Sophie was on time. I met her by the café in the park and we had a latte before walking the dogs. Starsky and Hutch knew me by now; jumped up and licked me when I arrived, sure of my loyalty. Part of the family.

I sensed Sophie's mood and we didn't talk much. The weight of Jason's crime hung heavily between us, unspoken. Neither of us was going to mention it; that wound was too raw to reopen.

She said that she and her mum were going away for a week or so. Leaving this afternoon. A quick break, she said, somewhere sunny.

I didn't need to ask why they were going away at such short notice. She said she'd see me as soon as they got back. We walked across the park and the hounds ran off, bounding across the grass. I saw that Sophie was blinking back tears and I put my arm around her shoulder. She leant into me.

"Eddie," she said, "was that really your dad the other night?"

"No, babe. Nutter. My dad's long gone."

She looked me in the face and her eyes took on that cold, blue Tommy Kelly look that I hated. She knew I was lying.

"I'm confused. Sometimes I think I don't know you at all," she said.

I pulled her to me to avoid her eyes. I was confused too. I fancied her to bits and I wanted to be with her, but I hated that she turned a blind eye to all sorts of things she didn't want to know about. Like class-A drug dealing and murder. So she could have a comfortable life without counting the cost to anyone else. Just like Mummy.

I kissed her hair, which smelt as good as usual, and she turned to kiss me back. We hugged each other tight and she put her mouth to my ear.

"I love you," she said.

"I love you, too." I think I meant it.

In truth, I didn't really know what I felt any more.

SIXTY-THREE

Donnie got the call nearly a day later than he'd expected. He preferred these things to move fast; to keep a step ahead of the machinery that pulled policemen from their beds and got detective inspectors out of pubs and back to their incident rooms. Twenty-four hours could bring a lot of things together. He knew that the mood in the firm wasn't happy and it made him jumpy.

He'd got the rods out and they'd fished in the muddy dykes that bordered the campsite. Killing time. The fatty bacon they'd used for bait had lured one, thin eel from the stagnant water. It had tied itself into slippery S-bends on the line and they couldn't unhook it. Donnie had beaten it to death with a shovel to stop its writhing. They didn't intend to eat it.

"Endangered species, eels," Jason had said.

"That one was," Donnie said, throwing the limp, slimy body back into the water as a warning to the others.

Later, they had got in the Merc and ventured inland as far as a grotty pub, where they sank fizzy lagers, smoked outside and watched Deal or No Deal on Sky Plus. The Nokia ringtone tinkled, muffled in Donnie's pocket, and he fished out the mobile.

"Hugh Jarsole," he answered. It was Dave Slaughter, who was in no mood for funny names. Dave gave him his instructions and rang off.

Donnie locked up the caravan, got Jason into the car and drove up to Chatham, where they switched the Merc for an undistinguishable silver Rover and headed on up the motorway.

The daylight was fading by the time I got to Kelly Towers. Paul Dolan was waiting for me, standing next to an anonymous Volvo. Dave Slaughter was sitting in another car, a BMW, with a young bloke next to him in the passenger seat. He looked like, but wasn't, Jason. A decoy.

I'd never seen either of the cars before. They were all newly hired and, more to the point, didn't have tracking devices planted in them.

Tommy came out of the house and slammed the door behind him. He looked solemn in his long, black coat, grey scarf and black cap. All the lights were off inside and there didn't appear to be anyone else at home. Cheryl and Sophie had gone and there was no barking – the dogs must have been kennelled. The house looked gloomy and dark. Sad and dead.

Tommy nodded at me and we got into the Volvo. I sat in the back and Paul drove down the lane. Dave followed in the BMW. No one spoke.

We headed towards Biggin Hill. I could see the airport lights and the woods where we were supposed to be making the rendezvous. I knew Jewel's Wood. I'd walked the dogs there with Sophie. But we drove straight past.

My stomach dropped. Already plans were changing, and I didn't know what they were.

We carried on along the country lanes, then took a fork to the left. More woodland appeared and we slipped off into the trees, down a muddy path. It was pitch-black and we were way off the beaten track. Dave turned off the engine and the lights, and we sat in darkness and silence. Five minutes later another car pulled up behind us and the driver killed the lights.

"Donnie," Dave said.

Everyone got out of the cars and grouped together by torchlight. Jason got out of Donnie's, wrapped in a blanket. He looked sheepish in the pale beam.

"Jason, get in the Volvo," Tommy said. There was clearly going to be no discussion or hugs and kisses. Dave opened the tailgate and Jason's shadowy figure hesitated. "In the boot," Tommy said. "Can't risk you being seen. There're some pillows in there. Keep your head down." Jason obliged and Dave gently shut the tailgate behind him. Locked it.

"You all sorted, Don?" Dave asked.

"Sorted," Donnie repeated. He walked over to the silver car and opened the boot. Tommy and Dave took a step forward and Dave shone the torch in. I craned my neck to see. Curled up in the boot was Saul Wynter. Or rather the twisted body of Saul Wynter, wrapped in clear plastic; I recognized him by the suit I'd seen him killed in just a day before.

"Right," Tommy said. He looked at his watch. I

checked mine: 7.30 p.m. "You go and sort Saul out, Donnie, and we'll get off."

Donnie got back in the car and drove off through the woods, taking Saul Wynter to his final resting place. At the bottom of some wet concrete, I imagined, with Donnie as his priest and chief mourner.

"Give us about half an hour, Dave," Tommy instructed. "Wait here, then head for Biggin Hill airport. We're not coming with you."

SIXTY-FOUR

"You're with us, Eddie," Tommy said. Paul Dolan opened the door for me and I climbed back into the Volvo. Tommy and Paul got into the front and started the engine. Jason was silent in the boot.

I was really beginning to panic now. If Tommy was prepared to sacrifice Saul, his oldest and closest advisor, no one was safe.

Based on my information, Ian Baylis would have a team waiting – at Jewel's Wood and Biggin Hill. All the details I'd given Baylis were what I'd been told after the meeting.

And we were going in completely the opposite direction.

We drove without talking, the radio tuned quietly to Classic FM. I couldn't tell where we were going and I could hardly ask why we hadn't met up at the appointed place, where we could be conveniently ambushed. We could be heading for Dover … or anywhere.

Ten minutes later we turned off the A20 and whipped

round a couple of junctions on the M25 before exiting at Dartford. Suddenly the landscape became familiar again. We cut down towards the river and through the industrial area, and instantly I knew where we were heading.

I slipped my hotline phone from the inside zip pocket of my puffa jacket and tried to feel it in the dark, praying that I had turned the keypad sounds off. I had, but the screen would light as soon as I pressed anything.

It would have to be a stab in the dark.

I held the phone to my leg while looking out of the window. I found the 5 with my fingertip, picked out in a Braille dot, then pressed the shortcut to text message. I closed my eyes and tried to visualize the keyboard, trying to work out my message by counting the number of times I'd need to press each key. I pressed 7 three times: R. Then 8 three times: V. I continued until I thought I had spelt out: *Rv chng long reach.*

It was a long shot, but I knew that tonight, any message from me would be carefully scrutinized. I pressed send and made a wish.

"Is that your phone, Paul?" Tommy asked. The interference of my message being sent cut across Classic FM. Paul wrestled his mobile out of his pocket.

"Not me," he said. I hurriedly pulled out my iPhone and waved it at Tommy and Paul in the front.

"Me neither," I said, and thankfully he let it drop.

We pulled into the industrial estate and stopped at the Specialist Paint and Varnish Co. Paul Dolan unchained the gates and drove in. On a trailer, just inside on the forecourt, was an RIB: a rigid inflatable boat about fifteen feet long, with a big outboard on the back.

"Give us a hand," he said to me. I got out and we attached the trailer to the back of the Volvo. "You all right in there, Jason?" he asked. Jason grunted a muffled reply. We got back into the car and headed down the bumpy track I had taken before, on towards the river.

We stopped half a mile further, alongside a wooden jetty. We all got out and Paul gave me the keys to let Jason out of the boot. Jason swore and shook his limbs, stamping his feet to return the circulation.

"Put on your waterproofs," Tommy told him. It was like he was telling a five-year-old Jason to put his coat on to go out and play. Jason did as he was told. Paul and I unhooked the RIB from the back of the car and swung the trailer round to the water's edge. "Right. Don't hang about," Tommy said. "The Dutch boat's leaving at high tide, so you've got about half an hour to get down to Denton Wharf and find it in the dock. It's the *MS Annette Danielsen*, a cargo ship from Rotterdam. They're waiting for you."

Tommy stood in his long, black coat, looking out across the slow, tarry river like a figure in a painting. Then, with the first sign of emotion I had seen from him in days, he hugged his son, patted and kissed him on the cheek while Paul struggled into waterproofs.

"Sorry, Dad," Jason said.

"I'll catch up with you on the flip side," Tommy said. "Once it's died down."

Paul Dolan and Jason got into the RIB and I helped push the trailer further into the water, launching the boat as soon as it was deep enough. I didn't have waterproofs and my feet slipped around in the thick, black mud, freezing water seeping into my shoes. It was a clear night and there was no traffic on the river; all that could be seen was the steady red and white twinkle of the necklace of cars crossing the Dartford bridge in the distance. Paul turned the fuel tap on the outboard.

Then his phone rang.

SIXTY-FIVE

Paul struggled with the zip on his waterproof, trying to get at the phone, finally pulling it from inside. He answered it and looked serious.

"Dave Slaughter's been pulled in at Biggin Hill," he said. "The place is crawling with armed filth." Tommy looked at me, then back at the boat.

"Go," he ordered. "Now."

Paul pulled the starter cord on the outboard. The motor spluttered in the damp air and failed. He pulled again, then again.

"Hurry up!" Tommy shouted. Paul was panting with the effort and Jason stepped forwards to have a go, rocking the RIB from side to side.

The tide was pushing the boat back to the shore and into the mud.

"Help me, will you?" Tommy snapped. I slopped through the mud and walked alongside him, trying to float the boat. My fingers were numb as I pushed against the wet hull and my feet slithered around beneath me.

The boat caught a wave and we pushed it back into the shallow water. Paul pulled hard on the cord once again and the motor finally roared to life.

"Go, go, GO!" Tommy screamed, pushing the RIB into the water, almost up to his knees in river mud. Paul cranked the throttle and the outboard churned up smoke and sulphurous green water before skidding off across the river.

Tommy turned and looked at me. We were both stuck in the mud, panting with the effort of pushing the boat out. He looked weak and defenceless without everyone around him. Like a tortoise out of its shell.

"It's you!" he shouted. "It's *you*, Eddie."

He looked as if he was about to cry. I had nothing to say.

"You're the only one who could have told them Biggin Hill. You're the only one we told. You grassed us up."

I had.

"I'm sorry," I said. I don't know why. But part of me *did* feel sorry.

"They say you should keep your friends close and your enemies closer," he growled. "Looks like I let you get too close. Left myself wide open because I liked you. I was training you up and you've thrown it all away."

In spite of everything that was going on, he made it sound like my betrayal was the worst thing of all.

"I didn't throw it away," I said. "*You* did. Saul wasn't doing you over, he was trying to protect you."

His face hardened; he didn't like to think that the failure might be his.

"You signed his death warrant, you cheeky bastard," he spat. "I treated you like a son. With Jason out the way, you could have been…"

He gestured out to the river and we found ourselves watching the vessel's sluggish escape as Tommy's words tailed off. The RIB was spluttering slowly across the tide, then the outboard coughed and stopped altogether. In the distance I saw Paul's silhouette stand up in the stern and pull fruitlessly at the starter cord. The current was pulling the boat back up the river and in towards the shoreline.

"Shit!" Tommy shouted and tried to yank his feet from the mud. They came out with a sticky, squelching sound and he grabbed onto my arm to keep balance. I pulled my own feet out and made for the shore with him, his hand gripping my arm so tight it hurt. I considered pushing him over in the mud and making a run for it.

If Paul Dolan came back ashore, I was dead in the water.

Tommy clearly had the same idea and he was using me to lever himself forwards. Then I saw his face light up for a moment by a beam that swept across the water. He held tight to my arm as he looked out across the river.

"Shit!" he shouted again. From the other side of the Thames, a police launch was heading for the RIB midstream. Its searchlight was sweeping across the river and a harsh, metallic voice was shouting through a megaphone, telling them to stop.

Now Tommy knew it wasn't just a case of getting Jason away.

He pushed himself away from me and found the solid

gravel of the beach while I slipped back into the wet sludge. He ran towards the car. I remembered that I had the keys and fumbled in my jacket, finding them seconds before he reached the car door. I pressed the remote. The hazards flashed and the car announced itself locked with a beep. Tommy cursed and looked around frantically then began to run across the marshes. I continued to slip and scramble in the mud before finally pulling myself to my feet.

Tommy was disappearing across the coarse grass and I could hardly see him in his black coat. I ran in the same direction and caught sight of him again, a black shadow against the night sky. My throat began to burn with the effort, but I gained on him and soon I was close enough to hear him panting. He tripped, and I threw myself into a rugby tackle, bringing him down in a pile of rubble and rusted barbed wire. He was winded; he lay on his back, breathing heavily, and the fight seemed to have gone out of him. It was horribly intimate. I was lying on top of him, my face to his, gripping on to his coat. I could feel his body heat and smell his breath coming fast into my face. Like we were lovers.

There were gunshots out on the river.

"I've been good to you, haven't I, Eddie?" he said. His voice had taken on a wheedling, friendly tone. "Give me the keys and let me walk away from this."

"I can't," I said. "You killed my brother."

Tommy's jaw dropped open in genuine surprise.

"Your *brother*?" he gasped. "Who the fuck's your brother?"

I was about to have the satisfaction of telling him but my hesitation gave him his chance. He snapped his head hard up into my nose and slammed his knee into my balls.

Weakened by the pain, I loosened my grip. Enough time for him to bite hard into my ear, tearing it, and to grab the car keys out of my pocket.

I had a painful taste of the street scrapper Tommy Kelly must once have been. The man who would shoot his best mate in the head.

He rolled me back into the barbed wire, which scratched across my face and snagged my jacket, trapping me. Using the momentum to push himself off and clamber up, he ran back towards the car.

I tore myself from the wire and forced myself back on my feet, running hard after him. I saw the hazards flash as he unlocked the Volvo from twenty feet away and saw his running figure in the orange bursts of light. He wasn't far away from me.

He made a final rush for the car and opened the driver's door, grabbing something from just inside the pocket. When I finally reached him, I slammed myself against the door so he couldn't get inside. Then I saw a flash of metal as he swung his arm around, and the curved blade that he had pulled from the car door sliced into the sleeve of my padded jacket, spilling feathers into the air. I grabbed his arm and kicked his feet from under him, causing him to slip into the thick mud, then I wrestled him away from the car door. He was awkward to get hold of inside his big, soft coat, and while I struggled to get a grip, he worked an arm free, thrusting his fingers into my eyes. His other arm thrashed wildly with the knife and I felt it cut through my jeans and slice into my leg.

It had become a matter of survival. As we rolled in the grit and mud by the car, I couldn't see a thing but could still detect Tommy's distinctive smell, mixed with the oily mud. I locked him round the neck with my left arm and reached into my jacket pocket with my right. Found a biro.

I clenched it in my fist and stabbed it into Tommy's neck. He screamed and dropped the blade as his hands went to his throat. I scrambled to my feet while he writhed in the sludge, and grabbed the collar of his coat, punching him in the face, hard, breaking expensive teeth. I lifted him by the wet coat collar and drove his head back violently against the wheel arch. It made a sickening clunk. I did it again, and again, and stamped on his face with my heel until he went limp. Then I dragged him up and opened the back of the Volvo, where Jason had been imprisoned minutes earlier.

He groaned as I wrestled him in and slammed the boot behind him. The first attempt brought the tailgate down on a thin, white shin that poked from his trousers, breaking the skin and splintering bone. I lifted the shoeless leg into the boot and slammed it shut again.

Then I grabbed the keys, switched on the hazard lights and locked the car.

Out on the river, the police launch was bringing the RIB back towards the jetty. Another searchlight stung my eyes, sweeping across the wet shore of Long Reach, picking out one of Tommy Kelly's expensive shoes, sunk in the mud.

I looked at my phone, at the text message I had sent from the back of the car. It read: *Rv jch6mg logrnjou*. It made no sense at all. Whoever had received it was either a mind-reader or they were tracking me.

Or someone else had tipped them off.

Armed policemen dragged Jason Kelly and Paul Dolan out the RIB, cuffed them and took them off in different directions. Paul was frogmarched up the beach, and as I saw him walking calmly towards me, his face caught in the orange hazards of the Volvo, I could have sworn that he winked at me.

I sat down on the damp grass, nursed my broken knuckles and began to cry.

EPILOGUE

It was nearly 3 a.m. by the time I got back to Deptford. I didn't want to go back to the flat, but I needed to pick up my laptop and a few bits. What I wanted to do more than anything was go straight to the safe house and sleep for a week.

I felt like something was over, but it didn't bring me any satisfaction or sense of relief. In a strange way, I felt bad about Tommy Kelly. I hadn't wanted to hurt him. In my mind, the fatherly figure who had taken me in and the street-fighting murderer who had half bitten my ear off were two different people.

I let myself in and went straight to the fridge for a beer. I flipped the top off and walked through to the sitting room, where I switched on the desk light. There was a loud pop and my first thought was that the bulb had gone and fused the electrics. But the force that hit me in the back and spun me round was stronger than that.

It was a bullet.

As I fell to the floor I saw that it had been fired by

Donnie Mulvaney. I dropped to my knees and put my hands to my stomach. Blood was pumping out through my fingers. The gun went off again and I felt a hammer blow to my chest, throwing me backwards, flat on the floor. I heard a door slam.

Then I passed out.

I felt myself being moved, gently. My eyes flickered open for a moment and I heard a voice that sounded a long way off.

"Eddie. Stay with me, Eddie, we're going to try and move you."

I felt a hand on my face. Smelt something familiar. I tried to focus.

Anna.

"Stay with me. I'm going to look after you," she said. "Listen to my voice. Stay with me, Eddie."

I tried, but her voice got quieter, and her face faded out.

Faded to black.

I opened my eyes. White ceiling. Tiles. I blinked and looked around. A hospital room. A nurse leant over to look at me.

"You're awake," she said, stating the obvious. I tried to say yes, but no words came out. It hurt to move. She went away.

A little while later, the door to the room opened and Tony Morris came in. He looked anxious but smiled when he saw me awake.

"Hello, son. How you feeling?"

I tried to speak again, but no words came out. I lifted my hand and felt my throat. There was a tube helping me to breathe. I held my hand up in front of my face and saw that there were a couple of drips plumbed into the back of my hand.

"Don't worry, Eddie," Tony said. "They'll have the tube out soon. You're getting better." I must have looked bewildered because he wheeled a medical stand close to my bed. There was a clear plastic bucket hanging on it, half full of foamy red liquid, attached to me by a tube. "It's a lung drain," Tony explained. "You got shot in the stomach and the lung. You've broken a couple of ribs but you'll be OK."

I lay back and closed my eyes. When I woke again a few hours later, Tony was still there. Ian Baylis was with him. He leant over my bed and I looked at his thin face sideways on.

"Well done, Eddie," he said. "You did good, and the great news is, you'll live. There'll be plenty of time to talk about all of this when you're back on your feet, but there's something I think you should know now. We've tried to – well – protect you a bit more. So we've put the word out that they were successful. We needed to keep you out of the way, for fear of reprisals."

I shut my eyes and rolled the thoughts around in my drug-addled brain. Successful? Reprisals? I *still* wasn't safe? I was confused.

I opened my eyes and looked at him again. It was like having a strange dream, made stranger by a bloodstream full of morphine. I went to lever myself up in bed, but the pain stopped me. I went to say something but couldn't. Baylis patted my shoulder and hushed me; leant even closer to my bed.

"You don't understand, do you," he whispered. "Eddie Savage is dead."

Scan this code to read an extract from
the next Eddie Savage thriller:

Get the free mobile app at
http://gettag.mobi

To discover other Undercover Reads, visit
www.undercoverreads.com

ACKNOWLEDGEMENTS

I am eternally grateful to uberagent Sarah Lutyens for her straight-talking, sure-footed advice and her push in the right direction.

To Mark Billingham for his long-term co-writing, inspiration, industry, support and encouragement – and for putting up with my endless descriptions of people's shoes over the years.

To Tommy Roberts and Justin de Villeneuve for their insight and education in the idiom, rhyming slang and ways of the duckers and divers. I have learnt many things at the feet of these masters.

Also to Gill Evans for her faith, enthusiasm and sound editorial taste in this and other projects, and to Emma Lidbury for making me look classier than I really am.

And to Davina for putting up with me at all…

Peter Cocks

was born in Gravesend, Kent and studied the history of art at UEA. He worked in interior design, antiques, fashion and performance art in London, New York and Japan before becoming a TV writer and performer in the 1990s. Peter has since performed in and written many BAFTA-nominated shows, such as *Globo Loco*, *Basil Brush*, *Ministry of Mayhem* and *The Legend of Dick and Dom*. He has also published a trilogy of novels with bestselling crime author Mark Billingham under the pseudonym of Will Peterson: *Triskellion*; *Triskellion: The Burning*; and *Triskellion: The Gathering*. Peter lives on the Kent coast with his wife, two children and three dachshunds. *Long Reach* is his first thriller.